# A SMALL DECEPTION

"Jon Marc O'Brien, are you backing out on our plans?"

"No, Beth honey. I'm not."

*Beth honey.* She liked it when he called her an endearment. It gave her strength not to keep arguing for a quick marriage, which would only serve to draw attention to how desperate she was to change her name to O'Brien.

That he had stalled about the wedding worried her, though. How long would he drag his feet?

"Anything I can do or say that'll make you feel more at home?" Jon Marc asked. "Or more welcome?"

*Get me to the church, big fellow, before I do or say something that triggers the truth about me.*

"I—you—you have welcomed me, sir. I'm relieved to have arrived." *You can't imagine how relieved. Or how daunted.*

Filling angelic Beth Buchanan's shoes? It would be Cinderella's stepsister jamming fat toes into a glass slipper.

How would Jon Marc react should he learn that she was not the lovely Beth, but Bethany Todd—daughter of a criminal, discarded mistress of a double-dealing lawyer? Oh, for a magic lamp to make a wish on! Bethany could think of a few things she'd ask for. Peace. Security.

Another maidenhead wouldn't be bad, either . . .

DANGEROUS GAMES          (0-7860-0270-0, $4.99)
by Amanda Scott

When Nicholas Barrington, eldest son of the Earl of Ul-
combe, first met Melissa Seacort, the desperation he
sensed beneath her well-bred beauty haunted him. He
didn't realize how desperate Melissa really was . . . until
he found her again at a Newmarket gambling club—being auctioned off by her father to the highest bidder. So,
Nick bought himself a wife. With a villain hot on their
heels, and a fortune and their lives at stake, they would
gamble everything on the most dangerous game of all:
love.

A TOUCH OF PARADISE          (0-7860-0271-9, $4.99)
by Alexa Smart

As a confidence man and scam runner in 1880s America,
Malcolm Northrup has amassed a fortune. Now, posing
as the eminent Sir John Abbot—scholar, and possible
discoverer of the lost continent of Atlantis—he's taking
his act on the road with a lecture tour, seeking funds for
a scientific experiment he has no intention of making.
But scholar Halia Davenport is determined to accompany
Malcolm on his "expedition" . . . even if she must kidnap
him!

# MAGIC
# AND THE
# TEXAN

## Martha Hix

Kensington Publishing Corp.
475 Park Avenue South
New York, NY 10016

Copyright © 1999 by Martha Hix

All rights reserved. No part of this book may be reproduced in any form or by any means without the prior written consent of the Publisher, excepting brief quotes used in reviews.

If you purchased this book without a cover you should be aware that this book is stolen property. It was reported as "unsold and destroyed" to the Publisher and neither the Author nor the Publisher has received any payment for this "stripped book."

Zebra and the Z logo Reg. U.S. Pat. & TM Off.

First Printing: September, 1999
10  9  8  7  6  5  4  3  2  1

Printed in the United States of America

## Zebra Books
## Kensington Publishing Corp.
http://www.zebrabooks.com

ZEBRA BOOKS are published by

Kensington Publishing Corp.
850 Third Avenue
New York, NY 10022

First Printing: January, 1998
10  9  8  7  6  5  4  3  2  1

Printed in the United States of America

*DEDICATION*

In loving memory of
Boney
the little fellow
who sat at my feet
from my first book
to almost the end of this one

Special thanks to
the ladies who make me laugh
and hold my hand in cyberspace—
my America Online pals
especially
Jeanne McBride of California

# Chapter One

*April 21, 1872*

> *There once lived a cowpoke by the Nu-aces,*
> *Who looked for a wife in pious places;*
> *He sought a bride with nothing to hide;*
> *What he got was a ride,*
> *For the nag done been put through her paces.*

Bethany Todd tried not to think of that rhyme—the sort she'd first encountered in the Long Lick drinkery—yet how could she not? Today she would face that cowpoke, and marry him. Deceiving Jon Marc O'Brien into marriage would be the biggest sin in a life of transgressions, slips, and lapses.

"Don't do it," Bethany whispered against the curled fingers that she pressed to trembling lips. No one heard her. No other passengers rode the stagecoach traveling south on the Old Spanish Trail, the other having met a tragic end seven days previously. "Just stay aboard. Don't step down. He doesn't know you from beans."

After a two-year correspondence, Jon Marc O'Brien had written to Kansas to ask for marriage. Marriageable ladies, Bethany had been given to understand, were as scarce as cobbled streets in the badlands that stretched southwest from San Antonio to the Mexican border at Laredo.

For some unmentioned reason Jon Marc had requested his mail-order bride's arrival to coincide with the day he turned thirty. Today. He expected chastity and a whole lot more, none of which Bethany Todd could provide.

Her curled fingers flattened on the bodice of a traveling suit that she'd fallen heir to from her sainted friend, the same one who passed last week to wherever saints went. "Just say you aren't Beth. Keep going. It's the right thing to do."

Jarred by more than a ride through Texas brush country, Bethany pulled curtains aside as the stagecoach vaulted over the bridge that spanned the river Nueces, approaching the settlement called Fort Ewell.

A cowboy stepped from beneath a sign lettered "Post Ofice," alighting the porch of a clapboard building that tilted slightly to starboard. Dressed in Sunday best—black suit, ruffled shirt, string tie, and polished boots—he wore a ten-gallon hat supported low on his brow.

He cast a long shadow, his step carrying a sensuality to it. She couldn't make out his face, but his shoulders capped a lanky frame. His litheness bespoke a hale, hearty man of the land—a physique honed from rounding up wild cattle and even wilder mustangs.

Was this Jon Marc O'Brien?

Jon Marc. Ranch owner. A man of means. The answer to a wretch's dreams. The man who could give her everything she wanted and needed, starting with respectability.

But why weren't two young men awaiting this stagecoach? There were two men at the post office, all right. But one had some years on him. The older man, grizzled and bearded, sat on the porch, a big dog at his side. That man couldn't be thirty.

When the stagecoach screeched to a halt, Bethany settled her gaze anew on the cowboy who ambled the thirty or so feet that separated building from coach. From the outline at the right pocket of his frock coat, she noted something sinister.

He packed a big gun.

She let go the curtain to shove her spine against the coach seat. Hopefully he wasn't a thief of horses, cows, and handbags—the Fort Ewell bandit gossiped about as far north as the Fort Worth stage stop, and no telling how far to the east.

The coach bounced once, when the shotgun rider jumped down to assist his passenger. But he didn't. The cowboy opened that door.

A hand browned by the sun reached into the interior. "I've been waiting all my life for you. Welcome."

He had a deep voice, a nice one. Could this be the answer to her dreams?

"Are you . . . are you Mr. O'Brien?"

"Yes, ma'am. None other. But I'd think, due to our engagement, you'd feel free enough to call me Jon Marc."

This was where good sense should have told Bethany not to get off the seat. Practicality mixed with desperation pulled her up, as if by marionette strings. Where else could she go? What could she do, and what would she do it with?

It had taken the last of her money, as well as her departed friend's, to get the poor dear buried with a decent marker. Bethany couldn't ride on to the next town, not without money for passage. Besides, she *wanted* what Jon Marc O'Brien offered.

Unable to eye him, she put her hand in his. Skin roughened by honest toil and a grip hardened by years of cowboying—these were what she felt. They bespoke honesty and hard work.

Having read and reread the stack of letters sent to court a bride, Bethany knew he had character. This was an honorable man. A man with an appreciation for the finer things in life, and he wasn't afraid to work for them.

In no time she'd gathered parasol and reticule, and was contemplating brown Texas dirt. Jon Marc stepped back. For that she could be thankful, since she needed distance to catch her breath.

Her nerves went from jarred to clattering like a tambourine at full jangle. Catch her breath? Impossible. Could she pull off this ruse? What if he saw through her? She might not measure up to the tintype sent last year. What if he flat didn't like her?

She dared a glance at him.

He cocked his hatted head, but the brim shaded his face. Even though he was a half head taller than Bethany, she found it impossible to assess either his looks or his frame of mind.

"You're even prettier than your picture, Beth honey."

Under normal conditions she would have smiled, compliments having been few and far between in her twenty years. Fear that he'd send her away froze the muscles around her mouth.

That was when he went down on a knee and brought her fingers to his lips. His gallant kiss launched a bounty of sensations up her arm, past her shoulder, and into her heart.

She almost dropped her reticule and parasol.

" 'For in my mind, of all mankind, I will love but you alone,' " recited the Texan.

Unfortunately, Bethany couldn't appreciate his gestures, nor smile at anything. Meeting his gaze? Dangerous.

"You sure are pretty." He drew to booted feet and brushed dust from a knee before adding, with either disappointment or suspicion, she couldn't judge which: "You're younger-looking than I expected."

She refused to admit falling shy of the twenty-two he believed her to be. Her gaze averted, she retreated a pair of steps and unfurled her parasol to ward off the afternoon sun. Or was it to put a barrier between herself and her prey?

He got close enough for her to see the tips of his boots and to smell bay rum. He said, "Please don't be frightened of me. I'm only out to love you."

Touched, albeit terrified of making a wrong move, she whispered in a kitten's mewl, "I know you are, sir."

Somehow Bethany collected enough courage to scrutinize the man she wanted to deceive. With the post office and the oldster with dog as backdrop, Jon Marc leveled those wide, wide shoulders. He had a charming yet disconcerting trait of looking into her eyes, as if the rest of the world meant nothing to him, as if she were the only person in it.

That had its advantages. If he kept his eyes on her face, he wouldn't get a look at her shoes.

His lips twitched as he met her stare. That was a manly mouth; Bethany had the urge to touch it and find out if it was as soft yet firm as it looked.

He wasn't pretty, not of features. Pretty didn't matter. This Texan was wonderful to look at.

Neatly trimmed, shining clean hair—the hue of a much-traded penny—grew thick and curled at his nape. He had nice, soft brown eyes with thick, straight brows that might have been tipped with gold dust. The best part? Those manly planes that made up his face.

Craggy, dipped by time and sun, it had substance and strength. No mustache, no beard. Shaven clean. Somehow he'd escaped the bane of redheads, skin that objected to sunshine. His nose was on the large side, but it complemented those crags and dips.

*Ain't no riddle when you get the diddle: big nose, long hose.* Bethany trembled anew, trying not to have bawdy thoughts.

Silence gathered, the only noise coming from the stagecoach boot, where the shotgun rider tossed her pair of valises to the bowlegged oldster who had gotten down from the porch to help. The old man complained about the weight of her belongings, and he hadn't reached the dowry offerings—boxes and a barrel of flour.

Jon Marc took the parasol from her stiff fingers to hold it at the correct angle. His voice rough with emotion, he said, "I may not be the answer to a maiden's prayers, but I'm healthy, I'm strong, and I'll always be good to you."

If Bethany had gone on instinct, she would have gushed about how easy he was on the eye and how much she wanted to please him. Unladylike behavior. Improper! A disgrace.

But why didn't he kiss her, just grab her up and slam his lips to hers? She knew why not. This rancher, born in Memphis but twelve years a Texan, was too good for grabbing a woman as if she were no more than a piece of meat.

"You'll do, sir," was all she dared reply.

The older man then toddled toward them. His sand-colored dog, missing a hind leg, hobbled beside him. The dog lifted his snout to bark, displaying a missing incisor.

"Shud up, Stumpy." His master nudged Stumpy's brisket with a toe of his boot. "If ya ain't barkin', you's gnawin' fleas. I swear, I'm gonna get shut of you, one of these days. It be into the Nueces for your lousy hide!"

"He's all bark and no bite," Jon Marc confided, his regard for the other man friendly. "And I'm not talking about Stumpy."

Bethany smiled.

"Howdy, ma'am. Welcome to brush country. I be Liam Short. Postmaster of Fort Ewell." Before she could muster the social graces, Liam turned to Jon Marc, scratching his white beard and saying, "Son, I thought you said her eye-uz blue."

"Why don't you get those thirsty horses a drink, Liam? Now!"

The meddlesome old coot shrugged, but imparted a superior look Jon Marc's way, before hitching up his britches to take off.

"You did mention blue eyes," Jon Marc prompted.

Bethany couldn't meet the curious, intense stare of her intended. This would be her first venture into what would surely lead to a host of face-to-face lies with the fine man who deserved honesty. "Did I say that? How very absent-minded of me. My eyes were blue, as a moppet. But they turned hazel."

"They're a pretty shade of hazel. Leaf-green irises with darker circles around them, like the color of a pecan. Looks mighty pretty with your black hair and heart-shaped face." His voice had a smile in it, despite the awkward moment. "Mighty pretty."

She sighed with relief, having covered her blunder.

Another copious silence puckered before Jon Marc said in a husky whisper, "You're sweeter-faced than your picture."

Having depleted her store of swift replies on the eyes error, she concentrated on his string tie.

"Beth . . . mind if I ask what became of your chaperone?"

"Mrs. Wiley had to be discharged in Waco. She was found in a state of inebriation, compromising her good name with the innkeeper. And, um, with the cook's assistant. I believe they were playing a game of cards that involved betting one's attire."

Jon Marc chuckled, the timbre deep and pleasant. Blinking and tilting his jaw just so, he clicked his tongue and grinned. His flirtatious yet boyish expression had a magnetic quality to it.

While he found mirth in Estelle Wiley's fall from grace, Bethany took comfort in his sense of humor about human frailties.

Maybe he wouldn't send her away.

Having gained some control over the tambourine of her nerves, she noted the riverside surroundings. A buckboard waited, festooned with roses, near the post office. No doubt to carry a bride and groom to the church, then to Rancho Caliente. What a sweet gesture, Jon Marc thinking of flow-

ers when few grew within miles of this stretch of Texas.
Where had he found them?

Not here in Fort Ewell.

The town barely fit the definition of one. A single
wooden structure, the post office. Cows on the horizon.
Chickens scratched dirt in front of a quartet of adobe huts.
One burro grazed next to a weathered oxcart, between
the river and what appeared to be a pen of pigs. A tiny
white church with a wooden steeple lay beyond what might
be considered the city limits.

Bethany also saw miles and miles of miles and miles. It
wasn't much, this town. But any place beat the place she
came from.

"Beth?" Solemn in both tone and face, Jon Marc asked,
"Would you like a lemonade before we ride over to the
church?"

"No." She couldn't have swallowed anything. "First,
where is Hoot . . . ?" Somehow she couldn't voice the outlaw's last name. But Hoot would be enough. From Jon
Marc's letters, and from gossip first heard in Fort Worth,
she knew the bandit to be an enemy to Rancho Caliente.
Her voice found, Bethany went on, "His half sister traveled
on the stage. Planned to make a home with him. We were
given to understand he'd meet her."

"He's not what you call dependable."

"I must forward a message to him." Grieved at losing a
friend—the women had formed a sisterly bond in a fort-
night of shared travel, one that Bethany would never forget—she whispered, "His sister won't be arriving."

"The postmaster spread it around, about Hoot
expecting kin." A frown shored up Jon Marc's mouth. "If
she's got good sense, she'll stay away. Hoot is bad news."

"So I've heard." Bethany moved her reticule to the
other perspiring palm. "I bring sad tidings. That lovely
lady succumbed to a rattlesnake bite, a week ago in Austin."

"She wouldn't have got much in him. Stinkingest varmint between San Antonio and Laredo, her brother. I

might as well give it to you straight, Beth honey. The closest lawman is in San Antonio. Outlaws cotton to La Salle County. But don't worry, not one whit. You won't suffer for ruffians. My word is law on the Caliente. I'll take care of you.''

Always, Bethany had yearned to hear such a pledge from someone like Jon Marc O'Brien. Her chest tightened. Before being handed the chance to become his wife, she'd had no life, no future, and had been betrayed by all she'd held dear.

But luck had finally smiled at her, through the benevolence of an angel and a twist of fate. Fallen she might be, yet she hadn't arrived with malice, and she still had worth, lots of worth. All she needed was a chance to prove it.

''I promise to take good care of you and your home,'' she said in a voice both soft and earnest.

She'd keep her word, but it wasn't by rights hers to make, and never had been. If truth be told, Bethany had been more than put through her paces. This saddle-broken miss wasn't even Jon Marc's mail-order bride.

Elizabeth Ann Buchanan, pious Catholic lady better known as Beth, was the one who got bitten by that serpent—not Hoot Todd's sister.

# Chapter Two

It was as plain as Jon Marc O'Brien's soap-ugly face: his bride-to-be didn't like him.

Still hurt that she'd barely looked at him, much less smiled, he set the last of Beth's valises in the beflowered wagon, then peered at the porch of the post office, where the postmaster—who didn't believe in marriage, sight unseen—stewed in a straight chair while braiding rawhide into a whip, Stumpy at his side. Mostly, Jon Marc saw the medium-tall lady, neither stout nor skinny, who hadn't accepted Liam's offer to make herself at home in one of the chairs.

Jon Marc had stared at her tintype, now tucked in a coat pocket, times too numerous to count. With a veil covering her face in the photograph, he hadn't been able to make out her features. In person she was more than he'd counted on. He'd gotten very lucky, just to have a chance with her. Lovely, just lovely was his Beth.

She wore a straw Gypsy bonnet tied with a ribbon beneath a sweet face of high cheekbones and a wide forehead, and the prettiest eyes and the smoothest skin in the

Lone Star State. Her hat rode atop midnight black hair
pulled back, tight as a tick, and skewered beneath her
bonnet. Her sea green traveling suit had a prim collar, but
the jacket stretched a tad snug across the bodice. Her
bosom caught his attention, secondary to Jon Marc's knowing this was a diamond of many facets.

She fit his requirements for a wife; her virtues met the
standards that poets spent their imaginations praising. Her
arrival on his birthday—well, it was magic. A gift. The
culmination of a wish on a magic lamp, made long ago by
his supposed aunt, Tessa O'Brien Jinnings.

Tessa, who had wished him a bride on this particular
birthday.

Unlike his two half brothers, Jon Marc had met magic
with planning. Careful planning. Knowing that today
would dawn, he'd made certain, before laying eyes on Beth
Buchanan, that his bride would be the cream of the crop.

Cream had never been creamier. Musical and poetic;
educated in a convent, and had stayed on after her schooling was over; daughter of the noble, recently deceased
Aaron Buchanan, cattle broker in Wichita. At her dying
father's behest, she hadn't returned to the cloister.

Although it had taken quite a bit of asking for her hand,
she had agreed to become a ranch wife, not long after her
father's death, and here she was.

But where was the feisty Beth of the letters, quick to
debate and speak her mind? She struck Jon Marc as young,
alone, and too scared to confess her heart by saying she
liked neither the town nor the man.

How could he ensure her happiness?

A poet would form the right words. Jon Marc wasn't a
poet. He was a brush popper with an appreciation for
verse, period. At this point in time, he wished—man alive!
how he wished!—he'd gotten more accustomed to the
company of ladies, as his two half brothers had done before
marriage.

Considering the mess he'd made of himself, his first

time out of the chute, with a certain San Antonio widow, he frowned. Persia Glennie had tutored him, amongst a host of lessons, to "take care how you kiss a lady, else you'll stick your big nose in her mouth."

Persia had smoothed a few of his bedroom talents, yet he remained green as grass in the areas of sweet-talking a lady. Like when he'd tried to compliment Beth. To disappointing results. He must keep trying.

Dusting his hands, he approached the porch and climbed the three steps. Beth retreated, a scant backward movement of her shoulders, as if she feared he might touch her.

"Y'all 'bout ready for the big event?" Liam asked from his chair, his brows wiggling at the bridegroom.

Jon Marc rubbed fingers across his lips. *I thought you said her eyes-uz blue.*

"Are you ready?" he asked her.

"Yes. Let's do go on to the church."

He blinked twice at Beth's suggestion. Several times in her letters, she'd objected to being wed by a "foreign" priest. Padre Miguel had been born in this area, and had more right to call himself a Texan than most who did. San Antonio being too far to travel to exchange vows in front of an Anglo priest, the Caliente too precarious to leave, lest Hoot Todd wreak havoc on the place, Jon Marc had begged her indulgence.

Apparently his argument had worked, but he wanted to make certain. "You're agreeable to Padre Miguel marrying us?"

She kept her head lowered while replying, "I have no objection. I want what you want."

"Ain't that peculiar, no objection?" Liam put in. "Sorta goes with the eyes."

Jon Marc studied the big hazel eyes that refused to meet his stare. Curious. Why had she fibbed about eye color? What stirred her to do it?

Apparently she'd rather be anywhere but here, yet she'd go through with the wedding. Why? Money, most likely.

Her father's last illness had destroyed the Buchanan fortunes. Jon Marc had sent funds for her trousseau and stage fare. Couldn't be much, if any, of it left. She might return to the convent, if she had the means to get there. Wouldn't come from him. By damn, he wouldn't spend hard-earned cash to expedite her leaving.

"It-uz me, I wouldn't've changed over to the Meskin church for no gal, 'specially one I never met." Liam squinted at Beth. "Iffen I-uz a gal, I won't marry no feller I ain't met afore. No tellin' what mighta been crawlin' under his saddle."

"It's Church of Rome, not Mexico City, and we couldn't have been married in the church, if I hadn't converted," Jon Marc came back, peeved. "Furthermore, watch your mouth."

"Thank you," Beth murmured to Jon Marc.

Liam lifted his half-braided whip to the sun, squinting at his handiwork but giving the bridegroom food for thought. "Y'all got a lot to learn, be what I think. Got the cart leadin' the horse, planning to marry afore ya even know if—"

"You do too much thinking," Jon Marc interrupted.

He then noted a flush of embarrassment in Beth's face, all the way to her slightly pointed chin. "Liam Short," he demanded, the timbre lifting Stumpy's ears to attention, "apologize to my lady."

Rheumy gray eyes filling with contrition, Liam did as ordered. "Beg pardon, ma'am. But I think a lot of your man. I worry. 'Fraid y'all be making a mistake. Hope ya ain't."

Lifting her chin with dignity, Beth replied, "You wouldn't be much of a friend, Mr. Short, if you didn't question my presence. I trust, as time passes, that I measure up, both to your standards and Mr. O'Brien's. Actually, I meet his. We have, you understand, been on friendly terms for a good while. By correspondence, granted. But does a couple ever really know each other until they've lived in marriage?''

Did she mean it, though, about wanting forever-after?

Jon Marc brushed her elbow. She started. The straw hat teetered on her head of black hair, reminding him of dark days gone by. When his mother flinched at her husband's touch.

Georgia Morgan O'Brien had gone into marriage with a disinclined heart, which proved it wasn't smart to push a woman in a direction she didn't want to go. Jon Marc realized something he should have considered months ago. He ached for a willing, perhaps even eager bride.

*Where the hell is that magic lamp when an hombre could use help?* A purely rhetorical question, since it was common knowledge, at least in O'Brien circles, that the lantern was no more.

He proffered a forearm for Beth to lay a palm across, which she did. ''Liam, if you see Hoot Todd, tell him not to look for his sister.'' Jon Marc lifted her parasol to ward off the sun. ''Miss Todd is with the saints.''

They quit the porch, strolling toward the buckboard with the lame dog Stumpy hobbling in their wake, two strangers about to pledge their troth to each other.

Jon Marc halted short of the wagon. Cost what it may, he couldn't bring himself to wrest a vow from a reluctant bride.

Or was it conscience? *I cannot be false to this woman.*

Taking the cowardly advance, he said, ''You don't have to go through with this.''

''I want to! We should proceed with our plans.''

Bemused, Jon Marc let the parasol tilt away. It just didn't settle, how she said one thing while her actions said another.

Of course, he'd promised to love her, when he didn't have the first idea what love was like. Surely it started with admiration and respect. He had those.

And a wild desire for her.

He crouched back on his heels to pet Stumpy, who snapped. "Beth, we've just met. We ought to get better acquainted. It could be this . . . *place* may not please you. Folks say God forgot La Salle County." But God had been good to Jon Marc O'Brien, right here in the badlands. "It must look pretty bad, you being used to mercantiles and recitals and the hubbub of town life. Hope you'll give it a second look, though."

"I've been looking for days, from a stagecoach window. I am here to stay, but . . ." Beth shuffled her feet, giving him a peek at pointed shoes.

Red shoes.

Why the dickens did a lady wear such shocking shoes?

She was saying, "I can't take accommodations when there's no hotel or boardinghouse. I can't stay in your home, either, not just me and you, us not wed. It wouldn't be proper. We should proceed with our plans."

Jon Marc had a word with himself. So what if she had a hankering for red footgear? Padre Miguel smoked cigars, brewed his own beer, and wasn't above cheating at cards. Any of the three would have gotten him tossed out of a Protestant church. Could be, Anglo ladies of the Catholic religion, even former novices, wore whatever they wished on their feet.

Jon Marc waved his hand in dismissal. He said, "If there's any place where you needn't fret over gossip, it's La Salle County. I'll pitch my bedroll under the stars. Till you're ready for the wedding. Or whatever. Will this suit you?"

"Do I have a choice?"

"No, ma'am." His lips twisted into a lopsided grin as he turned his head up, abandoned Liam's mutt, and took a long gander at the beauty fate brought him. "I'd love to make you mine, right away." It might be forward, spilling wicked secrets, but if there were to be no falsehoods between them . . . "Every night I've fancied me and you, alone in our marriage bed."

His blood raced even now, as it had on many occasions, not all of them at night.

Beth didn't appear shocked. In fact a hint of a smile tugged at her heart red lips, which Jon Marc decided to take as a good sign. That she hadn't been insulted, was there a chance that she might someday become a wanton in the marriage bed?

*Put it out of mind.*

"Beth, I've waited thirty years for a wife. I reckon I can wait a spell longer."

"I thought you wished to be married on your birthday."

Tired of gawking at bearded faces, sick of leading the lonely life of a bachelor rancher, Jon Marc had intended to marry her, first off. But just because the magic lamp brought a bride today didn't mean they must marry on his birthday.

Never in his letters to Beth had Jon Marc mentioned the powerful lantern that came into Tessa's hands in 1860, in a seaside town on the Mediterranean. And he wouldn't. Not yet. The pagan could scare his bride away. Being devout in religion, Beth might be further put off by knowing an all-too-human genie, at the behest of Aunt Tessa, had once been able to play God.

"No marriage," he answered. "Not today."

This time Beth looked at him, really looked at him. Feminine shoulders drooped, then straightened, like a schoolteacher with a mission. Was it challenge in those eyes?

"Jon Marc O'Brien, are you backing out on our plans?"

"No, Beth honey. I'm not. I'm insisting on time."

Beth honey. She liked it when Jon Marc called her an endearment. It gave her enough strength not to keep arguing for a quick marriage, which would serve only to draw more attention to how desperate she was to change her name to O'Brien.

That he had stalled in going through with the wedding had her worried, though. How long would he drag his feet? Would Liam Short's keen old eyes spot more inconsistencies?

"Anything I can do or say that'll make you feel more at home?" Jon Marc asked. "Or more welcome?"

*Get me to the church, big fellow! Before I do or say something that triggers the truth about me.*

"I—You—You have welcomed me, sir. I'm relieved to have arrived." *You can't imagine how relieved. Or how daunted.*

Filling angelic Beth Buchanan's shoes? It would be Cinderella's stepsister jamming fat toes into a glass slipper.

*Too bad I couldn't jam these feet into her dainty shoes.*

How would Jon Marc react, should he learn what had brought Bethany to both slippers? Bethany Todd—daughter of a criminal, long-estranged sister to his enemy, discarded mistress of a double-dealing lawyer—had let Miss Buchanan talk her into this ruse, "to save Jon Marc from grieving and being lonely."

The last full sentence Bethany recalled the tragic miss uttering: "You need him, too."

Yes, but what if Jon Marc discovered the truth?


Imposter and prey departed the post-office grounds, setting out in a rose-bedecked buckboard of antebellum vintage for the short trip to the church of Santa María, where Jon Marc would tell Padre Miguel to "douse the candles."

"Be right back," Jon Marc said, once they were braked in front of the wooden-steepled structure.

He strode toward the tall doorway, Bethany's eyes on his shoulders and lean hips. It was a grand appreciation she had for his form. If they ever got there, what would he be like in bed?

*Shy to his toes, when Mighty Duke arose.*

The minutes ticked by, one after another. Bethany fidg-

eted on the wagon seat. Why was it taking this long to tell
that Miguel fellow to douse the candles?

"I can't let anything go wrong," she whispered to her
wringing fingers. "Just can't."

She sprang from the wagon and started toward the
church, but hesitated. This was a Catholic place of worship.
Such had been the final ruin of her drunken father, when
he'd broken into one in the Red River town of Liberal,
thought it wasn't liberal at all, despite its watering hole,
the Long Lick Saloon.

Bethany didn't want to think about Pa or how he'd
broken her heart. Why she'd accepted his sole possession
of worth, a gold timepiece, was another thing she'd best
not mull.

"Señorita?" a small voice asked, causing Bethany to
glance down to the right. "Are you the bride?"

The question came from an olive-skinned girl of about
eight with hair the color of tea, her eyes every bit as hazel
as Bethany's. She held an orange in her grubby hand.

Bethany had no problem understanding the child. She'd
learned Spanish from the other hired girl at the Long
Lick, before Hortensia gave up cooking and dishwashing
chores to move to the upstairs section. Where bedsprings
sang, day and night.

Bethany bent at the knees to get closer to this child.
"Good afternoon, little one. Yes, I am the bride. Who are
you?"

"I am Sabrina." Frays at her sleeves, she offered the
orange. "This is for you, pretty bride. For your wedding.
Padre Miguel says I must give something for your special
day."

Although Bethany hadn't eaten for two days, nerv-
ousness having brought that about, she searched for a way
to honor and nourish Sabrina. She thanked the child, then
began to peel the fruit. Tearing a section open, she took
one bite and offered a large portion to the giver. "We will
share this."

Sabrina beamed. "Thank you, señorita."

The child devoured the rest of the orange. A smile on her streaked face, she rubbed her tummy. "I am glad you have a special day. That was very good."

"Where did you find such a lovely piece of fruit?"

"Señor Hoot brought it from Mexico. He gave it to my mother. Terecita is his friend. At the cantina."

Hoot Todd gave oranges to his "friend"? How sweet, Bethany thought snidely. "I don't see a cantina around here."

"It's not far up the river." Sabrina pointed northwest. "Señor Juan Marc won't allow a cantina near his land."

Good for Jon Marc. The farther Bethany was from saloons, the better.

"Where do you live?" she asked, not liking the idea of this child being exposed to a tavern.

"I live here. At Santa María. Padre Miguel watches over me and the orphans, Ramón and Manuel. He is very nice, the padre. He lets us take care of his pigs."

That was a relief, knowing Sabrina had been spared what Bethany knew too much of.

"I must go now. It is time to take care of the little ones. Jacinta, she has many babies." Before she took off, Sabrina said, "My mother would like to marry your *novio*. She told me so. But Señor Juan Marc will not marry her."

That so? Hmm. Jon Marc banished the cantina to the far side of Fort Ewell, but Bethany figured he knew a lot about the inside of it, as well as Terecita herself. That he had baldly asked Miss Buchanan about morality spoke volumes. He was typical of men. He expected chastity but hadn't practiced celibacy.

If worse came to worst in the marriage bed—should they get there—Bethany could counter his arguments with that Bible quote, so popular with Mrs. Agatha Persat, about "thou who art without sin, cast the first stone."

Albeit, Mrs. Persat had led the pack, chasing Bethany out of Liberal. So be it.

Bethany smoothed her skirts and entered the church. Dark, it was dark in here. Several moments slipped by, time in which she heard muffled male voices, before her eyes adjusted to the low light. Not only from those cloaked, unearthly sounding speakers—one a tenor, the other a baritone that had to belong to Jon Marc—she felt out of place, as well she should, in this peculiar place, banked by an altar lit with candles and a statue of a woman holding a baby.

Where was the church organ, or its piano?

Surely no one had stolen their keyboard, like Pa did the poor box at Our Lady of Perpetual Help.

Her experience being limited to a few Protestant services that Mrs. Persat had taken her to, Bethany wondered how to bluff her way through religion. They had all sorts of odd rituals in the Catholic faith, she knew from Miss Buchanan.

What she couldn't remember, she'd simply have to invent as best she could, and try not to stumble.

She followed those voices, walking down the aisle past empty pews. An odd-looking wooden box sat off to the side, the voices coming from there. Jon Marc was in that box with the preacher? *Did Miss Buchanan teach you nothing? They aren't called preachers, and you know it.* Why was he talking with a priest in a box?

"We confess our sins in a confessional," she recalled the serene brunette saying.

Was that a confessional?

What sins did Jon Marc have to confess, beyond Terecita?

Whatever they were, they couldn't be as bad as Bethany's.

If she were to confess her schemes and sins, would Jon Marc have it in his heart to understand her reasons? He might accept her "as is." Might even give her a chance to become his wife, somewhere down the line.

Never happen, the voice of reason screamed.

# Chapter Three

Bethany, having retreated to the buckboard already, breathed in relief when Jon Marc stepped out of Santa María and approached with a smile. The wedding wasn't off. Of course, it also wasn't on.

They drove down the trail gauges that led to his ranch headquarters, Bethany on the seat next to him. Neither spoke, until she said, "I met a little girl. Sabrina."

"She's a sweet child. Padre Miguel took her in, with the orphan boys, when her mother left a house of ill repute in Laredo to be with the child's father."

"I thought Terecita worked at the cantina."

"She dances there. Hoot Todd never saw fit to shelter the mother of his child, or the child."

Hoot Todd, Sabrina's father? That made her Bethany's niece. Didn't relations carry responsibilities? What did she owe that child? At least an occasional orange, if not more.

"I so like children." Beth hoped for a dozen of her own, be they from her body, or small children who simply needed a loving mother. She would never forget Mrs. Persat's many kindnesses, before her charge proved a disap-

pointment. "I hope you don't mind if I invite Sabrina to
drop in from time to time."

"Fine by me."

"Shall I ask Terecita to come along?" Bethany goaded,
unable to stop herself. "Sabrina did mention that her
mother had designs on you."

Jon Marc gave a snort of laughter, one that carried his
trademark click of tongue and arresting blink. "Designs
on me?" he echoed. "That's rich. She'd cut my throat,
given the chance. In the words of Congreve, she's 'a woman
scorned.' "

"Broken many hearts, sir?"

"I never encouraged Terecita. Never even shared a drink
with her. She looked for a rock to sun on, better than what
she's got with Todd. She thought my rocks were better
than his."

Bethany bit her tongue to keep from howling. *Do not,
under any circumstances, make something of that rocks remark.*
She concentrated on the countryside.

Cactus, cactus, everywhere cactus. Cactus and chaparral.
Mesquite. Oaks, along the river. And cattle—cows with
wide, wide horns sprouting above powerful spotted bodies
of several colors such as white, rust, and black. Lots of
cattle to drive to market . . . with no clear path to it.

The entirety of unremarkable little hills and cattle-
cluttered dales had turned summer green, as everything
had a tendency to do all over Texas in late April. But this
was not the Texas Bethany knew. This was a scary place.

But she'd made up her mind to love Rancho Caliente.
Love it, she would. From this land, from this man, she
would gain respectability, husband, children.

Yet, having come from the windswept prairie, Bethany
couldn't imagine cowpokes wrangling cattle in thickets of
brambles, terrain cut by fingers of the Nueces River. But
water ran in abundance, a luxury in Texas. It could be
worse.

"Sir, why don't you burn off some of this scrub?"

He shook his head. "Start a fire on dry land? Never. No way could livestock get to safety, not with the river branching this way and that. They'd be trapped. Or would drown. Disaster, that's fire."

Put in her place, Bethany tried different conversation. "Pardon me, sir. Didn't I read you employ but twenty cowboys?"

"You did."

"How can you manage thirty thousand acres with so few cowboys?"

He flashed good strong teeth. "Skill."

"So many cows . . ." No one had that much skill.

"More cows than a rancher oughta even wish for."

The Buchanan miss, Bethany had learned, checked into the O'Brien family, finding they were richlings from the Mississippi River delta. *If he's rich, why doesn't he employ more than twenty cowpokes?*

Jon Marc changed the mare's reins to one hand, placing his other palm on a knee. "Remember, I told you how the herd increased during the War, when there weren't any roundups? 'Course, they were partnership cows at the time. But now the Caliente belongs to me alone. To us. It's ours."

Ours. She loved the sound of that, even if this place wasn't a princedom with excellent amenities. As she eyed his land a second time, she saw challenge. Bethany liked challenge.

"You did mention how you'd bought out a partner." Between her departed friend's death and today, Bethany had read those passages several times. "I'd like to hear about your life here in Texas, from your voice. You left holes here and there."

Her interest pleased him. "I came to brush country in '60, to work for Drake Wilson. We made a deal. If the Caliente turned a profit that year, he'd sign over half the title. We turned a profit."

"You never said why Mr. Wilson sold his half to you."

It took a moment for Jon Marc to reply. "His, uh, his wife never thought too much of this area. When their house burned down last fall, she insisted they move to Laredo. He brokers cattle there, like your father did in Wichita."

Bethany knew how Jon Marc had come to know Aaron Buchanan. Three years ago he trailed cattle to Wichita, sold them to Buchanan. The men struck a fast friendship. When the cattle broker was in his last decline, his daughter, newly returned to Kansas after leaving a convent, had written to tell Jon Marc of her father's illness. Thus had begun a courtship.

"It bothers you, doesn't it, Beth honey? Don't let it."

What would Miss Buchanan say now? The dear girl had been plain-spoken, to the point, although kind and nice. "I think Mrs. Wilson should have asked her husband to build another house."

"You'll do fine, just fine in brush country."

"I long to become part of it. I can't wait to meet your men." Gracious! The last sounded rather come-hither, much like general conversation in the Long Lick drinkery.

"My men are away, except for Luis de la Garza and Diego Novio, and a few other vaqueros," Jon Marc answered. "Driving cattle to market."

Good. A cattle drive to Kansas was underway. Kansas, where cattle brought up to forty dollars a head. Forty dollars times thousands—lots of money for a secure future.

"I intend to carry my weight at Rancho Caliente," she said truthfully. "I won't be layabout. I can cook, clean, and sew."

She'd learned homemaking talents through the guidance of painted ladies gone West to seek fortunes, but had stalled at the Long Lick. Those same ladies shied from taking up for her, when her conduct was exposed as loose. But that was the past.

This was the present.

Thankfully, Miss Buchanan—her charm having radiated

from gentility, grace, and a pioneer spirit as it related to her upcoming role as a rancher's wife—hadn't been the sort to sit around studying her fingernails and barking at servants. Bethany would have found those even more difficult shoes to fill.

"I'm eager to learn ranching, too," she tacked on, filled with her own pioneering fortitude.

"No need to work your fingers to the bone."

To someone who'd rubbed lanolin into calluses three times a day, and had shaved the worst, lest her hands not match those of a refined young lady from Kansas, those were lovely words.

Bethany, nevertheless, wouldn't accept such coddling. "I should imagine you can use all the help you can get, sir."

"I'm capable of taking care of a wife."

Bethany knew she'd bruised his pride.

Catching sight of a dilapidated, obviously vacant cluster of adobe buildings, she tried to steer conversation from a touchy subject. "Good gracious, what's that over there?"

"The ruins of Hacienda del Sol."

As she knew *caliente* meant hot to the touch, she translated this ranch's name to Estate of the Sun. "It was once a grand place. Does it belong to you?"

"Yep. The *hacendado* abandoned the property, years ago."

Bethany found herself unable to keep her tongue in her mouth, as good sense cautioned, since she couldn't ascertain just how strong had been Miss Buchanan's opinions. "I should imagine the owner found it difficult to manage, far from civilization."

"He was forced out, once this stretch of Mexico became Texas. López gave food and supplies to Santa Ana, when the Mexican Army was on its march to the Alamo, in '36. Texans don't forgive folks who sided with that old rascal—remember the Alamo. Don Tomás López left in '48. The roof caved in after that."

Bethany's gaze settled on Jon Marc anew, catching a tightness in the jaw of his exceptional profile.

His voice as tight as his jaw, he then said, "I'll grant it's solitary and isolated out here, but I've loved this place since I first saw it, at eighteen."

Had she insulted Jon Marc by association? *Don't do it again.* "Meant no rudeness, sir. Honestly."

"Beth honey, I want you to think kindly toward the Caliente. Guess I'm kinda touchy."

"You needn't be. Although I must admit I feel daunted by the sheer size of your spread."

Wickedly, her gaze dropped to his lap. Yes, there was sheer size to his spread! *Bethany, behave.* "I was thinking how favorably you compare to that lapsed owner. You, sir, aren't the type to pull up stakes. Or to fraternize with enemies of the state."

A quick glance at his face told her she'd made him smile. He said, "You got that right, honey."

She didn't smile, having been tripped by her own tongue. *Enemies of the state. Enemies of the state.* "Your letters never mentioned local Indians. I've heard they're about."

"Comanches camp by the Rio Grande. I give 'em free range. And trade supplies, when they ask. They don't give headaches."

"Aren't you fortunate?" An awful chill went through Bethany. At four, she'd watched Kiowas in the Indian Territory give her mother more than a headache. They scalped her. Bethany would never forget the horror of it.

"Tell me they don't come around often," she pleaded.

"Haven't seen one in years."

The buckboard topped a rise; Jon Marc set the brake. He hitched a bootheel to the front rail and leaned into a relaxed pose, a forearm resting on his knee, as he gazed at his property. "I call this Harmony Hill. It's my favorite spot on the Caliente. Here, I see beauty."

The ranch's beauty lay in the flora that livestock grazed upon and the river they drank from, to Bethany's way of thinking. Fat cows and healthy horses brought in cash. No cow would go hungry on the Caliente.

He said, "Wish I were a 'painter of the soul,' to quote Mr. Disraeli. I'd love to put my own words to what's in my heart. Alas, I'm just a plain ole brush popper."

Bethany Todd hated poetry. The traditional sort, anyway. Lengthy versification on sunsets and birds and the sort of romance that surely no one west of the Mississippi had ever experienced didn't hold her attention.

Jon Marc's written quotes from the bards had given her a taste of the fruits of boredom, her sole reservation about spending the remainder of her life with him.

Bethany took a gander downward at the panorama. To the left ran the river. Ahead, civilization. Pecan and oak trees grew around an outcropping of buildings, all adobe. A small home built in an L shape, a red roof, probably of clay, above it; three chimneys bespoke three rooms. As well, there was an outhouse, a cistern, a smokehouse, and what looked to be stables, but . . . "What is that?"

Jon Marc frowned as he followed the direction of her pointed finger, to half-collapsed fireplaces and blackened rubble. "It's what's left of the Wilson house."

What a shame, that fire. Bethany's attention turned to a mockingbird perched on a mesquite branch. "Don't you have a bunkhouse for your cowboys?" she asked for conversation's sake.

"My men live in their own houses, scattered around the ranch. The nearest is the Marins'. Isabel Marin cooks and cleans for me. Her husband, Guillermo, is one of my vaqueros."

Bethany took note, not wanting to mistake anyone's name.

She studied the area between the burnt-out house and Jon Marc's home. "Could that be a flower garden?"

"It's Trudy Wilson's rose garden. It thrives despite neglect. All I know is raising cattle."

"I love roses, especially red ones." Bethany now knew

where he got blooms for the wagon. How could she couch appreciation without speaking lavishly, too much herself? She couldn't.

"I see you like red," he commented, "from your shoes."

Instinctively, she tucked the toes of these dratted shoes beneath her hems. "Yes, it's my favorite color. When I saw these shoes, I simply had to have them," she lied. Then held her breath after asking, "Do you think me terribly brazen?"

He slanted a grin at her. "I'd say you're unique."

She puffed out pent-up air.

"Beth honey . . ."

She sensed Jon Marc had something to say that didn't much appeal to him; she sensed correctly, for he wouldn't look her in the eye, and say, "It wasn't just a fire that destroyed the Wilson home. It was set. By Hoot Todd and his *bandidos*. But don't worry. They won't burn another Caliente building."

Jon Marc had bragged about his word being law. Few ranch hands about, no law nearby, how could he protect his home and run a ranch at the same time?

Goose pimples tightened Bethany's arms, but not in fear. If not for being forewarned, if not for changing places with dear Miss Buchanan, she'd have arrived at Fort Ewell, expecting a home with a criminal.

If she were to be honest, which she could not, she would admit something. She'd formed a dislike for the half brother not seen in seventeen years.

Since Fort Worth, where she'd first heard of Hoot's crimes, she'd transferred a lot of her anger at their handsome father to his only son. They were much alike, the Todd men.

No-goods.

Bethany didn't know what to think of Jon Marc's house, once she stepped up to it. While her feelings soared at its decent condition—not a shutter hung loose from hinges, and each had coats of real paint—the design was somewhat peculiar.

Passageways—Jon Marc called them dog-runs—separated each room; the parlor from the bedroom, the kitchen from the parlor. It didn't sport a courtyard, as many Spanish-style homes did. But this one was serviceable, livable.

Then she entered the parlor.

Good gracious!

Isabel Marin kept the place clean, but it bore the mark of a bachelor without much taste for decoration.

Bethany had seen the inside of but two homes with store-bought furnishings, the Frye residence and Agatha Persat's home. The only one Bethany cared to remember was Mrs. Persat's, although the schoolteacher undoubtedly didn't wish to be remembered.

"Make yourself at home," Jon Marc said and backed away. "I'll unload your stuff."

And where would they put those belongings? This parlor had so much furniture that it was difficult to maneuver in.

A round table, much like Agatha Persat's, stood in the center of the room, although this one lacked doilies.

A huge piano hogged one corner. Bethany had never seen such a piano. The one at the Long Lick went upright. This one spread like a calm, shining sea of black.

In another corner were a table and six chairs. Between the door to the kitchen's dog-run and that hog of a piano was a fireplace. The opposite wall held the clutter of a horsehair settee, a brocade sofa, a rocking chair, and more upholstered chairs than most house parties would require.

Every wall bore shelves, each shelf lined with books.

Many times Bethany had imagined being the chatelaine of a home with elegant furnishings. She'd never fancied it quite this cluttered.

She heard Jon Marc set down a box, and whirled around as he asked, "What do you think, Beth honey?"

"Uh, um, you are indeed blessed, having such valuable

property." She stifled a groan at her avaricious reply. Miss Buchanan, while practical, wouldn't have put a mercenary slant on replies. Being nice and being Bethany just didn't mix.

"Beth, do you truly like our little home in the West?"

"You've a grand spread." *Behave, girl.* Too timidly, she tried to make amends. "I've never seen anything quite like it."

He looked disappointed. "I'll leave you be awhile. Go check the mustangs. Why don't you take a nap?"

"I'm not weary in the least," she said, thinking about how she might rearrange furniture to spare stubbed toes.

"If you're interested in reading, I bought several new poetry works, special for you. Wish I had some poems of my own composition for you to read."

Yawn. She owed him more than that. Being decent and hardworking, therefore susceptible to attack by the nature of his goodness, Jon Marc merited a traditional Mrs. The answer? Bethany would learn to admire tedious stanzas. Could she?

Steering her thoughts to his remarks made during their drive here, she wouldn't allow him to belittle his many strides. "Perhaps your poetry is what you've made much of yourself, during your twelve years in Texas." Twelve years, minus the three he'd spent in Confederate service. "Or should I say nine years?"

"Say whatever's on your mind." A moment passed as he moved to her. "Beth honey, I'm glad to hear your spunk. I liked it in your letters. And feared, after you laid eyes on me at the post office, that I'd frightened the spunk out of you."

"You seemed to mind when I spoke of Hacienda del Sol."

"Guess I've got bridegroom jitters."

She couldn't help but chuckle. "Then, sir, we're in the same fix. Bridal jitters have attacked me, too."

"We'll get past them"—he touched a tentative hand to her wrist—"before the wedding."

"How . . . how long do you think that will take?"

"That, honey, is up to you. I want you comfortable with me, with the Caliente, before we take that big step."

"Sounds as if you've made it more up to *you*. Remember, you didn't give me a choice. Do you regret sending for me?"

"Never." His eyes were on her in that charming yet disconcerting manner of rapt attention.

Not up to his stares, she did, however, smile. She'd played her role to an acceptable degree. Miss Buchanan, an inspiration in reaching the marrow of others, would be proud. Yet Bethany hadn't acted in this instance.

As if swallowing ipecac, she managed to say, "I look forward to hearing you read from your collection of books. You have a fine voice," she added truthfully, these words rolling smoothly. "I should imagine you're a wonderful reciter."

"You'll plump up my pride, get me fat as a Christmas turkey." His long face angled to bookshelves. "Reading and having it come from the heart—two different things. I'm too much the brush popper to think in pretty terms. Guess you need to be pretty to think it." He laughed at himself. "Which brings me to your own poetic work. I'd love for you to recite for me. Tonight would be nice."

What! Her *own* poetic work? Why didn't the wooden floor open up and swallow her? Miss Buchanan hadn't said a word, although that was to be expected in a case such as hers, about being a poetess.

Of course, Bethany knew bawdy ditties brought home by her drunken father, who'd gone from barrooms to prison bars. Moreover, the painted ladies of the Long Lick had given her an education in twisting the tongue around ribald words.

Vulgarity had never passed Miss Buchanan's lips.

*I'd better find her own words, and reread Jon Marc's.*

"Will you recite for me, Beth honey?"

*Comes our wedding night, we'll turn down the light, and— my dear!—you will get a fright. The cherry you've expected, to tickle what you've erected, was picked by a very bad knight.*

Had but a year passed since Oscar Frye bartered his services as attorney for Pa, in exchange for her virginity as well as her servitude? It seemed more like a hundred lifetimes.

Had but three weeks gone by since the sheriff threatened the Long Lick ladies with jail, if they protested when the upstanding citizens of Liberal chased Bethany out of town?

She was no Beth, for certain.

Bethany, bold Bethany, closed her eyes, having lived too fully in two decades.

The fine, upstanding man who'd sent off for the Buchanan miss wanted to know: "Will you recite for me, Beth honey?"

# Chapter Four

Beth did not recite her poetry that evening.

When Jon Marc read from Mr. Shelley, she fell asleep in the settee that had been shoved up against the ebonized corner cabinet to make room for the grand piano Jon Marc ordered last Christmas, while in San Antonio.

He eyed the sleeping, exhausted beauty, then studied how pretty she looked. He tucked a blanket under her chin, tiptoed outside, and snapped open his bedroll. A lantern beside him, he reread Beth's poetry. It wasn't great poetry, or even good poetry, but it was written from the purity of her heart.

"Son?"

"What the heck are you doing out here, Liam?" Jon Marc craned his neck, making out two figures in the shadows. He tucked those poems away. "You spying on me and my lady?"

Moving through the rose garden, the postmaster toddled forward, old Stumpy staggering behind him. "Thought I oughta warn ya, son. Word has it Hoot Todd sold a mess of your cows over the border at Laredo."

"That's old news. You were spying."

"Maybe I wuz. Figgered to drop in for a whiskey, or maybe one of them poetry or pianer recitals ya been braggin' on. My eyes is wantin' to see iffen y'all is gettin' along. Worried me, when I found out ya sent a message to the preacher."

"Priest."

"Y'all gonna get married?"

"I don't know."

As the dog curled up on the ground to give his privates a bath, Liam reached into a back pocket to pluck a flask from it. "Have a sip, son. It'll do ya good."

It did.

"Beth be a purty thing," Liam stated moments later. "Cain't help but worry, though. Them eyes ain't blue."

Liam Short wouldn't have been Jon Marc's first choice in crony, but a lack of respectable English-speaking neighbors in La Salle County, and the absence of the Caliente strawboss, had made him one. Jon Marc confided, "She won't even look at me, not for more than a split second. The Caliente scares her, too. I know it does." He thumped his chest once. "Right here."

"La Salle County's run off many a gal. You know that, son. Like with Trudy Wilson. Why, she done got her man to sell out, nickel to the dollar."

It had taken a lot of Jon Marc's nickels to get title to this spread, leaving him in a bind, truth to tell.

"Beth knows about Trudy," he replied. "Took it like a true pioneer." But she'd eyed the Caliente like a city girl.

He glanced at the modest home that took more of those nickels to build and fill. "I tried to make it nice for Beth. But it's still a shack."

Having grown up amid wealth and privilege, Jon Marc knew the difference.

"Did she cluck over—dad burn it, Stumpy, leave them fleas be!" The toe of Liam's boot nudged the dog from the nasal serenade in concert with a chewing raid into his remaining canine hindquarter. "Did she cluck over them furnitures you barged in?"

"Nope. Not a word."

"That don't sound good," Liam said.

Jon Marc walked over to the hitching post, leaned his butt against it, and crossed his arms. "Figured she'd gush over the piano, her being a master at it."

"She didn't? Lordy mercy! And to think me and you, and your boys, near to broke our backs—" an exaggerated show of rubbing the base of his spine "—shovin' the biggest danged piano in the Lone Star State into your house."

Jon Marc grinned despite his disquiet, but said nothing.

"Son, what about that new outhouse we built her and you won't let nobody use, no matter how full a feller's bladder be?"

"She appreciated the privy. Matter of fact, she set some sachets in it." Her stores included a collection of dried flowers, pine cones, cedar shavings, and spices. "She put little bowls of po-porridge around."

"Potpourri," Liam corrected, not usually able to.

"Potpourri. Adds a nice touch."

"All ain't lost, then."

"Let's hope she's rested enough in the morning to appreciate the whole of our efforts. She was tired tonight," Jon Marc tacked on in her defense.

"That explains it. She wuz tired. She'll feel better, come morning. Just wait and see."

"If I didn't know better, I'd think you're on her side."

"I'd like to be, son. Ain't nothing'd make me happier than to see ya settled in with the purty little lady of your dreams. What you need is that magic lamp of your aunt's. A rub on two on it, and you'd be in high cotton."

Jon Marc laughed. "Too late for magic. Didn't I tell you it got blown up, when the *Yankee Princess* went down in '68?"

"Ya mentioned your brother Burke and his string of bad luck with his first two flagships."

Both the senior O'Brien brothers had experienced trouble aplenty in days gone by.

Connor, the eldest, had been a Union Army officer, until blue-eyed India Marshall of Louisiana, a miss who arrived at Connor's army post on the day he became thirty in 1864, got him in trouble as well as into a spin. They worked everything out, despite Jon Marc himself having unwittingly added to their dilemma in his capacity as a spy for the Confederacy.

Nonetheless, Connor and India eventually settled at Pleasant Hill Plantation in St. Francisville, Louisiana.

Then 1868 came to pass. That was when the second of the brothers, Captain Burke O'Brien of New Orleans, reached his fated birthday, amid treachery from within his steamship company. Add the problems of making Susan Seymour—snake charmer, kidnapper, accused murderess—his bride, well, Burke had had his hands full.

Every bit of the trouble Connor and Burke experienced had been complicated by the interference of a magic lamp.

Forewarned, *forearmed*, and eager for his own bride, Jon Marc hadn't and wouldn't fight the magic. It brought Beth here. If only magic were available to make her happy.

The postmaster lifted the flask to his own lips. "The genie's still around, ain't he?"

"Around, and married to Tessa, according to Pippin O'Brien." Jon Marc smiled while mentioning his adopted nephew. Now twelve, Pippin provided information by mail. "Eugene Jinnings lives like a regular fellow nowadays, in Memphis."

Liam scratched his beard. "Ya know, ya oughta mend fences with kin. Someday, you look up and it'll be too late."

"I'm not ready for peace. Probably never will be."

The last time he saw an O'Brien had been November first, going on four years ago, the day after a double wedding linked Phoebe O'Brien to brother Burke's first mate,

Throckmorton. Burke had also married Susan Seymour in that Presbyterian ceremony.

As if it were now, instead of long in the past, Jon Marc recalled the morning he'd left New Orleans, a dawn reeking with the sweet-rotten stench of the Crescent City.

"Uncle Jon Marc!" The boy's voice carried down the banquette fronting the St. Charles Hotel. It mingled with a pup's bay and the cathedral bells that beckoned worshipers to mass. "You going to Texas again without saying good-bye?"

Such had been his intention. Yet Jon Marc didn't keep walking. He had a soft spot in his ragged heart for Burke's adopted son, even though their acquaintance had been but weeks in the making. It was empathy Jon Marc felt for the boy. Both in bygone days had witnessed their share of the sordid.

"Gotta go, Pippin." Jon Marc notched the brim of his hat a mite lower and turned back to glance down at the freckle-faced child who toted a bloodhound puppy under an arm. "Time I got back to the Caliente."

He'd leave as he arrived, no closer to reconciling with the O'Briens. In a way Jon Marc was worse off for the trip.

"You promised to teach me another rope trick." A foghorn bleating from across the levee, Sham II wiggling to get free, Pippin O'Brien yanked the shelve of his uncle's yoked shirt. "You're making me and Great-granddaddy real sad, Uncle Jon Marc. That's what you're doing."

From the corner of his eye Jon Marc spied a man leaning on a cane, an aged bloodhound, tethered by a lead, at his heel. Fitz O'Brien, looking every day and more of ninety years, watched the exchange between Pippin and the last chance for Fitz & Sons, Factors to fall into an O'Brien brother's hands: Jon Marc.

Without doubt Fitz brought his adopted great-grandson

to the hotel as a ploy to keep Jon Marc on the Mississippi River.

The patriarch intended his establishment—upriver in Memphis—to stay in O'Brien keep, didn't have time to see the newest generation grow into it, and would settle for handing it over to an O'Brien he'd tossed out of the family home, in 1860.

On the night he'd given Jon Marc such a miserable present to celebrate his eighteenth birthday, Fitz had assumed Connor and Burke as heirs presumptive to the damned old warehouse that had sown the seeds of fortune.

*Fooled you, didn't they, old man?*

Neither Connor or Burke would touch it.

Facing his mortality, Fitz was now desperate.

"Uncle Jon Marc?"

As a street vendor pushed a cart down St. Charles Street and a carriage rolled by, Jon Marc pinched the bridge of his too-big nose and momentarily closed his scratchy eyes. "Pippin, you know more rope tricks than any other boy in Louisiana, I reckon."

"But I don't want you to leave."

It had been a mistake, this trip. *Loco*, that was what it had been, to leave brush country at the urging of Connor's wife.

India Marshall O'Brien had sought to bring Jon Marc into their family fold. Loneliness and the prospect of reconciliation with Connor and his family lured Jon Marc to the Mississippi. Then he'd gotten hogtied to Burke's problems.

Those worsened when Jon Marc picked off a villain, one Burke had sworn vengeance on.

Captain Burke O'Brien saw the light with Susan Seymour, then reclaimed the helm at O'Brien Steamship Company. But he still felt undercut, and resented Jon Marc's interference.

*No good deed goes unpunished.*

No doubt about it, Jon Marc was worse off for this trip.

"Stay, Uncle Jon Marc! Please, please." Pippin's freckles

became even more prominent in his ardor, his cowlick waving. "How can we be a family if you keep running away?"

Pippin had a habit of parroting remarks made by others. Simon-sure, "running away" came straight from the crimped lips of Fitz O'Brien, the old goat now inching closer and closer.

"Been away," Jon Marc replied. "Always been like that. Always will be. You folks are the river." He glanced at the man who used to be his grandfather. If he'd had any idea of running smack into Fitz O'Brien, he would have stayed put at the Caliente, where he fit in. The Caliente, the only place he belonged. Or ever had. "I'm the frontier."

"You don't wanna live on a nice plantation, like Uncle Connor does? You don't like the river, like Dad does? You don't want a family?"

Once Jon Marc got offspring, they would never know what it was like to be an outsider, always looking in. Sometimes at things no child should ever see.

"I'll get me a wife," he replied. "Once I reach thirty."

"Aye," Pippin said, sounding so much like Burke O'Brien. "Aunt Tessa's magic lamp will send you a bride."

Jon Marc patted the boy's shoulder, tugged on Sham II's ear, then scooted around the two.

"Ain't a family more than just your wife and kids?" Pippin shouted. "It's us, too."

"Gotta go, Pippin."

"Can I come visit? I wanna rope cattle and brand 'em, and sleep under the stars, and eat beans and cornbread."

An affirmative answer might bring a host of O'Briens to the one place where Jon Marc had found peace. "Pippin, what about joining your dad at the steamship company?"

"A fellow's gotta learn all kinds of good stuff, before he settles into a family business."

"You get grown, Pippin, you can visit. Not till then. When you do, come on your own. Alone."

"Great-granddaddy said you'd say that. Why don't you like us, Uncle Jon Marc?"

That wasn't the point. It had to do with bastardy. While Jon Marc carried the O'Brien name, he had no right to it. He'd sprung from an adulterous affair between Fitz O'Brien's daughter-in-law and a redheaded interloper, Marcus Johnson.

Their liaison had ended in Georgia's murder and her husband's suicide, although some O'Briens disputed whether Daniel put a gun to his own head, or if her lover spared him the trouble.

His red hair was branding him the interloper's get, and his corruption of given names was tying him to scandal as well. Jon Marc bent down to rearrange newly purchased poetry books in his favorite mount's saddlebags, then threw them over a shoulder. He caught sight of a livery hand leading the dun gelding León toward the banquette.

And his gaze locked on the original Shamrock, still hovering at Fitz O'Brien's heel. Sentiment yanked in his chest.

Shamrock had been his dog, his pal, when no O'Brien understood a youth's pain at being the ugly-duckling bastard child amid a family of handsome, legitimate brothers.

Jon Marc turned his back on the old man hobbling forward. "Gotta hurry, else León and I'll miss the steamship for Texas."

Jon Marc swung into the saddle. Just as he started to head in the wharf's direction, a cane handle grappled onto the reins, yanking them out of the rider's hands.

"Pippin," Fitz O'Brien barked, "be getting into the hotel lobby with ye and the pup. Stay there till I come for ye."

The child did as he was told. Shamrock the elder tilted his head, his sad eyes watering at his master of past. Fitz O'Brien stood firm, despite his many infirmities of limb.

Jon Marc clenched his teeth. "Let go those reins."

A frown marked a face creviced by four-score-and-ten of trying to make others repent, mostly Jon Marc. "Feeling good are ye? Makin' me suffer for one mistake, tearin' out me—"

"All I ask is to be alone." Jon Marc tugged the reins out of gnarled hands. "It isn't becoming of you to ask more."

"Ye've got aunts and brothers who love ye. *I* love ye, though I know ye canna see that."

"You didn't love me enough to give me Fitz & Son when I would have taken it."

He hadn't wanted it at eighteen. Never had. He'd offered out of love, had yearned to give peace to the man who brought order to the O'Brien orphans's lives. Back then, he couldn't have loved Fitz more, even if they were related.

"You flew your true colors in 1860, Fitz. Didn't bother you a whit, tossing me out, not a penny to my name, not a person or a place to turn to."

"I was wrong, Jonny. Wrong." Fitz hoisted his hand as if to touch Jon Marc, but rested his palm on León's mane instead. "Will ye be making me go t' a grave with this breach betwixt us?"

"I bear you no grudge for favoring blood kin. But I can't forget it."

The spark left Fitz's gray eyes. "Jonny, ye canna pretend the O'Briens doona exist. What about Tessa's wish for ye? Will ye be ignoring her wish?"

Before the double wedding, Burke's new wife had asked how Jon Marc would deal with Tessa's skewed gift of love. And skewed, as it had been for Connor and Burke, it was.

Those gifts came with baggage, since Tessa, feather-brained Tessa, hadn't had the presence of mind to be precise. Instead of mere brides, she should have asked for "peaceful courtships and the wisdom to appreciate your ladies."

Jon Marc clipped a salute at the nonagenarian before reining toward the wharf. He never looked back. Not then.

Not since.

In the near-to-four years that separated his New Orleans trip from now, his only contact with Fitz or his daughters had been to write and warn them to stay away while he got his bride.

And now he had one. Maybe.

"You being quiet," a voice, Liam Short's, said, slicing into Jon Marc's brown study, "I take it you got your regrets."

Jon Marc shoved thoughts of Louisiana aside and squinted up at the fine, moonlit Texas sky. His gaze lowered to Liam Short, who watched him closely. "I owe Fitz a thank-you for cutting me loose. He sent me to what I always needed. Peace."

"Ain't too late to thank him."

Jon Marc chuckled without meaning it. Hurt and a chill ran down his spine, still a rebuffed youth in his heart.

"You're cozy with family, in a roundabout sorta way." Liam offered another swig from the flask, an offer declined. "Ya hired your sis-in-law's nephew as strawboss."

"True. Catfish Abbott showed up in San Antonio." When Jon Marc had ventured up there for a poetry reading. "He was looking for adventure and a job. I offered both."

"Dang it, Stumpy. I'm gonna kick your butt!" Liam shook a peed-on boot at his beloved companion. Yet the postmaster got back to his mission: aggravating Jon Marc. "Ya been known to call on the widow Glennie."

"I never called on Mrs. Glennie."

India O'Brien's sister had chased him. Jon Marc was glad he had never mentioned his indiscretion to Liam. He might be a sinner, but some things didn't get told outside the confessional.

Jon Marc feigned a yawn. "It's late. 'Night, Liam."

The oldster took his leave. Jon Marc settled into the bedroll to spend the rest of this night wishing for wishes. That Beth would warm to him. That she'd love this land.

And that she'd never find out how far he'd gone with Persia.

If so, sure as hell, the pious lady of the letters would wash her hands of him. And he wouldn't have that, not over someone like Persia Glennie. Trouble was, he'd enjoyed the widow's bawdiness and lack of inhibitions.

He'd had a helluva holiday season last year in San Antonio, after Persia showed up in his hotel room, toting cognac and wearing nothing under her cape. Liquored up, he'd let her fiddle with his britches buttons. And more. But he hadn't enjoyed a good enough time to consider making Persia his wife. He wouldn't have a woman who spread her legs for men.

It wasn't that the idea made Jon Marc sick.

It was what a loose woman could do to those around her.

# Chapter Five

Beth, at breakfast, cooked like she had an outfit of cattle drovers to feed, using provisions brought with her. Food and supplies not seen on the Caliente since Trudy pulled up stakes. Some of it never seen, like dried flowers.

Jon Marc didn't scold her for wasting grub, even though freighters were scarce as orchids hereabouts. Damned good cook, she was, even if preparations went overboard. He wolfed eggs and biscuits, gravy and potatoes—ambrosia to an hombre accustomed to his cook's menu of chiles, chiles, and more chiles.

Mainly he filled his mouth to keep off the subject of that widow woman in San Antonio. Damned fool thing it would be, like when he'd let himself be drafted into the Confederate Army, if he yakked his way out of a poetess with big, alluring eyes.

He studied her. She sat opposite at the table in the room that served as both formal eating room and parlor. Her fingers filled with needle and thread, she sewed some sort of hankie-looking thing, probably one of her sachet sacks.

Beautiful in green calico was Beth. And he loved her

dark hair in that single plait down her back, to the middle of it. A powerful urge beset him, the need to unbind that braid and take off her clothes. Slowly. Like Persia had taught him. *Don't be thinking about such as Persia.* But if he could someday coax a few lewd words out of Beth's tender lips, more was the better.

*Straighten up. This one's been in a convent, not men's hotel rooms.*

Rooms. She hadn't uttered a syllable about the furnishings in this one, which hurt Jon Marc's feelings, but why make too much of it? Before Aaron's illness sent the Buchanans to the poorhouse, Beth had known better than what the Caliente offered. That Jon Marc couldn't return her to the style of her former custom bothered him more than her silence.

While Isabel Marin removed dirty dishes to the kitchen, he quit thinking on his failings. He leaned back his chair, patted his stomach, and asked, "What're you making? Sachets?"

"I'm redoing a blouse. I think with a few tucks here and there, and it'll fit Sabrina."

"She could use some nice duds for Mass."

"Does she get enough to eat?" Beth studied her handwork.

"She eats as good as any Mexican around these parts. Beans and chili, mostly. Tortillas when the padre is lucky enough to get ground corn."

"I'd like to share some of the supplies I brought. She needs greens to grow up sturdy and strong."

"Sabrina won't eat greens, bet you money. Unless the green is a *jalapeño* pepper." Not the funniest thing in the world to say, but it disappointed him when Beth didn't so much as crack a smile. "You hate this house," he accused. "You hate this ranch." *And can't stand the sight of me.*

Poking the blouse into a basket Isabel wove sometime back, Beth swallowed, licked her lips, and brushed an imaginary crumb from the table. "Not true, sir. This is a fine home. Quaint. Compact. Perhaps a bit too compact for so much furniture.''

Did he hear right? She complained about effects that most frontier women would kill for? Stuff that Jon Marc had cleaned out his strongbox for? Had put himself in San Antonio, and into the line of Persia's fire, to order?

Upon glancing at him, Beth must have read his chagrin. ''Oh, sir, I didn't mean to criticize. Honestly, I didn't. I'm simply not accustomed to fine things, having lived in poverty.''

Why hadn't he thought of that? Besides, she'd at one point been set on taking a vow of poverty, for the church.

''Sir . . . this residence is lovely, stupendously so. And it's home.'' Her lips softened. ''I've never looked upon a house and saw it as a home. Before, I was always in my father's home, or at school, or at the convent. Someday, hopefully, I'll be able to say this is our home. *My* home.''

He'd never thought about that, either. Having made his own place for years, he hadn't considered what it must be like for a lady to first see something as her own.

He had a lot to learn about women.

He just wished this one wouldn't refuse to meet his eyes.

''Beth honey, how about I show you Salado Creek this afternoon? Luis and Diego are breaking mustangs there.''

''I'd love it. How many horses do you own?''

''Two hundred. Not as pretty as you are, but beauties nonetheless. There is no prettier lady than Beth Buchanan.''

She blushed, shivered.

*Run her off by complimenting her, that's the way to do it.*

Jon Marc got somber. ''I recall you do ride.'' Had she meant English style, or what? ''Do you need a sidesaddle?''

''I can manage astride. If you don't mind, I'd like to stop by the church on the way, and say hello to Sabrina.''

''No problem.''

''Thank you. A ride would be nice. I would like to meet your cowpokes.''

"Vaqueros, or in our language, brush poppers," he corrected. "There's a difference."

"How so?"

"Vaqueros are like no other cowmen in the world, honey. They can ride and lasso and move cattle through hell. A vaquero can do it standing in the saddle, leaning on either side of it, or halfway underneath his *caballo.*"

"Amazing," she said, her rich voice filled with awe.

"*Caballo* is horse in Spanish."

"I know that." She left the table, turned her back. "I-I've picked up a few words, here and there."

That didn't strike him as peculiar. He, himself, had learned no more of the local tongue than necessary. "I guess Spanish came easy, your speaking French like you do. The 'language of Voltaire,' you called it."

"French? Oh, yes." She grabbed a rag to dust books. "*Mange moi, mon chou!* Lovely language."

"You're a lady of many talents," Jon Marc stated, his mind stuck along wicked paths. "What other talents do you have?"

"None."

Spurs jangling, he stepped in front of her, yet her chin ducked, a signal of indifference that he'd tired of. "Tell me something, Beth. Why don't you like to talk about yourself?"

"Hubris never lauds the speaker."

It was his turn to back off. Her answer made him feel about an inch tall, after he'd bragged about being a vaquero.

Retreating to dispassionate chatter, he said, "Meet me in the stable, say at noon." At her nod, he added, "You can't ride in that dress. If you'll look in the cabinet, in the bedroom, you'll find riding clothes hanging there. They're yours."

"Your generosity never ceases to touch me."

Beth swept out of the parlor.

Jon Marc scratched his jaw. What would it take to get on a more even keel with her?

*"Mange moi, mon chou.* Good gracious, why did I say that?"

Bethany shut her trap and charged into the earthen-floored kitchen. What did it mean, that French phrase? It couldn't be decent. Couldn't be, since it came via the sluttish Jeanne-Marianne de Vous, native of Paris, who made enough money at the Long Lick to return to her homeland to live in the style in which she had aspired. Miming Jeanne-Marianne could prove disastrous.

Frankly, Bethany didn't know how much longer she'd last, trying to be Miss Buchanan.

What if she behaved as herself? Never work. It just wasn't practical. She'd be telling bawdy stories, singing wicked songs, and manhandling the manly goods in no time.

What about the meantime? Bethany plopped down at the worktable and buried her chin in the palms of her hands. This morning Isabel Marin said something troubling. During the war, Jon Marc had served as a spy. A spy!

How long could Bethany fool a man trained in intrigue?

"To start," she muttered, "why not quit fretting to the point of disaster?"

Endeavoring for calm, Bethany spent the morning arranging dowry items in the kitchen, supplies once the property of dear Miss Buchanan, although the potpourri had been picked and dried by Bethany alone. Mrs. Persat started her on the hobby. From seeds given over by the schoolteacher, Bethany had planted flower beds, raising a truck garden as well, in the yard of Pa's hovel.

Before falling heir to Miss Buchanan's largesse, Bethany claimed little as her own; she'd been fortunate to leave Liberal with anything. Vigilantes burned her few belongings, leaving nothing but the shoes of a whore. Thankfully, Bethany had kept sweet-smelling clippings, vegetable seeds, and a jute sack of knickknacks—her most treasured possessions—hidden.

She ran, feet shod in red, with the clothes on her back and the treasures that included a hairbrush once her mother's; a package of needles, a dozen spools of thread, and sewing scissors that were gifts from Agatha Persat on the occasion Bethany had memorized each U.S. President. Luckily, she'd saved all the penny tips that the Long Lick ladies gave her, which provided stagecoach fare. And the means to bury a saint.

Why Bethany hadn't sold her father's pocketwatch, she couldn't fathom. She wanted no reminders of Cletus Todd.

Maybe she'd give the watch to Sabrina someday.

*You may need that watch to buy a ticket out of La Salle county, should your identity be revealed.*

That, she wouldn't consider.

As the morning progressed, Bethany found other chores to keep her occupied. The noon hour approached, and she dug through the armoire in Jon Marc's over-furnished bedroom, finding garb that might pass for feminine.

Frowning, she held the garments up before changing out of Miss Buchanan's nice calico. At least these tucks and darts had feminine lines, she later decided, while smoothing the material along her sides. It wasn't a proper riding habit.

Would Miss Buchanan have worn such a daring ensemble?

Marching to the adobe building that served as stables, Beth rather appreciated the freedom these clothes gave.

She found Jon Marc hatless and in the tack room, fitting out the pretty little pinto mare, Arlene.

For a moment Bethany forgot attire. She smiled at the mare. Never had she had a mount to call her own, yet Jon Marc had given her this one. Before, no man ever gave her anything but trouble, and red leather. Then luck brought her to Jon Marc.

Now, a mare. Clothing for riding, plus a dowry and more. Even her own outhouse. A *man*. Respectability. If only she had a new pair of shoes.

Which reminded her . . . "You think I should wear this?" She pointed to her apparel. "I've never heard of such a thing."

He smiled, which caused her to glance away, but not before she caught the glint of admiration in his toast-brown regard.

"There's no place for fashion around here," he said.

Wiping his hands on a bandanna, he stuffed it in a back pocket of his denim britches. Britches that were a mite on the tight side for manly fashion, but looked good on his lean frame.

*I wouldn't mind setting his spurs to spinning.*

"A lady needs to be practical," he tacked on.

*That's what I've been telling myself. Be practical. Yet I'm practically out of my mind with lewd thoughts.*

"Nothing's more practical than a shirt with pockets or a pair of britches. And they look doggone good on you. You're mighty pretty, Beth Buchanan."

If he hadn't tacked Buchanan on his compliment, Bethany would have reveled in his approval.

When she said nothing, he threw a tooled-leather saddle over Arlene's back. "Look beneath the hook holding that hackamore. There's a stack of stuff. Yours."

Bethany examined the pile of appeal. Holding up accompaniments to the wholly functional gear already on her body, Bethany surveyed buckskin. "Chaps?"

"Chaps. And a straw sombrero to protect your complexion. Don't forget your vest, either. And your gloves. Brush and branches will tear you up, if you're not careful."

No. The role of an angel might be her undoing.

"Let's ride," Jon Marc ordered.

\* \* \*

Bethany and Jon Marc reached Salado Creek, and she made up her mind not to think about something Sabrina had said during their stop in Fort Ewell.

Surely Jon Marc could explain not sending cattle to Kansas. Yet Bethany didn't know if she wanted to hear it. It might make her angry. Or scare her. She suspected Jon Marc O'Brien wasn't nearly as well off as one might expect.

*He's got a home and property. It could be worse.*

And he did appeal to her, as a man.

Focusing on Jon Marc, she succeeded in getting her mind off Kansas. Astride a fine piece of horseflesh called León, keeping close to the creek bank, Jon Marc rode ahead of Bethany and Arlene. No slouching in the saddle. A horseman born was he.

When he reached a barricade, he eased from León and looped reins around a mesquite branch, then strode, loose-limbed and confident, to the stone-and-wood barrier. With ease he hoisted rocks to make an entry. Bethany didn't miss his muscles flexing during toil. For a lanky man, he had excellent muscles.

Bethany, fidgeting and almost losing her sombrero, rode Arlene through the entrance.

Ahead, a half-dozen mares, three with colts, stared at the interlopers. One cropped from a chaparral, then nudged her youngster to leave, to join the herd grazing in the distance. The last mare flicked ears and whickered at the intrusion. Her colt simply nursed from beneath her.

These were broad-chested equines, shorter in leg than the more noble thoroughbred, yet they were noble in their own right.

Jon Marc offered his hand to help Bethany to the ground.

"I, I'd rather stay up here," she replied, somehow too much in awe of these wild horses.

His gold-dusted eyebrows drew closer together. "These mares won't hurt you. They're saddle-broken."

Still, Bethany didn't alight.

He angled away to stride toward the mama horse crop-
ping from that chaparral. Clicking his tongue and speaking
gently, he stroked the mare's shoulder, although she did
gave a warning neigh when Jon Marc got too close to her
offspring.

She was a beautiful beast, mahogany in coat with a blaze
of white on her chest. Her colt, a stud in the making, had
a hide as black as the inside of a cave. The little fellow
didn't seem to care what went on around him, so intent
was he on filling his belly.

How nice it would be, Bethany mused, to know a mother's loving protection. How nice it would be to become a
mother.

To grow a child, she must lie with a man. She'd done
too much of that with Oscar Frye, but he'd always spilled
himself into a handkerchief, or on the sheets. Which was
just as well.

What would it be like to have it fill her womanly cove?

Jon Marc ambled back toward León, who gave his master
a wall-eyed stare, as if jealous for losing out on attention.
But Bethany didn't keep gawking at the gelding.

Her eyes welded to the center of Jon Marc's groin. What
would he look like without denim and chaps? Good gracious, how those buckskin chaps did accentuate Mighty
Duke's bulge.

She squirmed, feeling lush urges. Her breasts itched to
be touched, to have Jon Marc's lips around them. Good
gracious for sure! He hadn't even kissed her lips, much
less her flesh, yet erotic thoughts clenched Bethany's teeth.
Should she wander outside tonight . . . and invade his
bedroll?

Yesterday, hadn't he said something about fancying her?
No. Jon Marc fancied Beth Buchanan.

Bethany Todd had to be careful, lest she'd expose herself
as a saloon dishwasher-turned-cook with too much experience.

# Chapter Six

Jon Marc grew tired of being ignored.

On their way home from Salado Creek, he walked León through the narrow *senderos* that cut through the brush, on a path toward Arlene and her rider, which pleased the gelding in spite of clipped virility. Leon did cotton to Arlene. Jon Marc, of course, wasn't thinking too much about horses. Beth still refused to smile at this soap-ugly redhead. *Why be surprised?*

Having allowed her sombrero to fall on its strings to her back, she presented an unencumbered profile. Such a stab of yearning went through Jon Marc that he felt it all the way to the toes. The side view of her face was just as lovely as the front, what with her fine nose and comely little chin showing a hint of determination. Beautiful Beth. Alluring in britches. Beth of the letters. More lovely than her picture.

Therein lay the problem.

*Something doesn't add up about her. You didn't spend three years undermining Yankees for nothing, you know. Use your head. Get some answers.*

He had to call halters to that thinking. It was no way to start out, interrogating her like Daniel O'Brien used to grill his mother. He wouldn't follow in family footsteps that had led to disaster. Setting out from the misery of Memphis, in '60, Jon Marc decided to settle in the solitude of Texas. Where he would *never* take a wife like the one Daniel O'Brien had settled for.

Living here had gotten old, real old, no use trying to deny the loneliness, but thriving in a secluded spot on the map took a certain attitude.

It didn't include asking for trouble.

Besides, he adored the lady of the letters. Did he? He wanted her, yearned to take her innocence and make them both breathless. He pined to be the first man, the last man to see her hair spread across a pillow, a smile of satisfaction in her eyes and on her lips.

What was love, though?

Right now he didn't know if he liked her. Beth, in correspondence, had been different. This Beth kept a part of herself to herself. Didn't she have that right? Any lady, especially a virginal miss, new to a setting as well as to a betrothed, would act demure to the point of silence.

"You're sure being quiet," he commented, seeking to bring her out. "You just keep looking and looking. Looking at the Caliente."

"Do I?"

"You do. What's on your mind?"

"You don't want to know."

"Don't underestimate me, Beth."

Not a muscle moved, until she ran a palm along the sleek line of hair at the crown of her head. "I was thinking about a poem you sent. '. . . dew tickles the leaves o' morn.'"

"Why wouldn't I want to hear about that?"

"It's not morning." She touched her knee to the mare's ribs, riding ahead of Jon Marc through the clearing.

Strange.

Giving León a nudge, he came abreast of Beth and her mount to grab Arlene's saddle horn. "You weren't thinking about poetry. What's the matter?"

"What was it like for you in the war?"

It took him aback, her asking about the conflict now seven years past. "I got lucky. I stayed alive."

"And how did you accomplish that?"

"I went in as a fool, linked to the doomed Confederacy," he answered slowly. "Foolishness at the utmost. When I was called, though, I went." Mainly to irk Fitz O'Brien, who was Blue to the core. "Spent most of my time behind Yankee lines, drumming up trouble on a one-to-one basis."

"You never said in a letter . . . but Isabel says you were a spy. You have to be astute, unsavory for the business of spying. Of course," she added briskly, "you are quite clever."

"Not clever enough at times." Like when he'd accused Beth of not liking the Caliente. And when he made hot water for Connor and the supposed member of the U.S. Sanitary Commission who ended up Connor's bride. Jon Marc didn't feel comfortable discussing kin, so he didn't.

Furthermore, from looking in a particular heart-shaped face, he figured his war record wasn't all that had Beth unsettled. "What else is bothering you?" he asked.

"Rockport."

Rockport. She needn't say another word for Jon Marc to know what was on her mind. Disappointment.

Hazel eyes drilled him. "It seems everyone in town, including Sabrina, knows you're shipping cattle to a town on the Gulf of Mexico. Why ever do you send cattle to that place?"

"To ship to Cuba," he replied.

"You'll make a fraction of what you'd get at the railhead in Kansas."

It aggravated him, the truth in her statement. Sent him on the defensive. Removing his hand from Arlene's saddle, he asked Beth, "You trying to tell me how to run this ranch?"

"Maybe someone—No. Of course not. I didn't mean to pry. Forgive me. It isn't my place to advise you. I have no right to tell you anything, us not married."

The way matters were going, Jon Marc wondered if marriage would be right between them. "I can't send cattle to Kansas this year. Costs too much money."

"What do you mean?"

"I mean I spent my cash. Near all of it." He studied a single strand of León's mane. "It was all I could do to rake together the supplies and salaries to get the vaqueros and the herd to Rockport."

He expected an argument, or disappointment. Instead, she guided the mare closer and reached to take Jon Marc's hand. "You spent too much money on furniture, sir."

"Wasted it," he muttered, yet liked the feel of soft skin against rough.

"I'd rather you spend money on making more. Poor people don't have a chance in this world."

She knew right where to slice pride. Instinct whipped his hand from hers. It took the whole of his restraint not to shout. "Those cows'll bring seven dollars a head, times three hundred. Besides, I sell cattle every year in Laredo. Plan a trip next week. The Caliente will get a herd to Kansas in '73."

She didn't have the impressed look to her.

He said, "You need to trust me, Beth."

"I do trust you." She fit the sombrero to her head, the brim shading her expression. "You couldn't have made a go of it these years if you didn't know what you're doing. Please know I don't mean to boss you. It's just that, well, money—or should I say lack of it?—troubles me. I've seen what can happen when you don't have it, when you need it."

She pondered. Somehow it didn't sit well with Jon Marc.

* * *

Bethany, at the house, could have kicked herself for cramming her foot down her big mouth over Rockport, irking Jon Marc. Bossiness wouldn't get a Mrs. in front of her name.

But why had Miss Buchanan lied to her about his being purse-secure?

Best to reread his letters. Bethany dug them from a valise, and curled up in a chair. Two things were missing. A six-month gap in time, from October of last year to April of this one. And no mentions of childhood or money problems.

Any number of things could have gotten written in the space of those six months. Where were Miss Buchanan's letters? Perhaps tucked away in the bedroom? "I'll look tonight."

For now, she'd address herself to homemaking.

Hands on her hips, she eyed the parlor area and its crush of furnishings, including a beast of a piano. Should she take the liberty of rearranging the room? Best not. It wasn't hers.

"Señorita?"

Bethany recognized the small voice that came from the open doorway. Smiling, she said in Spanish, "Welcome, Sabrina."

It was a joy, visiting with the eight-year-old. Sabrina took a chair at the eating table. Her hostess and aunt offered a handful of dried figs, and the hazel-eyed girl ate them. Recalling the orange they shared on her first day here, Bethany asked where Hoot Todd got tropical fruit. Apparently saplings could be had across the border. Would Jon Marc agree to buy a few, during his trip to Laredo?

As well, Sabrina agreed to try some canned turnips. And loved them. What would Jon Marc think about that?

"I have a blouse for you," Bethany said later, after fetching the folded garment. "Would you like to try it on?"

*"Sí, muy gracias."* Sabrina beamed as she ran a hand along lawn fabric. "This is nice, señorita."

"Sabrina, do you speak English?"

The girl nodded her head of tangled, tea-colored hair, replying in a variance of the Queen's English, "Señor Hoot, he no like me to speak Spanish."

"Do you see him often?"

Again the girl nodded. "When he no stealing the cattle and the horses, he stay at the house of my *mamí.* Terecita send for me. She say I need to know my papa."

"Is he good to you?" Bethany asked, worried for her niece, as she helped Sabrina slip thin arms into blouse sleeves.

"When he no mad, he good. He scares me."

From what Bethany had heard of the bandit, he stayed in a general state of uproar.

"Why don't I brush your hair?" Bethany offered.

While Sabrina scooted into position, as a child would with her mother, her aunt dug the late Naomi Todd's hairbrush from her reticule to pull the bristles through tangled locks. Winding a ribbon into braids, just as Mrs. Agatha Persat used to do for her, Bethany made up a ditty, keeping it clean. "There lived a young lady who was not content-a, when she wasn't feeding many pigs and a sow called Ha-sint-a." She tickled young ribs, drawing a squeal of delight. "But Sabrina had a friend—oh, my, I do contend!—who'll give hugs or kisses to no end. Be it spring, or summer, or wint-a."

Sabrina giggled and threw her arms around Bethany.


Jon Marc strode into the parlor in time to hear Beth recite a rhyme to Sabrina, their backs to him. He smiled, despite the aggravation that hadn't left him. Such a familial sight. By letter, Beth hadn't sounded anxious for motherhood, beyond a mention of, "It's my duty to present you with heirs." He'd taken that with a grain of salt, so this display salved the doubts he'd kept hidden.

The moment he started to make his presence known, Sabrina asked, "You are happy, pretty bride?"

He leaned a shoulder against the doorjamb, listening to Beth reply, "I am lonesome for the ears of another female."

He cleared his throat to call Beth's attention. As she whipped around, shamefaced, and lunged to her feet, the child scrambled to stand, and he said, "Sabrina, Padre Miguel will be looking for you. Go. Now."

The girl left, pausing only to grab her gift blouse.

Beth tried to leave, but Jon Marc caught her arm. "Don't be telling tales out of school," he warned. "I won't have my business reaching Terecita. She'll relay it to Hoot Todd."

"I was wrong to speak with the little girl."

"You got that right. Dam—" Scowling, he clamped down on the curse word, and tried to look into eyes that refused to meet his gaze. "Beth, if you've got woes, and you need to tell them to females, you've come to the wrong place."

She brushed his fingers away, then straightened. "What point are you trying to make?"

"You must accept the Caliente—and everything on it— as is."

"I didn't come here with the proviso that I interview for the position of wife." Arms crossed, presenting her back, she walked across the room. "How long, sir, will this test last?"

"Why won't you look at me?"

"This, sir, is a wretched time to ask that!"

Nose in the air, displaying a goodly portion of red shoes, Beth flounced out of the parlor, taking the open door.

At twilight Jon Marc asked Bethany to walk to Harmony Hill with him. Crickets sang, so did cicadas. From the distance a cow lowed, mingling with the sounds of river. It was a pleasant evening, lit by the last streaks of orange sunlight.

As they stared down at the Caliente, Bethany still didn't look at Jon Marc, this time out of aggravation. She hadn't gotten over their tiff. An out-and-out confrontation would have cleared the air; common sense warned her off. One thing would lead to another, and she'd be leaving brush country.

"Think we can get past this afternoon?" he asked.

"I'd like that." She broke a blade of grass and wound it around her fingers; curiosity got to her. "I'd also like to know about you, your childhood. Everything that's important to you."

"I wrote everything that needs to be said."

From the way he sidestepped her entreaty, she'd bet he had a few skeletons rattling in the closet, too. *No matter his truths, they can't be as bad as yours.*

Best to return to the benign. Thinking about the modesty of the supplies hereabout, she said, "With no garden, how do you get enough food to eat?"

"We've got pinto beans. And beef. Lots of beef. Fish in the smokehouse. I hunt rabbits and wild turkey. Buy eggs from Isabel—she donates chiles." He grimaced, but chuckled. "I sure wouldn't want to pay to set my stomach afire."

Bethany enjoyed spices. But she laughed with him, glad for the less formal, and certainly less fractious, moment. "How do you feel about sending to San Antonio or Laredo for supplies? A touch of this and a dash of that, and I'll place some marvelous dishes in front of you."

"Beth, you don't need to cook. I pay Isabel to do it."

Probably not well, Bethany bit her tongue rather than say. Isabel Marin, wife of a vaquero gone to Rockport, now washed dishes, as Bethany had done so many times at the Long Lick. Isabel would next set the kitchen for breakfast.

"Besides," he teased, "you cook for an army."

Bethany had a tendency to overcook, and knew it. After

serving meals to plentitudes of patrons at the Long Lick, she didn't know how to cook for two. Pa had taken sustenance through liquids. Or he'd gorged on pickled eggs and pig's feet, right at the bar. None of this, of course, would Bethany share.

Ducking her chin and yanking at another blade of grass, she varied the subject. "It's nice out here."

"Why don't you recite some of your pretty poems, honey?"

Where did he keep his letters from the Buchanan miss? Bethany needed to commit a few verses to memory. As she'd claimed yesterday afternoon and again last night, she said, "I can't think of one."

"Bridal jitters." He patted her hand; she almost jumped out of her skin. "Don't fret, honey. I've got just the ticket to lift your spirits. Longfellow's *Evangeline.*"

Jon Marc relaxed into the grass, propping on elbows and crossing one leg over the other. He began to recite from memory.

"Longfellow is a rather long-winded fellow, wouldn't you say?" Bethany could help but comment, no more than five minutes into the monologue.

"I thought he was your favorite."

"Of course. Of course, he is! But, well, I must be overtired, not appreciating all those"—she coerced a grin—"murmuring pines in the hemlock."

"I like your smile." He also grinned. "Say. I've got a new book. Maybe you'd enjoy—"

"Jon Marc, please don't." She couldn't take another moment of their mixture of uncomfortable silences and awkward conversation, nor one more word about mossbearded trees and their equivalents. "It's late, and I need to give my hair a good brushing before I turn in. Why don't we call it an evening?"

Bethany assumed Jon Marc would play into her hands. She was wrong.

# Chapter Seven

It did not warm the cockles of Jon Marc's heart, Beth cutting another evening short. Obviously she couldn't wait to get shut of him. Wouldn't happen, by damn.

Not without a fight.

Thus, he followed her down the hill and into the house. She didn't turn into the bedroom, but chose the parlor instead, since he said, "If you're going to brush your hair, by darn, I'm going to watch you."

Beth sat down in the rocker, ready to argue.

Black lashes settled against the crest of her high cheekbones as she stared at the small, dainty hands that were laced and rested on her lap. She seemed young, defenseless, a damsel out in a cold, lonely world. His virgin. His?

She *would* be his. He'd never let anything or anyone hurt her, especially some ole redheaded vaquero, but they had to get on a different plane than what was between them now.

"Beth . . . I'd love to watch you brush your hair. I love to look at you, period. If we've got a future ahead of us, you'd best get used to me looking at you."

Her chin rose. Her eyes widened.

"Where's your brush?" he demanded.

"In my . . . it's in my reticule."

He dug in the handbag, bristle prickling his fingers. His grasp on the handle, he asked, "Shall I stand or sit?"

"Sit, for pity's sake. Sit."

He eased back in the horsehair settee that he'd bought to please her, but had displeased her. Her gaze averted, she took pins from her hair; it cascaded past her shoulders. When she lifted her arms to swing the mass of those locks to one shoulder, Jon Marc got an ache of need in his groin.

He may have waited thirty years for a wife, but didn't know if he could wait much longer for Beth, not with passion and desire, deep in his veins. He yearned for her, his need building with each passing moment, as man wanted woman since Adam and Eve.

Beth put the brush to work. Lamplight caught the sheen of those locks. They were like the deepest of midnights, dark yet touched by sparks of blue. How many nights had he slept under the stars and worshipped the sky's hues? Poetry of the heart, midnight.

Poetry was Beth.

She was more than he'd ever dreamed of. Lovely, talented, poetic. Her presence brought light to dark.

Exactly how much *more* was she?

Her lovely hair recalled a question, one that nagged too often. Why didn't it curl? Why didn't a lot of things add up? Like why she hadn't squawked about the padre. Like why she'd written about blue eyes. This was not a stupid woman. Not the sort to be blind to the color of her own eyes.

Jon Marc couldn't quell his nosiness. *It's not suspicion. It's curiosity.* "Why doesn't your hair make little curls at your earlobes, as it does in the tintype?"

"Sir, don't you know about curling irons? Ladies use them all the time, especially before they sit for a photographer. A lady does seek to look her best for posterity."

"Sounds reasonable. Guess I don't know much about ladies," Jon Marc admitted slowly.

"What do you mean, you don't know much about ladies? Your letters were sensitive and sentimental. Every woman yearns for such. I'm surprised you don't know that. But maybe you do. Did you make jest with your remark?"

"I've lived a lonesome life, Beth honey."

She laid the brush aside. "You've been in company with women, surely."

"This may be the frontier, but it's not a monastery. There are ladies in La Salle County. None of them were for me."

"You were at war," Beth reminded him.

"War is for men."

"Not every moment."

"It was for me."

Beth gave up on that line. "What about the ladies who weren't 'for you'?"

He quit the settee and walked to the chair next to the rocker. "They're all señoritas."

"Good Catholic girls." Beth began to plait her hair. "Like Terecita."

"Terecita López is nothing to me. You know that."

Jon Marc wanted off the subject of women. He wanted off it. Bad. Clamming up might save a lie.

He went for diversionary tactics. "Did I tell you about the Mexicans who settled brush country? Most of them pulled out when the Anglos got claim to the disputed area between the Nueces and the Grande. This is the last part of Tejas to become Texas."

"Did any of the grandees stay here?"

"One or two. And a nest of Mexican bandits."

Beth wasn't a woman to give up. "I should imagine they have daughters and granddaughters."

"They go to Mass at Santa María."

"You found nothing attractive in the Mexican women?"

"Some of the prettiest ladies in Texas attend that

church," he answered honestly. "Rest assured, not a one is as pretty as you."

"Jon Marc O'Brien, you're thirty years old. Surely you've courted at least one lady!"

He fidgeted. And knew that he and Beth were nearing an area best left unmentioned. "I've never *courted* anyone but you."

"Are you saying you've never had a lover?"

Beth gasped at her own question. Eyes rounded. A flush blossomed in high cheekbones, a sure sign of embarrassment, even before she gave an even more telling one: covering her mouth with the fingers of both hands.

Several seconds passed before she said, "How very crude. Forgive me!"

He assumed it wasn't easy for a virginal plum like Beth to speak of the carnal.

"There's nothing to forgive." He then said something he felt in his heart, even though he knew it invited trouble. "A couple needs to be frank. What good would come out of muzzling our mouths?"

"Nothing." Gazing downward, she picked at a pleat of her skirt and moistened her lips. "I have a case of curiosity. Will you humor me with candor? Are you . . . untouched?"

A mantle of silence dropped. Jon Marc rubbed fingertips across his lips. Squirmed. This was the moment of reckoning. If he told the truth, he would lose Beth.

Just when Bethany decided the conversation had gotten interesting with Jon Marc, he again plunked down in a hideous chair, saying, "Maybe we shouldn't speak too frankly, us not married. Embarrasses me is what it does."

That was another thing. When was he going to set a date?

First, Bethany needed an answer to her question. "Sir, we must move past embarrassment. I'm not without some knowledge of the animal kingdom. My father spent his lifetime in the cattle business." When he wasn't drunk. "I know how calves are made." Beth Buchanan had said similar words, somewhere between Fort Worth and Waco. "You needn't be shy with me."

The oil lantern flickered, popped. Jon Marc sat straighter. He twitched his lips. Squirmed again.

Bethany felt somewhat guilty for putting him on the spot. Somewhat. "Are you untouched?" she repeated.

At last he said, "Fitz O'Brien, my grandfather of record, took me to a bordello to learn 'the sweetness o' lasses.' I was sixteen. I didn't take the 'lass' up on her sweetness."

"You've never been to a house of ill repute?"

"One. In Laredo. Terecita's old haunt. Didn't stay."

"You've never tasted forbidden fruit?"

He glanced downward, bashful as all get out. "Would I do something like that?"

Of course not.

Holding onto the rocker arms as if for dear life, Bethany had to swallow a groan.

A virgin. For pity's sake, the man was a *virgin!*


"Hellfire and damnation," Jon Marc muttered, reverting to his Calvinist upbringing. Had he out-and-out lied to Beth? No. But he'd led her to believe an untruth. How could he get out of the mess he'd made?

Gathered up in the saddle, making a midnight check of the herd, Jon Marc groaned. A familiar voice cut into his thoughts.

"*¡Patrón!*" The vaquero Luis de la Garza rode up, reining in. "The horses, they have broken out of the corral. It is too much for me and Diego. You must help."

It took two hours to round up the strays, a blessing in that Jon Marc didn't have time to think about his lie. Work finished, he headed home, where light spilled from the bedroom window. Beth, awake. He ought to tell her the truth.

As if choking life out of the reins, he turned toward the Nueces and walked León along the riverbank. Dismounted. Skipped a few stones across the water. "Damn Persia Glennie to hell."

After her husband choked to death on a chicken bone, that widow made a habit of finding ways to waylay Jon Marc.

He'd been in San Antonio, ordering Beth a piano and feeling sorry for himself at Christmas—both from spending yet another holiday with no one to share it with, and from being perturbed at letters filled with poetry rather than a definite answer to his proposed April wedding date. He let Persia lead him astray. Twenty-nine years of celibacy, out the window.

Up to that point he'd sworn to bring his own honor to the marriage bed. It hadn't been easy, keeping his pecker in his britches, but he'd done it, until Persia and her cognac and the black mood of a forlorn hombre did him in. As he'd mentioned to Beth, only a hypocrite asked for purity when he couldn't give it.

"I'm a hypocrite. Dammit."

He now kicked a stone into the water.

He'd lured a virginal bride here.

He'd lied to her.

The only way out was to hope that Beth would forgive him.

He climbed back into the saddle to head for the house, again seeing that light in the window, a beacon that urged him forward. To honesty. Wait. Why should he ask for trouble?

Beth hadn't been frank with him, yet he hadn't held dishonesty against her. But a little thing like eye color was just that, little. Confessing his sins was no small matter. She'd be done with him.

Maybe he'd get lucky. Maybe Beth had something to hide. Something big. A sin. Of the flesh?

Did she have something he could bargain forgiveness with?

Hellfire and damnation!

How far had he fallen that he would trade off the one thing he'd spent a lifetime looking for?

He needed help.

That was when he took himself off to the church of Santa María. Reaching the sanctuary, he let himself in the heavy wooden doors. Padre Miguel was nowhere to be found. Jon Marc lit an altar candle. Genuflecting in one of the pews, he asked for divine guidance.

When he left, he knew what he must do.

Tell Beth the truth.

About Persia.

About the other secrets that troubled him.

But he'd wait for the perfect moment.

# Chapter Eight

"Let not your heart be troubled," Bethany whispered
into the burrows of bed. Easy to say, not easy to do. How
did one comport herself in the company of a virginal male
of thirty?

She needed help, training, and more. Thankfully, she'd
found Miss Buchanan's letters to Jon Marc, in a box under
the bed. Read them, she must. By lamplight she scanned
all fifty, particularly the ones composed in the six-month
gap found in Jon Marc's dispatches. Reading between the
lines, Bethany detected hesitation on the Kansas beauty's
part. She'd packed these messages with poems, not plans.

Heavens.

These poems.

They were flat wearisome. Bethany figured she'd never
remember line after line of painted sunsets or blooming
flowers. References to religion sent her to chewing a
thumbnail. She repacked the envelopes and shoved their
box under the bed.

Additional letters were scattered around her, most unopened, the unread correspondence having come from

Louisiana and Tennessee. The unsealed ones were from Pippin O'Brien, apparently a youthful nephew. Why did Jon Marc treasure Pippin's words but ignore the rest of his family?

"Trouble," she whispered. "There's trouble in the O'Brien clan." Scrutiny of one particular letter from the youth confirmed it.

*Dear Uncle,*
*Great-granddaddy and the aunties agree to stay away from you, just like you asked.*

*Yours, Pippin*

Bethany wanted to explore Jon Marc's hurt, and try to heal it. Survival, unfortunately, was of the utmost importance. Miss Buchanan had flat-out said, "I'm pure of flesh."

There was no way Bethany could claim otherwise.

"Let not your heart be troubled," she repeated.

Mrs. Agatha Persat had given such advice, saying it came straight from the Good Book. Bethany didn't know whether to believe Someone up there looked out for the sheep of this earth, but He'd never done much tending the Todds.

Bethany did, however, believe that if a spirit could ascend to heaven, Miss Buchanan was up there.

"I wish you were here to advise me," she said, as if Miss Buchanan were in the bedroom with her. "You were so wise."

They knew each other two weeks, the Beths. Fourteen days in which many people mistook them for sisters. They became sisters of the heart.

As she had many times since Miss Buchanan was injured, Bethany cried for her sister and mentor. She wouldn't cry for herself. That would be selfish. But wasn't it greedy to lead a copper-haired rancher down the garden path?

Bethany rose to sit at the bedside. "A virgin, Miss

Buchanan. He's a virgin! You couldn't have known. He wrote reams, yet never said much about himself.''

How she did yearn to know the source of his silence. If she could get past the marriage bed, she'd give whatever support he needed.

"How the dickens am I going to handle the situation, when I have to account for my lack of purity? What am I going to do on the wedding night?''

What was the use of bemoaning milk that refused to spill?

He hadn't once suggested setting a date, but surely their present impasse wouldn't last forever.

"I'm not going to succeed, at the rate I'm going. Like he said I must accept him, he must accept me as I am. Do you think he might?''

When pumpkins turned to peaches.

Moreover, if she admitted a lack of virginity, it would be a sin against the departed, a mark against the Buchanan name.

How could she be more like Miss Buchanan?

Bethany quit the bed to pace and clutch her arms, as if it were January. "I respect Jon Marc—even if he isn't rich—and I want to be his, till death parts us. What am I going to do?''

Miss Buchanan's memory must suffer.

Bethany lifted her eyes. "Wherever you are up there, my friend, please listen. Even if it spells disaster, should Jon Marc dislike the 'real' Beth, you must become the scapegoat.

"I loathe sullying your reputation, but if I have any chance of a future with him, I must walk with my own shadow. It's begun. It's too late to back out. And it was your idea to start with, Miss Buchanan.''

Of course, Bethany hadn't argued too long. Broke and on the run, she'd sought a decent man. Hoot Todd.

Fort Worth, a stop on several cattle trails, had disabused Bethany of the notion about her half brother's decency.

Trail drivers from brush country had spread stories of the outlaw. Those tales spread like a whirligig through town.

Hoot Todd, even in absentia, frightened Bethany.

When she took passage on the stagecoach headed south from the Trinity River town, the other passengers were Miss Buchanan and her soon-to-be-discharged chaperone. Miss Buchanan, thanks to correspondence with Jon Marc, added to Fort Worth gossip.

Bethany had been beside herself, frantic.

"I don't know what to do," she'd confided to Miss Buchanan, a day after Mrs. Wiley got into that strip-poker game. "I have no money to set up my own home."

"Why not secure a position as a tutor? You're educated."

"Not that educated. I didn't even learn to read until I was nine. My pa and I moved around a lot, you see. When we settled in Liberal, a schoolteacher, Mrs. Agatha Persat, saw that I had books and pencils and the opportunity to learn. Mrs. Persat even took me under her wing outside the classroom, to improve my verbal and social skills."

Shame heated Bethany's face. Disappointing the schoolteacher hurt the worst. Agatha Persat had been kindly, friendly, motherly, but her strict moral code, and her protégée's lack thereof, had killed their friendship.

"Sounds as if you have enough training," the dark-haired miss from Kansas commented.

"One needs references for the noble work of tutors."

"You did leave a mess, Miss Todd. It's worse than . . ."

"Worse than what?"

Blue eyes got trained on a spot outside the window. "Worse than being browbeaten. I yearned to take the veil, but Father objected. He wanted me married, and well. When he became ill, I agreed to leave the convent. Just short of my vows."

"Your heart doesn't beat for your fiancé?"

"How could I love a man I've never met?"

"Oh." Bethany forced her mouth not to drop. "Well,

your father is in his grave. Can't you do that veil thing now?"

"It's too late. I promised my hand to Mr. O'Brien. He would grieve, should I disappoint him. So I won't."

"You're an exemplary woman."

"Enough about me. We were discussing you. If you don't feel comfortable with tutoring, you could take a job as a servant." Tucking a curly lock of hair behind her ear, the Buchanan miss smiled. "It's respectable work."

"I've been subservient. And ridiculed. It got worse after my father was arrested, accused of robbing a church. Anyhow, I loved Pa. I believed in his innocence. We had no money to hire any attorney, much less the best in the area. But the best offered his services." Tears trailed Bethany's cheeks. "Oscar Frye promised to defend Pa . . . if I'd become his mistress. I had no choice. It was my Pa's freedom at stake!"

Placing a handkerchief into Bethany's trembling fingers, Miss Buchanan let her do the talking.

"It got worse. Oscar insisted I work as a servant in his home, so his wife wouldn't get suspicious of how he got paid. You cannot imagine the indignities I suffered, serving Mrs. Frye by day, servicing Oscar by night. Then—From the witness stand, Pa confessed. My sacrifice was for naught."

"Poor dear," Miss Buchanan said, all heart.

"Losing the case infuriated Oscar. He stomped over to Pa's cabin. His wife followed. It was a terrible scene. Then she told a friend, who told a friend, who told a friend. It didn't take much to organize the outraged. Even Mrs. Persat got in on it. They burned my belongings." Bethany would never forget the castigation in the older woman's face. "Then the sheriff threatened the painted ladies, said if they helped me, he'd toss them all in jail."

Bethany sat back against the squabs, the coach wheels hitting a rut that matched her disquieted heart. "The part of me that hadn't already died over my disgrace died that day. It didn't have much to do with being drummed out of a town I hated anyhow. I lost everything. My virtue, my honor. I'm nothing."

"Oh, Miss Todd. You unfortunate girl. I believe, in the proper element, you'd live as Caesar's wife."

"If I had a chance, just one chance," Bethany uttered, dreaming of a fresh start. "It seems I am simply unlucky. When I left Liberal, I thought my father's son by his first wife might help me get established in southwest Texas. He can offer no more than what I'm running from. Disgrace. I wish I'd never written Hoot Todd. Would that he didn't know to expect me."

"You'd best steer clear of him. He's quite horrid."

"I have no other choice."

"If I were you, I'd take whatever chances came my way."

Skeptical to the marrow, Bethany said, "I don't think you'd do that. Not you."

"I am not you. But if I were, I'd do it. A desperate lady must go to whatever lengths to survive. Thrive. Prosper. It's only sensible."

"You're right," Bethany said in a shallow tone.

Several moments passed before she was asked: "What is it you'd like to have? Say, if you were given three wishes."

"A husband. Children. And land. Land is power. When you own a piece of this earth, no one can take it away from you. No one can run you off, if you're entitled to stay."

"Unless you don't pay your taxes," Bethany's traveling companion had interjected. "There's always a price to pay . . ."

Now, as Bethany huddled in the bedroom of a land-owning man who could give her children, she trembled. That piece of advice, delivered the day before Miss Buchanan went behind the bushes and had been struck by the rattlesnake that Bethany herself had killed with a ratty old parasol, had distinct significance. Distinct significance, over and above Bethany's intention to be herself as much as possible with Jon Marc.

What price would she pay for taking another woman's place?

"I won't pay," she vowed. "I'm not evil, just tarnished. I'll do Jon Marc no ill. Ever."

What she needed was sleep. A good night of it, and she could address a day of making a saint into a scapegoat.

Sleep eluded Bethany.


"Oscar lied. Flat lied."

Bethany Todd, arch liar, deceiver of the first water, had added to her sins. She played the Peeping Tom.

Thus hadn't been her intention. When she'd left the bedroom for outside, she'd meant to walk out her plans. A light from the kitchen had drawn her attention.

Jon Marc kept it.

Evidently he hadn't been able to sleep either, for he had filled the copper hip-bath and was bathing.

For a closer look Bethany climbed the live-oak tree that grew near the kitchen window. She moved like a monkey, gaining a heavy, low-growing branch. All right, it teetered, but she paid no mind. Her eyes were soldered to Jon Marc.

He stepped out of the tub and grabbed a towel to rub down the long lines of his body, yet she got another gander at his attributes. Saliva fell to the oak branch. Yes, Oscar Frye had told her a fish story.

Oscar had claimed his male gear was as big as they grew. Not so. Even soft, Jon Marc had him beat.

Musing over just how big this one got, Bethany trembled, goose bumps running up and down her arms and legs. The hem of her nightgown caught on something. She tried to free it.

That was when she lost her purchase.

An involuntary scream of fright carried through the night as she tumbled to the ground, landing with a thud. Thankfully on a patch of last year's leaves, yet she hurt just the same.

Her cry exposed voyeurism. Jon Marc, frocked in his birthday suit, shouted her name and jumped through the window, ready to rescue her.

Too bad her aching body forsook the opportunity to appreciate his manly delights. She rolled into a ball at the same moment he hovered over her.

"Beth honey, speak to me!"

"I'm okay." And she believed she was, especially since he ran his fingers along her limbs to check for broken bones. "Nothing injured but my pride."

"What the dickens brought you out here?"

An answer that concerned checking new leaf growth got abandoned. Besides, hadn't she decided to be more herself? "Natural curiosity, sir."

He laughed. "You never cease to surprise me, Beth."

"I hope that doesn't displease you."

"No. Not at all." A moment went by, a second in which he leaned his face toward hers. "I like you more this way."

Good.

She liked it even better when his lips brushed hers. Her fingers floated up to settle against his ribs. Then he kissed her, really kissed her.

His bath made him smell like soap—his lips tasted like bliss. His body felt lovely against hers, even though she hated that the nightgown came between them.

*Have you lost your mind, girl? Keep this up, and he'll know you're not a virgin. Will never take you to the altar.*

Bethany pushed Jon Marc's face away. Flipping as fast as twinging muscles would allow, she rolled to her side, then shoved to stand. With as much dignity as she could muster, she limped to the bedroom, and was relieved he didn't follow her.


As the first shard of dawn lightened the day, Bethany faced the morning. Faced Jon Marc O'Brien. She expected to answer for tree-climbing, or at least field a question about her injuries, which were none, thank goodness. Not so.

Her intended wasn't all Bethany faced.

A quartet of mounted *bandidos,* clothed in Mexican hats and a wealth of silver, surrounded them on three sides.

Jon Marc had a six-shooter leveled at the leader.

The square-jawed Anglo, astride a black stallion, looked about thirty-five. Wearing a sombrero on his dark head and a bandanna at his neck, he might be considered handsome, in a cutthroat way. A black patch covered one eye, with a jagged scar running above and below it, about an inch in both cases.

Her heart stopped. Partially because he had a pair of pistols aimed at Jon Marc. Partially because she didn't have to wonder his identity.

Bethany faced her brother.

# Chapter Nine

"Get off my property, Todd. Now."

"Not till I talk to your woman, O'Brien."

Fearful for her man's safety, as well as ruffled at the thought of what could come out of a discussion with her long-lost brother, Bethany crept toward Jon Marc.

"You don't have any business with Miss Buchanan." His aim stayed on the leader of the ragtag band. "Get gone."

The foursome didn't turn their horses. The three Mexicans, bandoliers strapping broad chests, sat impassive, their sombreros shading crusty, brown faces. Hoot Todd continued to point a pair of gun barrels at the Caliente's owner.

Bethany brought clasped hands beneath her chin. "No hostility, please!"

"Go back in the house, Beth honey."

At the name "Beth," Hoot Todd flinched, and Bethany didn't need to wonder why. What she wondered was why she'd been foolish enough not to realize, before now, there might be a problem. Hoot had expected a Beth.

"Jon Marc, I'm willing to talk with these gentlemen."

Gentlemen? A vulgarity against respectful address. She

barely remembered Hoot Todd, her best recollections having to do with their now-departed grandfather's tales. Grandpa, many times, mentioned how happy it used to make Hoot, when Naomi Todd baked lemon pies for the family.

Who would have ever thought that the nice young man of yesteryears would become crooked as a dog's hind leg? Well, blood showed, and he had their father's.

She glared. "What is it you want?"

Hoot twirled six-guns before holstering the pistols and slipping a thumb behind his silver belt buckle. "Talk."

Jon Marc, his gaze never moving from the outlaws, lowered his trigger finger. "You hustle my cattle and horses across the border to Mexico, but you want *talk?*"

"That's right. Talk."

"Anything more," Jon Marc promised, "and I'll put your other eye out."

"You scare me spitless." Hoot sneered. "Even if you did half blind me."

Bethany gasped. Jon Marc had maimed the infamous Hoot Todd?

"You'd be smart to stop stealing my livestock, Todd."

"I never stole your friggin' horses or cows."

"Watch your mouth, Todd. There's a lady present."

"My apologies, ma'am." Hoot Todd, grinning like a false face, removed his sombrero.

Bethany was struck by how much he resembled their father. Struck disgusted. Even though she'd always love Pa, would she ever get over his betrayal?

"Meant no insult," Hoot said. "What I'd like is a cuppa coffee and some answers about my little sister."

Bethany would rather go back to Liberal than to discuss anything with Hoot Todd. Unworkable. The best course was to get the matter of Bethany Todd buried, once and for all.

"Will you allow it?" she asked Jon Marc.

"You don't have to talk with him. I don't want you to."

She stepped to Jon Marc's side and laid her palm on an upper arm taut with muscles and the need to offer protection. "If your sister had died," she said, "wouldn't you want to know what happened?"

"I don't have a sister."

Said Hoot, "I'm not here to steal the dishes or your woman. Or your cows. I just want some neighborly coffee and a few words about my kin."

She tightened her fingers on Jon Marc's wonderful arm and forced herself not to recall last night. "It's for the best."

"For you, I'll do it." He next said to Todd, "I've got a pot of coffee in the house. Get shut of your *bandidos.*"

The outlaw gave a hand signal; his cohorts turned their mounts to ride away. The trio of Bethany, Jon Marc, and the brother she'd rather forget sat at the kitchen table, with the prospective lady of the house pouring coffee and giving answers.

While she did, Jon Marc kept his arms folded over his chest, his glare on Hoot. The bandit planted forearms atop the table and lowered his head.

"I arranged for her burial in Austin," Bethany said at the end of her monologue. "She rests in a Baptist church-yard."

That was a lie. Bethany had arranged a proper Catholic burial, in accordance with Miss Buchanan's faith. And she used the last of the dead girl's money, as well as her own, to buy a marker to read: "E. A. Buchanan, 1850–1872." Why let it be known the Catholic cemetery was in Round Rock, north of Austin?

"Which one?" Hoot asked.

"I don't recall the church's name. I had to catch the stage before the funeral, else it would've worried Mr. O'Brien, had I not arrive as planned. Have no fear, every-thing was quite proper and fitting."

Hoot downed the rest of his coffee. Wiping his mouth

with the back of a meaty hand, he said, "Okay, now I know."

"I'm sorry, Mr. Todd," Bethany said.

"Don't make me no never-mind, beyond curiosity. Haven't seen her since she was a brat. Couldn't care less about her."

His attitude stank. Bethany felt as if she had a dig coming, both for herself and his neglected daughter. "Poor Miss Todd counted on you for a home. It's almost a blessing she didn't have to depend on your mercies."

"You mean that minx expected me to take her in? For good?" Hoot's disfigured, yet handsome face contorted. "Figured she was after money and movin' on. I tell ya. Women're always after what they can gouge out of ya. She can go to he—Hades."

While Fort Worth had set Bethany straight about Hoot Todd, and Sabrina confirmed it, she couldn't stop the sting that burned her veins. But who was she to judge? Love hadn't poured from her heart at the sight of this criminal, either.

"Nice way to think of your kin," Jon Marc remarked.

"You criticize me, O'Brien? Talk says you got brothers. Ain't never seen none of them callin' on you."

Had Jon Marc's letters mentioned the older brothers? No. There could have been a mention in the missing posts, of course.

He stood. "You got your answers, Todd. Now leave."

"Fine by me. Never could stand the sight of you, especially after you and the sheriff of Bexar cornered me in '61." Hoot just happened to turn to Bethany. "Fights like an Injun when he wants to, your man."

"Get gone, Todd."

Hoot strutted toward the door, but halted to turn around and inquire, "Lady, did I hear him wrong earlier? Didn't I hear him call you Beth?"

"That is my name. Beth Buchanan."

"Ain't that something—you and my sis had the same name."

"Not really," Bethany replied, quickly enough not to rouse Jon Marc's suspicions. She hoped. "Beth is a much-used nickname for Elizabeth."

"That explains it." He slapped his sombrero back on his head. "My sister was called Bethany."

"*Adios,* Todd." Jon Marc ambled to the door, opened it.

Just as Hoot was about to pass the host, he sneered. "By the by, asshole, it's a good thing you're getting a wife. Your coffee tastes like horse piss."

"Some of these days you're gonna learn something about me—I don't warn any man but once on a subject." Jon Marc drew back his fist and slammed it into Hoot's nose. "I warned you not to cuss in front of my lady."

Bethany's brother went down, out cold. In one lick. Blood from his flattened nose trickled into his mouth and beneath the black patch.

As if he were lifting no more than a sack of potatoes, Jon Marc picked Hoot off the floor, carried him outside, laid him across the stallion's saddle. The horse reached around to bite Jon Marc when he gave its rump a swat, but a stern "Whoa, Diablo" settled the mount. Another swat sent Diablo and cold-cocked burden on their way.

Bethany would have clapped, if not for impropriety, which had nothing to do with mores as they related to the late Miss Buchanan. She despised Hoot Todd. That Jon Marc would fight for her honor lifted him yet another notch in her estimation.

Right then he did something out of character. Dusting his hands, he crossed over to her, grinned in his uniquely appealing way, and snaked a forearm behind her waist to pull her to him. She looked up into his velvet gaze, startled. Yet she didn't pull back. A whiff of soap mixed with his particular scent enticed her, just as the feel of his strong body.

"Nobody messes with me or mine," he growled, then planted a hard yet too brief kiss on her lips.

He let go his hold and turned to walk away, leaving her astounded. Staggered, yes, and cautious. He wasn't modeling clay to be formed in whatever image Bethany pleased. A smart woman wouldn't toy with a man like Jon Marc O'Brien.


"I'm gonna get that son-of-a-bitch." Hoot Todd could barely talk, his broken nose hurt so much. "Gonna get O'Brien good."

Across the table in the empty cantina, Terecita López shuffled cards. "You always say that, *chico*. It has been two days since he struck you, yet all you do is talk."

Hoot ran the side of his hand across the table, disturbing the cards. "Can't do nothing till I'm able. But I'm getting my strength back. This time he ain't gonna get by with damaging my person. For the second time."

His mouth quivered, so deep did Hoot despise O'Brien. The Caliente should have been in Todd hands. Hoot had gotten here first, had been the first to be hired by Drake Wilson. Once that greenhorn kid from Tennessee showed up, Wilson fired Hoot, just because he pilfered a few dollars from the ranch strongbox.

Hoot had just needed an advance till payday, so he could buy a new dress for a señorita, but Drake Wilson hadn't understood why Hoot borrowed money without telling anyone. At least that had been the old goat's excuse. That O'Brien piece of cow shit turned Wilson off Hoot, sure as the world.

It had started war. Until he got shanghaied, Hoot gathered his buddies; they took his slight seriously. Not only did they steal big from the Caliente—including a whole *remuda* of the best horses—they expanded their enterprise, as any prospering establishment would, to include stage-coaches, mule trains, and the few Army patrols that had dared cross into Todd territory. Hoot grinned, even though his nose hurt like a sunzabitch. Yep, hadn't been nobody safe. Heaven help the lone carriage that meandered into brush country.

Then that bastard O'Brien, at Wilson's urging, laid a trap, and Hoot ended up losing an eye and getting sent to prison. Those seven years behind The Walls? Couldn't call it a tea party with fancy sandwiches and stringed music, no sirree, but it honed Hoot's direction. He figured to give the Caliente and its owners their own seven years of bad luck.

Now, four years into his plan, how sweet it was, stealing from the Caliente. Couple of times, Hoot had even lowered his sights to skin the odd horse or cow—that sort of high jinx was best left to lowlifes—just to foul the Caliente's stretch of the Nueces. He'd been drunk on each of those occasions.

He'd been drunk when his man Peña burned Wilson's house to the ground. Got lucky. The brush didn't catch afire. Wouldn't have been no fun, watching cows or land go to blazes.

Hoot believed a bandit ought to have a code, and stick to it, but Peña turned out too deep into tequila to listen. Well, the results were good, even if the fire was downright shameful. Drake Wilson did go. Ran like a spooked rabbit, which brought a speck of satisfaction in itself. But not enough. Hoot figured to keep Jon Marc O'Brien dangling for three more years.

After those years were up, look out, O'Brien!

Which was why Hoot didn't drink anything stronger than milk nowadays.

Hoot reared his chair back on two of its legs. "O'Brien is shore gonna get his."

"Do it." Terecita stood and raked fingers through her cat's-ass black hair. "I will get you another glass of milk, *chico*. Drink it, have a siesta, then plan your attack."

"Got it planned."

"What is it?"

"That's for me to know and you to worry about."

Terecita rolled her black eyes.

"Don't gimme that look, girl. I know what you're after. I know you want me to put O'Brien in his grave."

"You know me well."

Too well. Hoot was sick to death of Terecita. She was like a sore that festered, always coming around to bother him, even when he'd been doing hard time in Huntsville. Of course, he hadn't complained, even though it took cheating a prison guard in a game of monte to get her smuggled into his cell. Well, pussy was pussy, and a tom too long away from the prowl . . .

Didn't take too long for Terecita to accuse him of getting her in the family way. What rot. Sure, his remaining eye matched the color of Sabrina's pair of eyes, but hell. Terecita had been letting light-eyed men into her cabbage patch since she first sprouted cabbage.

Well, anyways, Hoot sort of liked her little girl, when Sabrina wasn't nagging for oranges. He did his best not to get close to the girl, though. Getting tight with anyone didn't appeal to Hoot. *You get close, you get hurt.*

Terecita, always the nagger, butted into his thoughts. "When will you make Juan Marc suffer?"

"Never did understand what you saw in that skinny bastard. His face ain't good for nothing but scaring crows. 'Sides, he'd never give no Meskin girl the time of day, much less a good screwin'. You know that, from your days at La Barca Puta in Laredo. When you couldn't even pay him to lift your skirts."

She got one of *those* glares and tugged up the bodice of her low-cut peasant blouse. "I would take a stiletto to him."

"Go get me that milk."

She whirled away, the hems of her red skirt swishing.

Good—he was shut of Terecita. Hoot had thinking to do. It wasn't about his plans. As he'd told the Mexican harlot who passed herself off as a dancer, he knew what to do.

He just wished he could blow his nose.

Since he couldn't, he considered how to use O'Brien's woman to an advantage. He'd been smart, letting her think him dumb about that Elizabeth/Bethany business.

Hoot Todd had a long memory. As if it were yesterday, he recalled his stepmother. Naomi Todd had been a pretty thing, not but a trio of years older than Hoot himself. Came from a good family, not that it did her much good, since she got disowned for marrying beneath herself. Cletus and his child bride had been like a couple of kids, in love and happy. When Cletus suggested they try ranching in the Indian Territory, though, she'd been fretful enough to turn over a pint-sized velvet sack filled with sparkling jewels to her stepson "for safekeeping."

He still had those baubles.

The saddest day of his life had been when the Kiowas lifted Naomi's scalp. Even now, sixteen years later, he still got an ache in his chest. She'd been good to him.

Baking lemon pies, mending holey socks, laughing at a young man's piss-poor jokes. Trusting him with her worldly goods. He'd loved her, dammit. Loved her with a youth's unrequited fire, but most of all, he'd adored her because she'd been good to him.

The day after she died, he left home to join the U.S. Cavalry, ending up here in La Salle County. Rings, brooches, and reasons for joining the Army were neither here nor there. That Beth who planned to hitch up with O'Brien was a dead ringer for Naomi Todd.

Didn't that pop the corn? "I bet they're one and the same," he muttered, "O'Brien's Beth and my sister."

Hoot wasn't up to revenge, but he could damn sure sit a horse to Austin. He had some grave-searching to do.

# Chapter Ten

In the three days that went by after Hoot Todd got divested of his tar, Jon Marc noticed a change in Beth. Little things. She was freer with herself, which pleased him. Her gaze met his, steady and straight, though occasionally wary. Every once in a while she even laughed. But not often.

Mostly she acted edgy, as if she feared her betrothed, at least Jon Marc decided as much, then pegged her trepidations on that set-to with Todd. Refined ladies didn't like brawls. Of course, they also didn't climb trees at midnight. He grinned, enjoying the idea of her climbing that tree.

In the kitchen, where Beth wore a bibbed apron over her britches and was in the process of making pot cheese this afternoon, he said to her, "Wish I didn't have to leave you here alone while the boys and I herd cows to Laredo."

"Do what you must. Strike while the iron is hot, as blacksmiths say."

"Sure you don't want me to ask Isabel to stay with you?"

"I'll be fine by myself."

Stubborn woman. What good would it do to insist on

company? What he wanted was a good-bye kiss, since he
kept remembering, and grinning, about the night of the
tree.

Wouldn't ask for a kiss; no, he wouldn't. In spite of
warming up a mite, she'd probably prefer to kiss a pig.

"You needn't worry about Todd." If Jon Marc didn't
have it on good authority Hoot Todd had ridden north—
Sabrina had said so—he would have insisted Beth make
the Laredo trip with him and the rest of the outfit. "He's
left the county."

"That's good." She laid aside cheesecloth, and got a
strange look in her face. Gazing down into the bowl that
captured the liquid from pot cheese, she said, "Something's been bothering me. What did you do to put Mr.
Todd's eye out?"

How easy it would be to whitewash the truth, but Jon
Marc wouldn't. He picked up a pecan and cracked the
nut's shell in his palm. "I carved it out."

After a visible flinch she again hooked cheesecloth above
the bowl and squeezed curds. "Why?"

"He had it coming. He'd been stealing horses, causing
general havoc. No law around here, Wilson and I rode up
to San Antonio, got in cahoots with the sheriff. The three
of us laid a trap on the banks of the San Antonio River.
Todd almost got out of it. But he didn't. It was his gun
against my knife."

"What happened to your gun?"

"The fight wasn't going my way."

"Would you have killed him?" she asked, her face pale
as she abandoned her work.

Jon Marc rejected a snap answer that would sting Beth's
tender sensibilities. On the other hand, he'd done enough
lying. "If it came down to it, I'd take his life."

Beth wiped her hands on a hem of the apron. "Have
you ever killed anyone?"

Several, none of which Jon Marc could take pride in,
not even when he'd taken out the murdering pirate who

would have added to his list of victims in the form of
Captain Burke O'Brien and his wife, Susan.

Jon Marc sidestepped a lengthy discourse on family.
"That's a cruel question to a fellow who's been to war."

"It is, was. Forgive me." Beth hurried to him, halting
an arm's length away. "Some things are better left unsaid."

Just as Jon Marc started to agree, Padre Miguel walked
up to the flap window. "Good day, my children," he said,
in the magnanimous way of priests.

The padre entered the kitchen, Jon Marc introduced
him, and they engaged in three-way chitchat that went
pretty well, since Beth, in person, didn't seem to mind the
"foreign" priest.

The padre, a medium-sized fellow of forty, folded his
arms level with the rope belt of his cassock, and muffed
his hands under the coarse brown material of its sleeves.
He asked, "When should I expect to hear your vows as
man and wife?"

Beth glanced at Jon Marc, her expression blank.

"We haven't set a date," Jon Marc answered, his conscience kicking in. *You need to 'fess up.* Wouldn't do it, not
until the Laredo trip was over. No way would he not be
around to keep her here, should she try to bolt.

"You will, you will set a date." Padre Miguel smiled, and
from the twinkle in his eyes, Jon Marc suspected a crafty
mind atoil. It came as no surprise when the cleric hinted,
"How nice it would be, having piano music to accompany
your vows."

"Yeah, well, who would play it?" Jon Marc came back.
Ever since Beth's grand piano arrived in La Salle County,
the priest had been on a campaign to get it moved to Santa
María. "My lady can't play for her own wedding."

That was when she bumped her hand against the pot-
liquor bowl, sending it crashing to the kitchen's dirt floor.
Both Jon Marc and Beth bent to clean up the mess.

As they finished, Padre Miguel eyed Beth's shoes and
lit a cigar. "Terecita López is a pianist. Her grandfather,

the grandee who owned Hacienda del Sol, hired a tutor to train her.''

Jon Marc tossed a dirty rag into a refuse can. "She was six years old when the *don* headed south, taking his piano and leaving his son's family to their own devices. Not likely Terecita is a virtuoso."

"A little practice, and I'm sure she would do fine."

"No way." Jon Marc infused an adamant tone. "No way."

"As you wish, my son." The priest took the opportunity to admonish, "I am disappointed you two did not attend Mass today."

"I had cheese to make." Beth set another crockery bowl under the dripping cheese. "Isabel milked cows Thursday, had more than she could use, and if I hadn't done something with that clabbered milk, it would have wasted."

Funny, Jon Marc had never heard anyone out of the southland use the word clabber. Probably picked it up from him, or somewhere between the state line and here.

"It is a sin to waste food, Señorita Buchanan, but it is also sin to neglect the church."

Her eyes blazed with defiance. "If I burn in hell for making cheese rather than prayers, so be it."

This, out of a former novice? Jon Marc would have chuckled, if not for the audacity of it. Beth was a Catholic of a different breed than he'd met in La Salle County, his past association with those of the faith being nil. Everyone here lived in fear of making a move against the church. Maybe Anglo Catholics were different.

Beth was different, no doubt about that. Last Friday, when she'd served roast beef instead of fish, and he'd been shocked by it, she'd scoffed, saying, "Jon Marc O'Brien, I don't like fish. Especially smoked fish. It's religious rot, decreeing we eat fish on Fridays."

Yes, Beth was different.

* * *

Bethany's eyes scoured the area around Fort Ewell's post office, the morning after the padre's visit. Having ridden to town with Jon Marc, to meet a mule train of supplies, she hoped they wouldn't run into God's man in La Salle County.

It was difficult enough, dealing with the religious issue without having Jon Marc present for it.

Bethany's program to be herself hadn't hit snags, but in the aftermath of that business with Hoot Todd, she had big reservations about Jon Marc O'Brien.

*The cowpoke who rode the Nueces, broke a nose in many places; for no more than a cuss, he made a big fuss; Then his lady . . . well! he again showed no saving graces.*

She'd bet each and every walleyed fishy monster hanging in the smokehouse that Jon Marc would be a holy terror, once he learned Bethany profaned everything he believed in.

Awkward position to be in, wanting to become a man's wife, yet fearful of it at the same time.

Soon, though, and it looked like tomorrow, Jon Marc and his vaqueros would leave for Laredo. She looked forward to his absence. Time was what she needed to gather her wits and plans.

"What all do you want?" Jon Marc asked, once they had reached the trio of supply wagons.

"Sugar. Lemons. Lard. Honey, if available. Do you have cinnamon sticks?"

"Got ever'thing but lemons, little lady." The wagon master spat a stream of tobacco juice to the ground. "You got the money, I got the stuff."

"We have the money," Jon Marc answered, yet Bethany worried about spending too much of it.

Worry, she did, yet something made her bold. "Do you carry shoes, sir?"

"A few," the wagon master replied, while Jon Marc looked aghast.

"These shoes are worn out." She wrenched a smile.

He winked. "Get some new ones."

This just might be her lucky day!

The purveyor marched to the rear of the train, Bethany went past big-eared mules, and caught sight of a woman approaching. She had a lot of hair. Black hair. Wearing a white peasant blouse and a mulberry skirt embroidered with braid, she swayed hips as she walked. Dollar to a peanut, that was Terecita López.

Bethany guessed correctly.

Eyes as dark and as cold as a winter's night glared, first at Jon Marc, then at Bethany. Terecita's hands went to hips; she tossed her head. "You!" She addressed Bethany. "Do you think I cannot clothe my child?"

"Now, Terecita," Jon Marc tried to placate her. "Don't get your dander up."

"Shut up, skinny *pelirrojo*. I do not speak to you."

Bethany didn't like having Jon Marc called skinny or a redhead; it seemed too personal. She also didn't like Terecita López. Yet she understood the dancer's bruised pride. Mothers sought to take care of their children, on their own, if possible.

"Meant no offense, giving the blouse," she said to Sabrina's mother. "I like your daughter. And I have extra clothes."

Bethany believed Miss Buchanan's estate should be shared, and felt that the unfortunate beauty would agree. Thus, she had been tailoring several outfits. The biggest task would be cutting down a winter coat. If luck held, she'd have it finished by winter and would be around to help small arms into it. Never having known what it felt like to wear a coat, Bethany would take a vicarious delight in its warmth.

"Would you allow Sabrina to accept a few pieces of clothes?" she asked.

"Lópezes do not take charity!"

Understandable. If memory served correctly, Terecita sprang from a grandee forced into Mexico. The rich, even when they'd gotten poor, still had their standards. Bethany knew that much from living in Liberal.

Too bad for Terecita.

Sabrina needed clothes. If Bethany could provide them, she would. "Señorita López, I intend to give your daughter gifts from time to time. Best you don't find a problem with that."

"I do find a problem!" Terecita took a step forward, getting way too close to Bethany's face for comfort. "Stay away from my child."

Jon Marc stepped between the two women. "There won't be any more gifts."

Didn't he have a nerve, taking Terecita's side? Bethany called him on it, once the dancer huffed away.

"I didn't appreciate that," she said.

"Look, Beth. Sabrina isn't your responsibility. Let her mother take care of her."

*She's my niece, and I will see to her needs!* That, of course, couldn't get said. How could Bethany get it across to Jon Marc, what it was like to do without the necessities of life?

Opportunity slipped away. The postmaster, his dog staggering at his side, approached. Liam Short had a suspicious glint in his gray eyes.

Padre Miguel hadn't shown up to cause trouble, but this visit to Fort Ewell might end up a complete failure, anyhow.

Despite the joy of owning brown, high-top shoes.

"I fail to see what that's got to do with anything," Jon Marc said to the postmaster, while Beth took her leave to speak with the wagon master.

Liam scratched his beard. "Them eyes ain't blue. She ain't played that pianer, ya said so yourself. Have ya heared any poetry outta her?"

"Mind your own business."

"Ya oughta check up on your gal, is what I be sayin'."

Jon Marc turned his back and went to load supplies into the buckboard. Yet it nagged him, Liam's reminders of the inconsistencies between Beth and what her letters had conveyed.

Several things nagged him. Religion. Like why that López girl was so important to her. Like why poverty scared her. The Buchanans had fallen on hard luck, but that luck hadn't lasted long enough to shatter a lady's outlook. Had it?

Could be, Jon Marc should go with Liam's advice.

Jon Marc and his vaqueros pulled out for Laredo, Bethany's reminder to buy orange saplings going with them. She blew out a sigh of relief that had to have reverberated south into Mexico. Last night, and again this morning, he'd asked nosy questions.

He suspected her—she felt it in her bones.

Her plan wasn't going well, not at all. She might yearn for Mighty Duke, might respect Jon Marc, might want all he could offer, but Bethany was getting nowhere.

Even burning those red shoes didn't cheer her.

She considered deserting the Caliente, a clear lane of retreat at hand. She could take off with Arlene—was it thievery to steal a gift?—and be gone before Jon Marc's return from Laredo. Excellent idea. Her troubles would be over.

Where would she go? What would she do? And could she really say good-bye, without a fight, to the Caliente and its soft-eyed owner with his shock of old-penny hair?

As the days passed, she found herself wanting to share inconsequential tidbits with the absent Jon Marc. Strange, how she missed moss-bearded trees and dew on leaves of green. Every bite she put in her mouth, she wondered what he would think of the dish. She pined for conversation, even if it meant the unenviable game of being herself yet a different woman entirely.

Besides, if she left, she wouldn't be able to keep an eye on Sabrina, who grew more precious as each day passed.

During it all, chores kept a lonely woman busy. And she worked on Sabrina's coat.

With Isabel's help, Bethany dug a shallow trench from a branch of the Nueces and planted vegetable seeds, where they would get excellent sun but not so much to burn leaves.

Most of all, whenever the bell tolled for Mass, she made certain to be there. It didn't take much to ape the motions made by the worshipers, and Bethany began to get comfortable with the strange ways of Catholicism.

Seeing the error of her ways from that day in the kitchen, she made it a point at church to be cordial to the padre. Padre Miguel was a nice enough man, when he wasn't making broad suggestions about Jon Marc's piano.

That monster ought to go to the church. But Bethany was in no position to give anything away. Thus, Bethany kept Padre Miguel's hints at bay.

And, at last, two weeks after his departure, Jon Marc returned.

# Chapter Eleven

Just at dusk's onset, Bethany saw Jon Marc and heard the ping of spur rowels as he entered the stables, where she was currying Arlene. She dropped the currycomb in her delight.

"I bear a gift," he said first thing, then tossed his hat to the floor and set a sack on a ledge. "Peppermint candies."

She loved peppermint, but would have preferred to taste his lips instead. He looked tired, yet good to her, standing in chaps and gun belt, vest and bandanna over britches and shirt as black as the devil's heart.

He held out his arms; Bethany flew into his embrace. He smelled of horse, sun, sweat. Nothing had ever smelled better to her—it felt good to be there. Forever it seemed, she'd wanted him to touch her, as a man greeted his woman.

Yet he didn't kiss her.

"Why don't you kiss me?" she asked, bold as brass, all Bethany, purely Bethany Todd.

"I'm not sure you'd welcome me."

Her palms flattened against his vest. "What sort of invitation are you waiting for?"

"Guess that's enough."

His lips parted. Yet he said an odd thing. "Don't you dare say anything about my nose getting in the way."

"That wasn't what I was thinking. I like your nose."

Startled, he dropped his arms. "You do?"

"I certainly do," she reassured him, suspecting his reticence about a wedding date. She'd done little or nothing to express her feelings. It was time for honesty. "You couldn't look better to me." She took his hands and placed them where they belonged, at the small of her back. "I would've told you when first we met, if it had been the proper thing to say."

A smile, broad with relief, lit his face. "I wish you had, honey. I do wish you had said something, 'cause I've died a thousand deaths, thinking you couldn't stand the looks of my mug. Guess I'm touchy about this ugly face and honker of a nose."

She touched the side of the member in question. "You know what they say—" *Don't get carried away, girl. Remember you're Miss Buchanan.* Bethany style, but still a Buchanan.

"What do they say?"

"Oh, Jon Marc!" At a time like this, what else could a girl say but: "Just kiss me."

He did.

Peppermint lingered on his lips—he'd been sampling the gift, undoubtedly. But he didn't sample her lips, not deeply. That was disappointing, even though she hated tongue-kissing, or at least she used to hate it, when Oscar forced his tongue past her tonsils on its foray to her toenails. This was a chaste kiss, as one should expect from a man of innocence.

The time for innocence had passed. "I read in a book about a kiss that employs the kissers' tongues." True. She had read such in a contemporary English novel on the shelves at the Frye residence. "It was a naughty book. Are you shocked?"

A flush of red crept above Jon Marc's shirt collar. "I've read a few banned books, myself."

"Do you ever think about doing that with me?" She smiled hesitantly. "You know . . ."

"You mean like this?" That was when he yanked her to him. His lips covered hers. There was nothing chaste about the way he moved his mouth, or the way he tangled tongues.

Theirs was a spiritual blending, as different from Oscar's invasions as rotgut was from cognac. Too soon it was over.

"Thank you, ma'am."

"Jon Marc, is that usually done? Thanks after a kiss?"

"Will be in terms of me and you."

Her eyelids felt heavy, her cheeks warm, she murmured, "You kiss as though you're a man of experience. Not a tentative thing about you, sir."

"I can cut the mustard."

She considered his statement's full import. He wasn't suave, like a knave in Liberal, but Bethany knew enough about men to sense his potential.

*He claimed to be a virgin, never tasting wicked sin, but when he chomped the wedding meal, his lady gave a squeal—"Milord willna cut the cheese, but he sure can cut the mustard!"*

That sort of thinking had to stop.

The practical seemed neutral ground, so she asked, "Did you get my orange trees?"

"Yep. Better not plant 'em till winter, though."

Would she be here, when cold weather rolled in?

He tweaked her chin, unaware of the pain that went through her limbs at the thought of not being here in winter.

His head tilted toward her neck. "You smell like vanilla."

With a forced chipper tone, she replied, "A dab or two of vanilla, why, sir, it's almost as good as French perfume, don't you think?"

"You don't need anything to smell good."

Taking the liberty of cuddling just a little bit closer to his strong chest, she said, "I bet you'll find something to like in the crock in the kitchen cupboard. I've been baking. Cookies. Do you like cookies?"

His eyes rounded in bemusement as he held her away. "I told you in a letter how much I enjoy cookies."

Probably one of those missing ones. "Jon Marc, how can you expect me to remember every line you wrote?"

His fingers squeezed her waist. "Arrogant of me, assuming you would."

Her fingers trailed to the curls at his nape. Such warm skin. She felt a ripple of excitement as it fluttered through his veins. Or were they her own?

She stroked his cheek. It felt good to her touch, those dips and crags. He both surprised and delighted her when his mouth moved against her palm, his lips touching the center of it.

Yet he stepped back. "Beth, over in Laredo, I ran into a fellow—an acquaintance of Aaron Buchanan's. In case you don't know it, your father bragged on you. He did some bragging to that rancher, too. Aaron told him you play beautiful piano. 'Like Chopin.' How come you never play the piano for me?"

Oh, dear. The monster. Rather than look Jon Marc in the eye, she turned to Arlene's stall and stroked the mare's shoulder. It wasn't that Bethany lacked appreciation for the big, beautiful beast that hogged the parlor, sitting like a too-large rider in a too-small saddle.

She simply couldn't play it.

It seemed as if she need lie not only about Miss Buchanan, but also about her father, too. "It was Father's pipe dream, that I could play. He paid for lessons. But I never learned."

Bethany steeled herself for the worst from Jon Marc.

* * *

Jon Marc studied Beth. Silence as heavy as a certain grand piano settled through the stable. He rubbed his mouth. Not halfway to Laredo, he had abandoned the idea of checking on Beth Buchanan. It just didn't seem right, such an investigation. It reminded him too much of Daniel O'Brien's ways.

Yet Jon Marc suspected Beth had something to hide.

Hadn't she 'fessed up about the piano? *And when are you going to be honest?* Not at the moment. Not when the issue of Aaron Buchanan's scruples hung in question. Beth's father had been one of the most respected men in Wichita. Why did he fib about his daughter's aptitude at the piano, unless he was ashamed of her lack of talents?

He said, "I figured Aaron Buchanan for an honest man."

"For pity's sake, you didn't know him that well. A couple of dinners and a business exchange do not a friendship make."

"Reckon not." Jon Marc watched her knit fingers and rub one thumb with the other. "Strikes me funny," he said, "Aaron not dwelling on your talents as a poetess." *Can you blame him? Well, you bragged on her, why wouldn't Aaron?* It wasn't awful poetry, it just wasn't great. Nothing to be ashamed of. "You do speak three languages. If I had a daughter, I'd center on her strengths and keep my trap shut about her weaknesses."

"You would. You being you. But you aren't he." Prying her fingers apart, Beth said, "I can't answer for Aaron Buchanan. Nor should I be called to task for his words."

"True." He decided not to dwell on Aaron Buchanan, or on that too grand piano.

Besides, it was happiness he felt, not only with a successful drive to Laredo behind him. Beth had assured him that his looks didn't revolt her. They had shared a deep kiss, one that still tingled his veins. A few more kisses like that, and his hands would be everywhere, not to mention other things aching to be other places. What he and Beth needed to do was make plans for the future, and not tarry.

Which meant honesty on his part.

Somehow he couldn't imagine *ever* admitting to a certain situation that arose in Laredo. Curious about that French phrase Beth had used, he'd repeated it to a sister at the church, a native of France. Must have recalled it wrong, very wrong. The nun's face had turned chalky, then she slapped him. Hard.

He now heard a rustle of paper but chose to ignore it.

"Why don't we stop by the kitchen, pick up those cookies, then retire to the parlor?" he suggested. "I'll read you some poems I picked up in Laredo." *Then I'll lay my heart open and plead for a chance to take your hand.*

"No more moss-bearded trees. No more dew on the leaves." Beth, her skirts swaying gently, crossed to him. Planting both hands on his shoulders, she reached on tiptoes to look him in the eye. "Where exactly do we stand, sir?"

Before he could suggest they head straight for the parlor, she said, "If you've read those naughty novels, you may be under the impression men are expected to perform at a, um, certain level. Are you . . . are you afraid of our wedding night?"

He almost swallowed his tongue. Quite an evening, this one. In that Beth had read bawdy literature might mean she had a wild streak in her. Climbing that tree spoke volumes. The more he thought about it, the more he liked the idea of wild romps with an even wilder woman.

His voice an octave lower than normal, he asked, "What do you expect out of my performance?"

"Kisses. Caresses. I don't know the rest, beyond those novels. Somehow I couldn't lose myself in the prose. I should imagine gentleness and respect would go a lot further in pleasing a woman than some of that mad frolicking about."

Well, hell. So much for wild romps.

"You'll get kissed and caressed. All with the utmost respect." He cupped her jaw between his palms, trying to show integrity. "You have my word on that."

"Sir, what *exactly* have you done in your limited experience?"

He shook his head in exasperation. "You're a single-sighted gal when you get something on your mind."

"I'm single-sighted. Curious, too."

The moment of reckoning upon him, he let his hands fall away from her smooth face. He paced. Ran fingers through his hair. From the stable's far side, he admitted, "You need to know something. I have gone beyond the proper with a widow."

"Went how far?" Bethany asked, her voice quiet.

"I can handle our situation, when the time is right." He retreated to the corner, folded into it, and rested a forearm on a bent knee.

Beth followed him. Hands on her hips, she canted downward, her hair drifting toward his mouth. "Tell me something, Jon Marc. Did you thank that widow lady?"

"You're making this hard for me." Hell, even though Beth did reject carnal romps, his nerves were springing like a pond full of frogs on a summer night, his rod getting harder and harder. He wanted to put some novel ideas to jumping.

Her eyes were squarely on him. "Did you save yourself?"

The tips of her hair brushed the top of his hand. How could he think at a moment like this? Confessing seemed secondary to seducing Beth out of her questions.

"How improper did you get with that widow?" Beth demanded to know.

His eyelids heavy, he brushed a fingertip across her bottom lip. "I'd prefer to show you."

"That's not the talk of a proper gentleman," she chided. "How many of those books did you read? Or did that widow tutor you to the best of her abilities?"

"Gracious, honey."

A crunching sound drew their attention. It came from Arlene. Quick investigation uncovered the mare, helping herself to the gift sack of peppermints. Her long tongue darted out to lap a pink-stained muzzle, before she eyed the gift-giver as if to ask for "more, please."

Her antics drew chuckles from the onlookers. Beth stood straight and said, "So much for your present."

"True." He had something better to give her, anyhow. A wedding present. To go along with the ring that he would keep hidden until the marriage ceremony.

Arlene might have broken the tension between the humans, but it didn't last.

Beth proceeded to park fists at her waist. "Tell me true, sir. *Did* you save yourself?"

No longer could he put off the inevitable.

"My late mother didn't set a good example—her willful behavior brought tragedy. Much grief. I vowed not to take a bride like Georgia Morgan." He paused. "Women like my mother tear their families up. She did ours."

"What . . . exactly are you trying to say?"

"That I insist on a virgin bride. Because of Georgia Morgan. She's why I was particular about choosing you."

"You demand a virgin, yet you haven't been celibate?"

"That, uh, about sums it up."

Dropping her gaze to the floor and hugging her arms, Beth shook with what had to be disgust.

"I'm sorry," he whispered. "I'll never do anything sinful again. And if you'll forgive me, I'll spend the rest of our lives making up for my lapse."

"Help yourself to the cookies, sir. Good night."

"Beth, listen—"

"Don't, Jon Marc. Just don't!"

She rushed into the night; he lunged to his feet to chase after her. Up to the house and into the bedroom, she hurried. The door closed in his face, and he knew in his heart why. She needed distance, else his tarnish would rub off on her.

Give her the evening to recover from shock, he decided. *Don't push a lady in a direction she doesn't want to go.*

He had plenty to keep busy with, to train his thoughts from trouble, although he'd prefer to stay and placate his sweetheart. Couldn't. León being winded from the Laredo trip, Jon Marc saddled a fresh horse, then swung laden saddlebags over the stallion, yet his mind was too occupied to stay off Beth.

If she could get past his confession, surely the rest of his admissions, would be child's play.

*If* Beth could get past Jon Marc's sins.

He'd never get past her sins. Would never forgive and forget. Jon Marc didn't have it in him to understand.

Bethany dragged in huge gulps of air, as if she'd been running instead of listening to a man's insistence on purity. She paced the bedroom floor, up and down, up and down. Didn't he have good reason for insistence? Undoubtedly it had taken much for him to dredge up the hurts of yesteryears.

"If I hadn't been such a coward," Bethany said, as if to Miss Buchanan, "I would've dug in my heels and done something to show my support. But, no. All I could think about was myself."

What kind of woman didn't succor her man in time of need?

*All you do is run. First from Liberal, now from Jon Marc. You can't keep running, Bethany Todd. Be brave. He needs you.*

It took a while to find him. It meant changing into riding clothes and setting out by moonlight in a direction given by Luis de la Garza: to a limestone hill called Roca Blanca.

At last, she found man and mount. The stallion's reins ground-tethered, Jon Marc used a shovel to dig into the rocky ground at the foot of the hill.

"Jon Marc!" Bethany called out. "I must talk with you." Her voice echoed through the night.

Night riding wasn't a favorite of Hoot Todd's, thanks to his limited vision, but he'd set out to follow that tart who called herself Beth Buchanan. Near to lost her, his right-hand man being about as useful for tracking as a Pekinese dog.

But her voice calling to O'Brien was like a beacon, drawing Hoot and Peña in its direction. What in tarnation was she doing at this hour of the night, at Roca Blanca?

Since she shouted for O'Brien, no doubt she'd followed him here. There was only one explanation, as near as Hoot could figure, why that pair was skulking around in the dark. O'Brien had to be burying the money he'd gotten in Laredo.

Well, O'Brien would need it, since Hoot and his men had waylaid the Caliente outfit on their return from Rockport.

"Don't that just pop corn?" he said to Peña. Chuckling—the action aggravated his half-healed nose—Hoot sat straighter in the saddle. "Now I've got two things in my favor. I know what O'Brien does with his money, and I know for damned sure he ain't fixing to marry no Beth Buchanan."

"*¿Mi jefe?*" That growl, calling for his boss's attention, hung heavy in the night air. "Do we steal the money now?"

"Naw. No need to steal it. I'll just get my little sister to give it to me. Be more fun that way."

# Chapter Twelve

" 'She walks in beauty like the night—of cloudless climes and starry skies—and all that's best of dark and bright . . . meets in her aspect and her eyes.' "

Such poetry on Jon Marc's lips, well, that particular passage wasn't half bad, yet Bethany sensed he meant to butter her up. After all, he did consider her chaste, and he had admitted to cavorting with some widow.

By stars above, he set down the shovel and extended a gloved hand, palm up, to beckon Bethany forward. A little butter went a long way, as if he needed it, desperate as she was for peace.

She wound around chaparral, there being no trail here, and went to him, but stopped short of his arms.

"You fit those words," he whispered above cricket creaks.

Jon Marc's compliment seeped through Bethany, causing a bittersweet smile to boost her lips. How she wished she could have come to him, pure. Unsullied. Meeting his expectations.

"Beth, can I take your following me as a good sign? Can you see past my mistake in judgment?"

"To err is human."

He slipped off his gloves and took her hand between his roughened fingers. "Will you forgive me for lying?"

"Let not your heart be troubled. By anything. Jon Marc, I came out here for a reason. Your mother hurt you, and I want you to know—I want to help you over it. Talk to me."

"Not here. Let's get back to the house."

"Why not here?" The cloak of night might help, should Bethany say more than she ought to.

"Can't chance Hoot Todd finding us. He'll be after our money, Beth, if he knows where to look. Let me finish burying these bills in the strongbox, then we'll ride back home."

As he shoved earth and rocks over the small iron safe, she asked, "Why don't you keep your cash in a bank?"

"Todd works the road between here and San Antonio. I'd hate to have to kill him over a few thousand dollars."

She didn't take those words lightly, his threat sending chills down her spine. *Don't make too much of it. His was big talk, not a serious threat.*

And they had serious talking to do.


A half hour or so later Jon Marc and Beth reached their adobe home.

Still dressed in riding clothes, they settled into the parlor, Jon Marc taking the armchair and Bethany the settee. Neither made a move to light the lamp. He sure wouldn't. Relieved he might be over her acceptance, he had more admissions to make, none of which would be easy.

"Tell me about your family," she prompted, her face lit by the glow of moonlight that beamed through an open window. "Tell me everything."

"I'm a bastard."

She laughed, the sound tinny. "Don't be ridiculous, sir. You are anything but a scoundrel."

"I mean literally a bastard." Bastardy being the next thing to felony in these modern times, Jon Marc fixed his gaze on the ceiling support beams. "My mother may have been married at the time of my birth, but a devil named Marcus Johnson sired me."

"Don't you keep whiskey in here?" Beth thumped the ebonized cabinet. "How about a glass of something stiff?"

"Don't spare the horses," he answered dryly.

Beth poured generous portions.

Lord, did it feel good going down. It gave Dutch courage to tell about scandal, death, and being rebuffed. "Georgia Morgan took up with Johnson again, around the time I turned six. She figured to desert her sons—even Johnson's get—and take off with him. Daniel O'Brien put a stop to that."

"How awful that must have been."

"Not as bad as witnessing the final argument between my mother and her husband. When he killed her." Eyes slammed closed, yet visions of blood and death remained. "The next day Daniel took me with him to Johnson's house. Figured to pawn me off on my blood father. He turned the gun on himself. Blew his brains out." Jon Marc downed the dregs. "I saw it happen."

"Poor darling," Beth whispered, her sympathetic tone downplaying the platitude. Rising from the settee, she refilled his glass; handing it to him, she curled at his feet. "What happened to Marcus Johnson. Did he not do anything to aid you?"

"Turns out Johnson wasn't planning to take Georgia Morgan anywhere. He moved on, even before the smoke had cleared."

"How could he do that to his own son?"

"Apparently with ease. Leastwise, he was out to save his neck, since he might've gotten blamed for Daniel's death."

Beth rested a cheek against Jon Marc's knee. "How awful your childhood must have been."

"It had its good moments." He stroked Beth's head idly. "Daniel's father took us in, me and Connor and Burke. Daniel's sisters raised us." Contrary to the pain of recounting the doomed triangle of his mother and her men, Jon Marc felt a smile lifting his facial muscles. "Tessa and Phoebe never favored any of us. We were all the same in their eyes."

"Then why do you never open their letters?"

"Ah, ha." He tugged on Beth's ear, not feeling anywhere near as jovial as his light reprimand, when he added, "Better not let me catch you going through my things."

"I'm red-handed. I saw unopened letters from a Tessa Jinnings and a Phoebe Throckmorton. I wondered who they were."

"Now you know. I suppose you read Pippin's letters?"

"Seems he's your nephew."

"Yes. Pippin's a good boy. Reckon someday he'll visit."

"What about the aunts? And your brothers? What about your, well, your grandfather?"

"It's best they stay on the Mississippi. I like it that way."

"Why?"

He told her everything, save for the magic lamp that seemed too ludicrous to bring into such a serious discussion. He brought up the alienation from his half brothers; from Connor, who'd never been close; from Burke, who resented Jon Marc's interference with Rufus West. "Burke pins a pet name on everyone. He even got Connor to calling me 'Jones.' When I was little, I assumed I got that name 'cause I had no right to O'Brien. Was thirteen before Burke set me straight."

"How straight? Tell, Jon Marc. I want to know."

"It was just a corruption of Jon. That's all. Made me feel a damn—darn—sight better, knowing the truth."

"Are you doing the same thing now, making too much of your brother's stance toward you?"

Jon Marc assumed that if any O'Brien, save for Pippin, thought of him at all, they did it with disappointment. Each seemed to demand more than he could give.

"I would like for them to think kindly toward me, but I can live without what passes for family. Had twelve years alone. Whatever's left to me, I can take the same way."

"I think there's more to it than what you've told me. You wouldn't have left Memphis, simply because you and your brothers didn't see eye to eye."

"You got that right, honey."

He next told her about the rift between him and Fitz, ending with, "Up to the moment he tossed me out of his home, I thought he cared for me. Like I was his grandson. But he drew himself up—no mean feat, considering his rheumatism—and rattled his old silver-handled cane. His eyes were like pieces of marble, they were so cold.

"'Ye're wet behind the ears, laddie,'" Jon Marc mimicked in his best impersonation of the immigrant O'Brien. "'Why would I be wantin' t' give me company t' ye? 'Twill rightly go t' Connor. And if he willna have it, Burke will take Fitz & Son, Factors.'"

"But they didn't?"

"They didn't. Connor had an army career, early on. Burke's been a steamboat baron since he turned eighteen. There's no one to take the factor house, not until Fitz's great-grandsons are grown, which won't be for a goodly number of years. It's doubtful Fitz will live to see the day. How 'bout another shot of whiskey?"

Beth poured; Jon Marc guzzled.

He spoke in a voice that began as a rough whisper but evened into a monotone. "Fitz may have sent a scared kid into the cold of night, yet he thought I'd forget all that. I can't."

Beth put her hand over his. "Would you like to be close with the other O'Briens?"

"I tried." Jon Marc scooted out of the chair to sit on the floor next to Beth. He slid his arm around her shoulder, hugging her with a closeness that asked for understanding, not carnal promise. "When Connor's wife needed help to get out of the mess I'd made for them, I had no interest in seeing anyone named O'Brien again. You see, I'd undermined Connor and India, although I didn't know it at the time. India—she's Connor's wife—ended up being court-martialed. Phoebe—nobody's fool, that one—figured out I played a part in the intrigue. She sent a letter, begging me to help. I gave a deposition. Lost my cover as a Confederate spy over the incident."

Beth said not a word on the subject.

"He's got a nice wife, Connor," Jon Marc allowed. "Once the war was over, India discovered I was living here at the Caliente." Her sister, Persia Glennie, had been the one to tell India where to find him. That came after Jon Marc attended a poetry recital in San Antonio, where the now-departed Tim Glennie served as reader. "Then India asked me to visit their plantation in Louisiana. Guess I was lonesome. I went."

"What happened?"

"I landed in a hornet's nest. Made the mistake of stopping in New Orleans to call on Burke, is what I did. Had thoughts of mending fences with him, too. Instead, I got involved in his problems. That came to a bad end. I tried to save Burke's hide, and his wife's, by shooting the man who would've killed them. Burke wanted his own revenge."

Beth tensed. "You shot a man for your family?"

"Like I once told you, I protect what's mine. The O'Briens aren't, but I didn't stop to think. Anyhow, Burke is my brother. Blood tells, you know. Even if it's Georgia Morgan's."

Beth got quiet, very quiet.

In this far, Jon Marc wanted the rest of it out. He must mention how he couldn't be free of them, since Tessa and her genie played a part in getting Beth here on his past birthday.

But she asked, "Why do you read Pippin's letters?"

"I'm fond of the boy."

"You need children of your own."

"Do you *want* children, Beth honey?" Frankly, Jon Marc was relieved at the chance to talk about the present, not the past. Her ways with Sabrina recalled, he suspected she'd make a willing mother. He would find out for sure. "From your letters I think you see motherhood as wifely duty."

"You are wrong. Beth Buchanan may have felt that way in Kansas, but I don't. It's a woman's prerogative to change her mind, you know. I want children. Several. I wouldn't mind adopting a needy child. But I mostly want your children." She laughed gently, then teased, "And they better all have hair like old pennies, or we're sending them back with the stork!"

A smile jacked up Jon Marc's face. "Then I guess we'd better do some serious talking with the padre."


Bethany awoke by dawn's light, cuddled on the floor with Jon Marc! The drinks must have gotten to them last night. Not a minute after he suggested talking with Padre Miguel, he had dozed off. She, too, had closed her eyes. And here they were.

Still, Jon Marc slept. She leaned up on an elbow to gaze into his remarkable face. He appeared younger, innocence itself. Yet he'd known suffering and heartache, disappointment and rejection. He needed a woman devoted to giving him a family to be proud of. A family who would be proud of him.

Beth brushed hair from his brow. *I'll be twice the wife you'd have gotten with Miss Buchanan, who would've preferred the veil.*

"I love you," she whispered from the bottom of her heart.

* * *

Had he heard right? Was that Beth whispering love? Or was this just a dream? Surely a dream, surely. Beth, smelling like vanilla, all cuddled up close. He disliked vanilla. But he did like Beth. She was soft where he was hard. Very hard. Hair tickled his nose; a breast, his midsection. Wonderful dream. Jon Marc snaked out a hand . . . and got an armload of woman.

That was when he opened his eyes.

This was Beth, dewy-eyed and mussed and smiling. She was a dream come true. Comely, diligent, never afraid of a challenge. Perfect for the Caliente. And for Jon Marc.

"Kiss me," was what she said.

He tightened his arms around her shapely form, his hands crossing over her back to cup her behind and bring it closer to the hardest part of him. His lips met hers, soft at first. Then with more insistence. Hands were everywhere, both his and hers. He moved his lips to her cheek, to her eyelid, to her ear.

He uttered a sweet nothing into that flesh-hued shell. The devil made him nip her earlobe; she didn't complain. In fact Beth grasped the hair of his head, keeping him at his task.

"You might claim not to want any of those book frolics, but I think you lie," he murmured and traced the tip of his tongue down the column of her throat.

"I lie."

"Well, ma'am, I'm glad about that."

# Chapter Thirteen

"Then do it—have your way with me," Bethany whispered, her entreaty defying the silent voice that begged for reason.

"Do you think I play tiddlywinks?" Jon Marc, growling a chuckle, blew a stream of breath across her collarbone that sent her to more shivers of expectation.

Her laugh sounded near to a giggle. "Don't stop."

Yet he listened to his own silent voice. He stilled, here on the parlor floor. His mouth stretched taut, his eyes closing, his grip lessening on her hips. "I must . . . I promised—"

"Hush," she whispered, not wanting to think what might happen after this was over. "Don't deny what we want."

"Crazed foolishness, woman. But . . ."

His fingers set her shirt buttons free, his lips trailing to the rise of her breast. Drunk with need, she pulled material away, baring one mound to his gaze. A strong browned hand circled the fullness as his lips descended.

Goose bumps rose on her flesh when his stubbled face tickled tender skin. She bowed toward the juncture of his groin, as he gave full attention to the aching need in that breast. She yearned to give everything to the man she loved.

Her hand pressed his head to his task. "Yes," she hissed through clinched teeth. "Feels so good."

And he wanted her. She knew it, even before he guided her leg over his hip. Full and ready for her, Mighty Duke pressed her inner thigh, nudging in the rhythm of lovemaking. A smile wide with desirous contemplation hovered on her lips.

Yet honor got the best of him. He rolled to his back and rubbed a palm down lips white with control. "Promised to treat you with the utmost respect. Gotta get you to the padre."

What he said had reason to it. *I don't want reason!* But it had to prevail. That didn't make it any easier for Bethany, stopping short of fulfillment, but she, too, must collect her wits. "We . . . ? Shall we discuss wedding plans?"

"I've got a brick between my legs." He was breathing hard. "Can't think, much less talk."

"What do you suggest we do?"

"Don't know about you, but I'd best get myself to the river for a quick cooling off."

He jackknifed to his feet, but bent over to press a kiss to her forehead. "Thank you, honey."

He loped outside the cabin.

"I love you, *querido,*" she whispered to his shadow. "You peculiar mixture of rascal and gentleman, I do love you."

She rolled into a ball, hoping to retain his lingering warmth. Dear Jon Marc. Her darling. Her beloved. A man much maligned by life. He deserved better than a woman of experience. But a woman of experience was his destiny.

"I'm tired of lying," she bemoaned to parlor walls. "But if I don't lie, I'll hurt him."

How much could she tell, without wounding him?

\* \* \*

Bethany took care of her toilette, then went to the kitchen, where Isabel was preparing a breakfast of *huevos rancheros,* fried eggs with a slathering of tomato-and-jalapeño relish. A sample proved to hold enough hot peppers to turn a mouth inside out, even Bethany's.

As she set the worktable with cutlery, Jon Marc strode indoors. In dry clothes, his hair damp.

He ordered the quiet servant to leave, which she did.

Pouring coffee, Bethany swept her free hand to indicate he should sit down. She stole a peek at his expression, wondering if he, too, were thinking about their moments in the parlor.

"There's more," he clipped out.

"Excuse me?"

Their past intimacy, and breakfast, got ignored.

"Before I get down on my knee and ask you properly to become my wife, you need to know everything," he said.

Sitting down, she studied his strained expression. "Are you guilty of a crime?" She tried to prepare for the worst, yet had too much faith in him to expect an affirmative reply.

"I'm no criminal. You just need to know what needs to be known about me."

"Maybe you ought to keep some things to yourself," she suggested. "I've heard it said that marriage is better, if you keep a part of yourself a mystery."

"Secrets lead to trouble."

This wasn't what she needed to hear. But she'd decided to be as honest as possible. "I have something to confess."

He shoved his plate to the middle of the table. "What would it be?"

"I don't like poetry."

His coffee-brown eyes grew puzzled, a muscle in his jaw

twitching. "How so? How can you write poetry, yet dislike it?"

Bethany was tired of lying, but what else could she do but pose a scenario that she would have employed, had she been a talentless Miss Buchanan? "I knew you had an appreciation for rhymes. So I paid a schoolteacher to write them. They were pretty awful, I thought. But anything was better than nothing."

The laugh that heaved his chest brought with it a shake of head. "Those poems won't be remembered as classic."

"Are you . . ." She swallowed. "Are you disappointed?"

"A mite. But if that's all you need to confess, you can breathe easier. I can, too."

If she'd believed in prayer, she'd have given one in thanks for his temperament, but how far would good humor stretch?

He reached for his coffee cup, asking over the rim of it, "What about the day I overheard you speaking with Sabrina? You had a rhyme on your lips."

"Verses with odd twists appeal to me," she replied, never more honestly.

"Does this mean you don't enjoy *hearing* great poetry?"

She laced fingers on her lap, aligned her shoulders with forthrightness, and eyed him with as much dignity as she could muster. "I have no rapport with pastoral prose."

His features showed a myriad of emotions. "I'll be doggone."

"Jon Marc, I am not the woman who wrote all those nice things in letters. I have defrauded you. And I have lied to you. I am not the Beth Buchanan you sent for."

There. It was out. Bethany felt better. Arguably, she'd told the truth. Vagueries didn't express the whole truth, of course, but he could never say she hadn't warned him.

He reached across the table to caress her cheek with the back of his knuckles. "Honey, you've overlooked my sins. I'm willing to overlook a few white lies."

That was the best she could hope for. Now, if he'd only overlook the rest . . .

He gazed across the table at the lady he would marry. Luck and planning brought her here. He, a man too often ill blessed, counted himself lucky for her forgiving heart.

*Beth isn't a poetess.* Jon Marc found it odd, trying to reconcile to that news, but, as he'd said, he'd look past it. After all, her aversion to poetry, and her prevarications along that line, didn't compare to his wild romps with Persia Glennie.

*It almost got wild this morning.*

His eyes went to the swell of Beth's bosom, a surge of desire hitting his sensitive places. How good she'd tasted. How good she'd looked to him. How superb she'd made him feel, once he got a sample of her passion. Yes, he was one lucky fellow.

His head spinning with anticipation of the rest of their lives, he quit the chair, walked around the table, then went down on a knee to take her hand. Looking up into long-lashed eyes, he asked, "Beth, will you be my bride?"

"Yes. Oh, yes!" She smiled, with worry? "When?"

"As soon as Padre Miguel will marry us." Jon Marc folded her into his arms.

They kissed deeply, lustfully. His veins afire for more, he didn't want to stop, but smarts—and a sense of honor—had a word with desire. Wouldn't it be better if they consummated their union in a fitting manner?

*You didn't tell her about Tessa and the genie.*

Later.

Jon Marc and Beth were headed for the church.

Bethany and her bridegroom set out on León and Arlene for Santa María Church. Neither figured vows could be read without banns, unless the old ones would do. Thus, they were dressed in riding attire. Halfway to Fort Ewell, they crossed paths with a rider on a broad-beamed mount, the codger Liam Short.

His odd-looking dog—Bethany seemed to recall it answered to Stumpy—slumped between Liam's lap and the saddle horn. The dog wagged a tail and, head up, barked.

Reins in one hand, waving an envelope in the other, Liam brought the chestnut to a halt in front of Jon Marc and Bethany. "This here letter be for you, son. Fitz O'Brien done wrote you."

Bethany glanced at Jon Marc. He blanched. Turned white as writing paper.

*Just what he needs, reminders of his uncaring family.*

If she'd had her if's, she would have snatched that document out of the old man's hands and torn it to bits before Jon Marc could be hurt by the contents. Not that he'd open it. But its presence caused pain, and his pain was hers.

Recovered from the shock, Jon Marc said, "Funny, your delivering mail, Liam. Got a case of nosiness?"

"Got business with ya." The oldster tipped his hat at Bethany, while the snaggletoothed mutt lolled his tongue, panting over the warm day, no doubt. "How doin', ma'am? When's the weddun?"

Bethany didn't trust him, and felt the feeling mutual.

"We're on our way to talk with Padre Miguel," Jon Marc answered.

He and Liam were friends; she wanted amity with the postmaster. "We won't send written invitations, Mr. Short, but please know we want you in attendance."

Jon Marc added: "Will you be my best man, Liam?"

"Nice of ya to ask, but I ain't never set foot in that Meskin church, and don't intend to. Thank ya, anyways."

Bethany fretted over the look of disappointment on her man's face. *He's too easily hurt.*

Three-legged dog listing to starboard, Liam righted the

mutt, patted Stumpy's head with reassurance, then said to Jon Marc, "Coupla vaqueros come into the post office, 'round noon. Said old Hoot is roarin' to get ya, 'cause you landed him a good one. He's back. Vowing to make you suffer this time."

"Let him try. He's got one more eye to lose."

The postmaster scraped a fingernail into his beard. "Your boys is gone for the most part, don't forget."

"They'll be back soon. Even if Catfish and the vaqueros are delayed, I'm not worried about the likes of Hoot Todd."

Easy for him that might be, but Bethany didn't feel quite as confident. Hoot Todd might leave something to be desired as a brother and neighbor—or as a human being!—but she disliked the idea of his tangling with Jon Marc.

She didn't want anyone or anything causing trouble. *That's not all, girl. You know there's more.* Jon Marc's streak of violence disturbed her. He had killed for his brother. For some odd reason she didn't want him to kill hers.

"Thanks for bringing the letter," Jon Marc said facetiously, took it out of Liam's hand, and shoved it past his vest and into a shirt pocket. "You're a real pal."

He kneed León and motioned for Bethany to follow in their charted course. They rode in silence toward Fort Ewell. Before reaching the town, Bethany could hold her tongue no longer. "Are you going to ignore Fitz O'Brien's letter?"

"Yes."

She brought Arlene to a halt, calling to Jon Marc's back, "I am not going another foot until you can walk into church with a smile on your face."


Jon Marc found a good spot on the ground, on the riverbank. How could he smile, what with that letter in his pocket? Nonetheless, he sat down, next to Beth.

"Read the letter," she ordered, softly yet insistently.

"No."

"There could be important news. Someone could be sick. Could have died."

"I doubt it."

"You don't know for sure."

"I know what's in it. Nosiness. Nosiness about our marriage, and probably another plea for me to return to Memphis." Turning his face toward hers, Jon Marc scowled. "You see, a few months ago, I wrote Fitz as well as the aunties. I told them to stay back while I got myself a bride."

"Jon Marc O'Brien, you confound me. You claim to ignore your family, yet you told them about me? Wait. Did you write to the boy, Pippin? Is that how they knew to begin with?"

"They've known about you for years."

She appeared confused. "You need to help me here, sir."

He should. And got worried. What if something had happened to Tessa or Phoebe, or one of the others? He plucked the letter from his pocket, wanting to tear it in half and toss the pieces to the sky. He handed it to Beth instead. "Read it."

Beth scanned the contents. "Fitz O'Brien is on his way for a visit. Doesn't say when to expect him."

Jon Marc rolled his eyes. "They promised not to interfere."

"Doesn't say anything about 'they.' It says, 'Make up the spare bed. I'm on my way.'"

Jon Marc uttered a foul oath, silently, saying aloud as if to himself, "Just couldn't leave well enough alone, could he? Just had to know what April twenty-first brought me."

Beth slipped the folded piece of paper back in its envelope. "Don't get upset. We'll simply offer a night's accommodations, then send him on his way."

"He'll put up a fight."

"It's two against one." She grinned impishly. "If he gives us any trouble, we'll just steal his cane."

"Steal his cane?" Jon Marc knew she was making light to quash tension. It worked. He laughed, feeling good for the first time since Liam delivered the mail. He'd found a fine woman. An excellent bride. Reaching to hug her shoulders, he said, "How the dickens did I live thirty years without you?"

They went on to the church, visited with Padre Miguel, and learned the previous banns were still in place. Jon Marc suggested vows be exchanged the next day, Beth agreed, and the padre said, "Be here at two in the afternoon."

Knowing it was bad luck for the bridegroom to catch sight of his lady before they reached the altar, Jon Marc arranged for Isabel Marin to spend the night with Beth at Rancho Caliente. The groom would put up in town, where he could collect items for a special wedding repast, with intentions to surprise his lady.

Before he tied his bedroll to León's saddle, he decided he had to speak, one more time, with Beth. With Fitz advancing, he *must* tell her about the magic lamp.

Before Fitz did it for him.

If the old man arrived. Chances were good he couldn't make such a long trip at his age. He'd turn back, sure as shootin'. Jon Marc came to a decision. No more would he worry about, or even think of, a visit from his supposed grandfather.

The machinations of a magic lamp needed to be told, though. More sure than shootin'.

Beth having retired already to the bedroom, he knocked on the door. Light spilled from a single lantern when she answered in a green wrapper. Gracious, how she did look good to him, black hair flowing below her shoulders, her face scrubbed to a glow, a minimum of clothes outlining her curvaceous body.

He almost forgot his purpose, but she reminded him of it, saying, "Don't tell me. There's more."

"There's more."

She swept a hand to indicate the bed that he intended to make love to her in, tomorrow night. Or tomorrow afternoon, if he got his if's. Jon Marc wandered over and sat down on the edge. She sat next to him. She smelled like lavender soap.

Soap was not the issue.

"Beth, do you believe in magic?"

# Chapter Fourteen

"Do I believe in magic?" Jon Marc's odd question was even more confusing than his vague references of this afternoon. Bethany answered, "When I look in your eyes, when you hold me in your arms, when you're your sweet self, it's magic."

"I'll grant it's magic I feel when I gaze at you, and during the other. But . . ." Roosted on the bed's edge, Jon Marc rested forearms on thighs, and dropped his hands toward the floor. "I'm talking about magic lamps."

Had he been tippling? She leaned toward him, but didn't catch fumes. Besides, he didn't appear drunk. She knew the signs. "No, Jon Marc. I don't believe in magic lamps."

"One brought you to me." He tipped his jaw toward her. "My aunt Tessa made a wish on a lamp. Three wishes, forsooth. Brides for nephews. Each to meet his lady on his thirtieth birthday. Connor got India. Burke got Susan. And I got you."

Poppy juice. That had to be it. "Any Chinese peddlers been running the Old Spanish Trail?"

"Beg your pardon?"

"It's laudanum. Where did you get it? Jon Marc, if this is why you've been strange here lately, it's good this came out before we wed. You must straighten up. I won't have a man who depends on invisible crutches, not with my father the way—"

She'd almost slipped. Well, if Jon Marc had a penchant for things of a nature to twist his mind, she'd have to leave, love or no love. *You won't leave. You love him enough to see him through any crisis. Just stand beside him through triumphs and tragedies, girl. No matter what his weaknesses may be.*

"Beth, I don't take medicinals."

"I think you'd better explain yourself."

Jon Marc squinted up at the ceiling rafters. "Tessa bought a lamp in France, when she and Phoebe were touring the Continent. The summer of '60. The lamp came with a genie. He's pretty much an ordinary fellow, except for the gold earring and tooth. She's married to him now."

This did not inspire confidence. *"Querido,* what makes you think the lamp and its 'genie' are real?"

*"Querido,"* her darling repeated. "I like that."

"Jon . . . Marc!"

"All right, all right." He waved a hand. "My brothers met their brides on their birthdays. And you arrived on mine. It's as simple as that."

"No. You *sent* for your bride. You made certain she'd arrive on the twenty-first of April. That wasn't happenstance. It was planning."

"I did plan. Once I knew about Tessa's wish—After I saw the trouble my half brother's got into with mere luck, and fighting it—I made up my mind to find the perfect bride, beforehand, and have you here at the proper moment." His hand, cooler than usual, settled over knuckles that seemed to have no warmth in them, thanks to her shock. "Beth, I wasn't going to take any chances on luck."

Worry began to yank at her. What were the implications?

He continued to speak. "I knew what I wanted in a wife. You were right for me. Magic is the reason I was set on not meeting you till my birthday."

Bethany felt as if she were being dragged behind a runaway wagon. "Did . . . did it have to be Beth *Buchanan?*" Her voice had a squeak to it, which she worked to even out. "Did your aunt have some sort of crystal ball? Did she see a Kansas girl? Did initials float through the air?"

"She just asked for a bride. Apparently the magic picks the nearest available candidate and goes from there."

What a relief! But, thinking on it, Beth realized that if—a large *if*—magic ordained Miss Buchanan for the post, it would have gone awry at the poor angel's death.

What if she hadn't succumbed? The real Beth, pious as she'd been, would have been outraged. It probably would have sent her flying to that veil. After all, it was un-Christian, believing in hocus-pocus. Even Bethany knew that.

She said, "You've confessed all this to Padre Miguel?"

"Why should I? It's not a sin, it's a miracle. Nothing's better than a good Catholic miracle."

Good Catholic miracle?

Bethany raked hair behind her ears, nervous as a whore in church, as Pa used to say. But Padre Miguel had told her about the Lady of Guadalupe and the miracles she'd done for Mexico. Maybe there was something to that magic business, and maybe not. Probably not. Whatever the case, Jon Marc believed in magic. What rot out of a seemingly sane fellow.

*There once lived a gal named Bethany; just before she would wed came an epiphany: he sounded right as rain, but how he did feign! The cowpoke wasn't sane, 'twas plain to see.*

Nevertheless, Bethany allowed a moment of her own lunacy. If there was such a thing as bending fate, a person could do many things with magic. It boggled the mind to think about it. But she could think of a few things she'd ask for, boggled though she was. Peace in La Salle County.

Security of purse. Another maidenhead wouldn't be bad, either.

"Any chance Fitz will have that lamp with him?" she asked.

"Not a chance."

"What a shame."

More than anything, she could have used that maidenhead.


Quite a few minutes after two the next afternoon, Liam Short snuck into the narthex of the simple Mexican church. He took off his hat, because that was the sort of thing his mama would have slapped off, had she been around. Mama being three decades with her Maker, Liam still remembered to be respectful, even though it had been thirty years since he'd entered a house of worship. He hadn't planned to be here today. But he was.

Before the mailbag arrived, Liam decided to take Jon Marc up on his offer to be best man, even if it meant going into Santa María. Friends did for friends. But it was too late for standing up. It was also too late to stop the wedding.

That preacher was deep into intoning a foreign tongue. Didn't sound Mexican. The bride and groom knelt before him at the altar, she in a lace mantilla borrowed from Isabel Marin and an ivory gown, he in Sunday best. Their guests sat behind them. Wives and children of the Caliente vaqueros on their way to Rockport. Sabrina. The orphans, Manuel and Ramón. Spiffed up like he was going to a dance, Luis sat next to the boys.

Isabel, crying into a scrap of cloth, served as matron-of-honor, or whatever one called it in a foreign church like this. Luis's partner, Diego Novio, was doing what Jon Marc had asked Liam to do: he stood up for the groom.

The preacher raised a robed arm, said a few words to Jon Marc, then did the same with Beth. They started praying, then did that thing Mexicans did whenever they reckoned they were in deep shit: touched their foreheads and chests with fingertips.

*Well, son, you are in deep shit.*

"You may kiss your bride," the priest said in English.

Beth appeared to be shaking. Jon Marc looked proud, flushed with triumph, as he swooped down to sweep his new wife into a kiss that could have blistered varnish.

*Damn dumb cowboy, no smarter than that horse of his. He didn't know he'd gotten sold a bill of goods.*

Best he never knew, Liam decided. It was too late for sense-talking. Too late to stop a wedding that should never have taken place.

Liam Short had done what Jon Marc didn't. He'd sent word to a friend in the telegraph office in San Antonio. Just minutes ago, word had arrived from Kansas: Beth Buchanan had blue eyes, and there was no disputing it.

Torn up like he was, Jon Marc might lose his head, should he find out his new missus couldn't be that Kansas girl.

*The moment has passed for anything but well wishes.*

Married.

At last.

Mrs. Jon Marc O'Brien.

The day finally began to draw to an end. Bethany didn't know whether she was more overwhelmed by the gravity of becoming a wife, or if having been too nervous to eat beforehand had given her such a light-headed feeling during the ceremony. Something strange had happened in the Church of Santa María.

Even now, as she waited for her husband to round the buckboard parked in front of their home, she still felt unsteady.

*You lied to God, girl. If there's a hell, you're going to burn in it.*

Her golden wedding band, filigreed with leaves and

hearts, captured a ray of sunlight when she moved nervous hands. Never before had a ring graced Bethany's finger, yet this one felt comfortable, as if she were born to wear it. Incongruous, her feelings of right laced with wrong.

"Mrs. O'Brien?" Jon Marc's voice rolled tenderly, yet holding ultimate promise.

He was happy, anyone could see it. His tanned face showing high spirits, his eyes dancing, he slipped one hand under her knees, the other around her ribs. A rush went through Bethany at his touch, the rush quickening when she laced her arms around his neck, and detected the scent of bay rum mixed with the particular scent of her new husband.

As if he were lifting no more than a feather, he carried her, but not into the house. They ended up on Harmony Hill, under a pecan tree, where the sun dangled low in the blue sky to the west. A thick blanket spread on a bed of leaves, a picnic of sorts had already been laid.

Tequila awaited them—sliced limes, and a cellar of precious salt. As well, a hamper held slivers of ham and hard cheese, delicacies. Sitting, then reclining, they ate their fill, stopping to kiss between bites that they fed each other. They toasted their marriage, although Bethany remained unsettled by their trip to the church.

*You've got enough to worry about without adding the gravity of religion to it.*

"I brought you out here, 'cause I've heard ladies like this sort of thing," he murmured. "Do you like it?"

"I most certainly do."

Finishing her second shot of tequila, she smiled at Jon Marc. The Mexican liquor, along with the promise of completion to the act that would finish uniting them forever and ever as one, had loosened him up. His hair was ruffled, his coat gone, and the top two buttons of his shirt undone.

She yearned to touch the flesh at the V of that shirt.

As if he could read her mind, he took her fingers and pressed them to his warm skin. The gaze that had unnerved her at the beginning now soldered to her eyes, and she loved it.

"This is the heart that beats for you, dear wife."

He'd never declared love; she wished he would. Deep in her heart, she believed he loved her. His actions spoke the language of love.

Yet he levered from a prone position, scooting over to brace against the pecan trunk. Reaching for her hand, he settled her between his legs, her spine at his middle. What she'd wanted, for what seemed like forever, was solidly at her back. It felt good, so good, to be here.

She nestled her head against his shoulder. "I love you, Jon Marc."

"I know." He brought her palm to his lips and kissed it gently. "Why else would you take a stray brush popper like me, unless it was for love?"

She would have preferred an avowal of love, but who was she to have preferences? If they got past tonight, she would know he loved her, would never need a reassurance of it.

"And now we are one." He kissed her ear. "Forever."

She touched a tentative hand to his shaven cheek. "There's nothing to stop us, not tonight."

"That's right. Nothing."

He slipped his hand to her breast, kneading it gently and evoking a murmur of delight from Bethany.

"I don't know quite where to start with you," he uttered.

"You're doing just fine." Yet she found herself unsure about what they should do next, as well. Both had done this sort of thing before, but apparently Jon Marc hadn't done it a lot. And she'd just as well not repeat her past experiences.

"Could you start like you did with that widow?" Bethany asked shyly.

His hand went still. "Beth honey, will you do me a favor? Would you not throw that up to me? Ever? What we have is between me and you, no one else. I'd like to keep it that way."

"I was simply trying to help," she said, albeit she had no interest in having his mind on the widow, when his hands were on his wife.

"You can help by telling me what you'd like to do," he said. "To start with."

"How would I know?" How should she know? With Oscar, it had been his call, each and every time. *Don't think about him.* How could she not? He didn't compare to Jon Marc, but it wasn't easy to forget the past. "The folks got right to it in those naughty books. But they didn't seem to be real, as far as I could tell. They didn't have much fullness of heart."

"True."

"Will you take me under this tree?"

"If you like."

She tilted around to look up at him, orange streaks of sunlight cutting a sky now turned turquoise. "What would you like?"

"I'd like for you to unbutton ... I'd like to see you naked. I'd like to be naked with you. Beth honey, getting married is new to us both. I don't want to rush you. I don't want to offend your modesty, either. You'll be better off, if we're in our bed. You might feel more comfortable in a nightgown. I-I've heard there's pain and blood."

Blood. This wasn't the first time she'd thought of that, but this was the first time Bethany worried about exactly what she'd say, when there wasn't any blood.

Rubbing her arm, he smoothed a thumb across her bottom lip. "I don't want you to wake up tomorrow with tears."

Did she ever not want to wake up with tears in her eyes! Not a half second later, they both heard hooves in the distance. By the time they got to their feet and straightened their clothes, each saw riders on the horizon.

"Catfish Abbott and the rest of my men," Jon Marc explained. "You know, he's my strawboss."

"Yes, your *segundo*."

"He's nephew to India O'Brien."

Jon Marc had basically a family member in his employ?

Eleven riders rode up, headed by a brown-eyed young man wearing a ten-gallon hat that he, as well as the other men, doffed. Catfish Abbott was dust-coated, his eyes tired, and the bracket at his mouth befitted an older man. Bethany would bet anything he brought news other than the successful completion of his drive to Rockport.

Jon Marc made introductions. Bethany noted from his expression that he wanted to ask what the devil had delayed them.

The brush poppers, an equally dusty lot of vaqueros still astride their horses, bade the new mistress of the Caliente a warm welcome, and best wishes to both on their marriage.

Jon Marc promised a hoedown with a proper *barbacoa*. "Soon as the wife and I settle in to married life, I'll call for guitars, we'll barbecue a steer, and drink plenty of tequila."

Several gazes moved downward, to the half-full bottle that lay on the blanket.

"Right now," Jon Marc tacked on, "I want y'all to go to your homes. Let your *señoras* and children welcome you there."

The vaqueros left, but not India's nephew.

Catfish Abbott, his lips grim, crossed gloved hands on the pommel. "Jones," he said, using the family nickname, "we ran into trouble. Got ambushed in Duval County. Hoot Todd and his cronies stole a sack of the Rockport money. Thank God I divided the money up, or he would've gotten it all."

Bethany had a sinking spell.

Fury, deep and hot, marked Jon Marc's face. His

clenched fists went white at the knuckles. "Anybody get hurt?"

"Nothing we didn't get over. Except for pride. We took a licking. Did you know someone broke Todd's nose?"

"I know. I did it. He'll wish he'd left well-enough alone, once I catch him." Jon Marc gritted his teeth. "I'll kill the son-of-a-bitch. I am going to get my rifle, saddle León, and find Todd. And kill him."

This was no idle threat, Bethany knew. A cold chill shook her despite the warmth of twilight. Marshaling nerve, she stepped over to her husband. "No, *querido*. No."

Catfish wiped a forearm across his brow. "I, uh, I'll be moseying on over to the stables to rub Arrow down. You decide what you want to do, Jones, you can find me at my place."

The strawboss reined his horse away from the pecan tree. The stallion descended Harmony Hill, his tail swishing, his rider hurrying him onward.

Jon Marc stood, eager to exact revenge.

*Don't let him leave. Do what you must to make the wedding bed a success. Make him so terribly happy that he won't put himself in peril with Hoot.*

She curled fingers on his forearm. "You have two choices, husband. Saddle up and ride out. Or you can stay. I want you to stay with me. In the morning, if you'd like, we can discuss how to get your money back."

"If I let Todd get away with it, he'll cause more trouble."

"Whatever means you employed in the past didn't work. What's wrong with taking a night to form a new plan?" She cozied up to what she expected to become a very hot iron. Matter of fact, Mighty Duke seemed to grow hotter from their close contact. "I can't stand the thought of anything happening to you."

Squinting, Jon Marc scratched his jaw. "That has the ring of ultimatum to it."

"I'm simply pointing out your choices." Bethany slid her palms up the solid bastion of his chest. "Earlier, you mentioned naked. I'm not opposed to that, if you give me enough time to get used to it.''

Her husband's hands splayed over her behind, pressing her to that heating iron. His voice a husky whisper, he said, ''Wife, you don't give a man much of a choice.''

# Chapter Fifteen

The bride began with a pale green nightgown that brought out the verdant hues in her eyes. Her bridegroom, having changed in the parlor for the sake of her modesty, chose his only nightshirt; it sported black-and-white stripes, much like a convict's pajamas. Truth was, Jon Marc didn't care about clothes, except how to get green cotton tossed aside.

Less than an hour had passed since Catfish brought bad news; thus, Jon Marc couldn't get shut of plans for vengeance against Hoot Todd, but as Beth had advised, tomorrow would be best for that. Why let Todd ruin a wedding night?

"I'll just, um, slip between the sheets," Beth said, her long-lashed eyes now shuttered as she pulled aside the coverlet.

He watched her climb into their marriage bed, his attention centered on the curve of her hip. He asked, "Shall I put out the lantern?"

"Only if it pleases you."

"It wouldn't please me."

"Of course it wouldn't." Beth brought the covers under her chin. "You're wanting nudity."

He winked, hoping to set her at ease. "It's a heckuva place to start, everything tucked in and shrouded."

"You don't mind giving me a little time to get used to this, do you?"

"I don't mind." What a lie! But he had to think of his wife's sensibilities. "Would it be rushing you"—he picked at one stripe—"if I took off this nightshirt?"

"Do I need to watch?"

"Only if you have a mind to."

She blushed, her lashes falling to half staff. "I've been admiring the looks of your legs and knees."

He glanced downward. This nightshirt didn't amount to much; it didn't cover knobby knees or the sprouts of red hair that grew on his shins and calves. "You makin' fun of me?"

"Not in the least." She grinned. "I've never seen a man's knees, save for yours. I like the looks of them."

He decided not to give her too much to gawk at, not yet, so he turned his back to shed stripes, then spread fingers across his tools to spare her reaction and slid between the sheets. The warmth of her side radiated to him, which he liked. A lot. A hint of vanilla wafted to him, yet he wouldn't tell her not to wear it again, that it was favored by the whores of Laredo.

He vowed to buy Beth a big bottle of French perfume, next time he went to town. If he crossed one, on his way to finding Todd—*Forget him. For now.*

Jon Marc thought about the gift he'd bought in Laredo. Should he give it to her right away? No. He'd wait until later, when they were in the afterglow of bonding their marriage.

Just before he started to cant to his side and kiss her, she said, "I lied. I've never seen your knees before."

His hand caressed her hip. "You do lie. Wicked woman, you climbed a tree to get a look at my legs."

"I wasn't looking at your legs."

"What were you gawking at, hm?" he teased, knowing full well she hadn't climbed that pecan to stare at the kitchen.

She gave a breathy little sigh as her fingers walked under the sheet and over to his most-male member. She stroked it gently. "This."

Immediately, it swelled. Damn shooting, Jon Marc had a wildcat for a wife. And she had a tiger by the . . .

Concerning male equipment, he had nothing to be ashamed of. He was as well-equipped as his brothers, if not better.

"So . . . what did you think?" he goaded, enjoying their intimate conversation.

" 'Tis a Mighty Duke, ain't no fluke."

"That rhymes."

Her eyes closed momentarily, then opened wide to gaze at him. "As I told you, I enjoy a twisted word or two."

"Let's hear another."

"I can't think of another."

He nudged his expanding rod against her palm. "Then . . . what are you thinking about?"

"How much I want you to kiss me."

"Think no more."

Jon Marc, tangling arms and legs with hers, pressed his lips to the heart-red mouth that had long intrigued him. Citrus from limes lingered on her tongue. Needing to feel her, yearning for more, he explored her spine. She didn't cry modesty when he inched her nightgown up the back of her legs.

Nor did she complain when he freed the ribbons attached to the nightgown's bodice. His teeth drew material aside. Her skin was translucent, beautifully clear with a faint network of blue veins that showed the delicacy of her flesh. No man's eyes had ever before feasted on these breasts, and the mere thought of that gave Jon Marc an even more urgent desire to mate with her.

His mouth sought the tan circle at the peak of one sizable breast. The circle, along with its pebbled heart, puckered against his tongue as he suckled deeply, as a babe would. What did she feel? Did her blood race, like his? Did she have a need to merge together in the primitive yet eternal act of joining?

Passionate she might be—her breath issued in short spurts of exultation; her fingers curled into his hair urging him onward—but he knew not to rush her.

With the greatest regret, he pulled his lips from her breast. Her eyes widened as if to ask why.

*Because the pump must be primed, honey love.* Thus, he set out to do that. "Gracious," he uttered and swept fingers to her flesh, "you have soft skin."

And she did. It was like cruising his hands on satin, as he canvassed a plump hip, a smooth thigh, and an even smoother inner thigh. His hand advanced to the thatch of hair at the crown of these legs. A middle finger delved deeper . . . caressed the nub, his massage bringing her hips off the mattress.

"What . . . what are you doing to me?" she cried.

"You don't like it? I'll stop. If you tell me to."

"Won't . . . tell you that."

"Didn't think you would." A grin pulled his mouth wide and flared his nostrils. His fingers slipped deeper into her moist femininity. Oh, Lord. Oh, saints above! She felt tight, wet, and hot. His—what had she called it? Mighty Duke?—was stiff enough to come apart at the seams, if it had seams. The urgency in his lower back demanded release.

Proud he might have been at the size of Old Duke, he wasn't proud, not at all, at his critical straits. Could he last through slow lovemaking?

No. He couldn't. Just couldn't.

Not like this.

"I need you, Beth. Now." He rocked her back to the mattress, swung atop her, fitting himself between her legs. His manhood nudged at its goal. "Open to me."

He felt her yield, a subtle lessening of tension. He thrust forward. She sheathed him. The muscles of her womanhood clasped him, squeezed him tightly.

His palms slid beneath her back, his fingertips meeting at her spine. He ached to surge forward, to press in to the hilt. Yet something stopped him. It wasn't a maidenhead. He wasn't a master at taking a woman's virginity, but he'd heard plenty of men talk about being the first with a woman. This was not a virgin.

"Goddammit to hell, you've been with another man."


"Pardon me if I don't say thank you."

Bethany ought to let his hurtful statement go. Couldn't. "If that's the way you feel, why did you spill your seed in me?"

Jon Marc didn't answer, not that she expected he would. His had been angry lovemaking, fired by accusations she couldn't deny, but didn't explain, even as he'd reached an explosive climax that his new wife had met with her own carnal release.

It had been her first.

At least he'd been first on that score. She now knew that what happened with Oscar—even though she'd thought it moderately satisfying—hadn't approached the intensity of making love with Jon Marc, even angry love, charged with hurt and disappointment on his part.

Not that he would appreciate hearing that.

While she made no attempt to straighten her nightgown, she did pull the covers up under her armpits. The musk of their mating clung to the sheets, the sting of sex still burning her insides, both reminders of his furious yet rousing assault.

She ached all over, but not from the act that had made them one forever. Every joint wrenched. Even her toenails hurt from destroying her husband. The biggest pain converged in her heart, where a solid block of smoldering coal burned.

Jon Marc, his face glum, continued to yank on clothes. Plopping down on the bed, as far from her as possible, he tugged on first one boot, then the other.

"Where are you going?" She feared for the future.

He eyed her in that disconcerting way of his. But for the first time, she saw a cold stare, not unlike the marbles he'd claimed to have seen in his supposed grandfather's eyes.

"I've slept under the stars every night." His voice was as cold as his eyes. "Why should tonight be different?"

"Because we're husband and wife."

He shook his head. "You are not the wife I expected."

"You've known that for a while."

"Not all of it."

"Do you want me to tell all?"

"Hell, no."

His language marked disrespect; perhaps she had it coming, but she would not be cowed by the past. "You're going to hear it. I was blackmailed into another man's bed. I had no choice, no money, nowhere to turn. I had to try to save my father. But he was beyond saving. Just as you had to kill that man who threatened Burke and Susan, I had to sacrifice for family."

"Bullshit." A tic beneath his right eye went along with a bearing of teeth. "Those red shoes should have warned me. A lot of things should have. You've whored yourself."

Bethany threw back the covers, pulled her nightgown down, and sat up. Afraid of losing him, she couldn't delight in his naked form. All she saw was a face filled with fury and disgust. " 'Thou who art without sin,' " she said, " 'cast the first stone.' "

He raked fingers through his hair, saying not a word.

"Jon Marc, I love you. I always will." *Don't bawl, girl!* "I'll do anything to make it up to you."

His upper lip curled. "Seems to me you do what needs

to be done, hang the consequences. No telling what you might do, left to your own devices.''

"That's unfair.''

"Don't talk to me about fair.'' Once more on his feet, he glared down at her. "Not in the same breath you speak of prostituting away what was rightfully mine.''

She could argue, could say she'd made a mistake to get involved with Oscar. If she had her Liberal days to live again, would she have done differently? Hindsight might be clear, but she'd loved Cletus Todd enough to sacrifice for him. With love came the willingness to sacrifice.

She had but one argument: "I wasn't yours at the time.''

"I don't wanna know whose you were, but your training speaks for itself.'' Leaning over, he braced palms on the mattress. "Repeat it. That French phrase you used once.''

Taken aback, ashamed to the pith of her being, Bethany uttered, "I don't remember.''

"Liar. Repeat it.''

*"Mange moi, mon chou."*

"That's exactly as I recall it,'' he said bitterly.

"I don't know what it means.''

"Likely story.'' His back to her, Jon Marc went over to a pair of britches that hung in the wardrobe. Pulling something from a pocket, he closed his fist around it. Swung around. Tossed the object. It landed on her lap.

A bracelet, it was.

"I believe it's customary for a man to leave a token after he's scr—That should be sufficient.'' On the crest of his words he stomped out of the bedroom.

Bethany glanced down at the burnt offering, tears stinging her eyes. Tri-colored gold, the bracelet had been fashioned into a braid of leaves and hearts. It matched her wedding band. He'd bought it with intent to honor his bride.

"Jon Marc,'' she moaned twice. "I have done you so wrong.''

Tucking the bracelet away, she never wanted to see it

again. But she must find her husband, must know his intentions. Rushing barefoot into the night, she stepped on one sticker after another; nothing kept her from his path.

She found her disenchanted husband at the river, throwing blanket and picnic leavings into the rushing water.

"Will you throw me away, too?" Bethany's voice carrying through the night air, like the mournful cry of a wounded animal.

# Chapter Sixteen

"Jon Marc?" Beth repeated, "Will you throw me away?"

He wanted to be done with her.

Yearned to toss her into the river.

He hungered to scream an "Argh!" to the night sky and ribbon his flesh with knife wounds, as the Comanches did at time of loss and grief.

Jon Marc longed never to see Beth Buchanan again. But she wasn't a miss. She was Mrs. O'Brien. In the eyes of God and the State of Texas. Having married in the Catholic Church, having been unable to stop himself from plunging into her body, time after time, they were bound. Until death did one of them in.

He squinted up at the stars, not wanting to look at the deceiver who was his wife. "Go away, Beth. Go back to bed."

"I-I can't."

"Dammit! Go, before I lose my temper."

"I can't," she repeated. "Not yet."

Then he would go. The night promising no sleep anyhow, why not collect his vaqueros to ride after Hoot Todd?

Jon Marc did an about-face, meaning to get the hell away from the riverbank. He stopped short. Beth had one knee bent, had a foot in her hand. Even in starlight, he could see blood. Blood that should have flowed in the marriage bed.

While he almost hated her at this moment, he couldn't watch her bleed and do nothing. "I'll help you."

"Thank you," she whispered.

He had no choice but to carry her to the house, where a lantern would light the chore of picking stickers from her feet. How different it was this afternoon, when he'd carried her to the river. Yet a damnable hunger for her still raged in his veins.

Sex and cheap vanilla clung to her nightgown. Before he'd stomped down here to get rid of picnic reminders, he'd poured the flavoring into the ground and tossed the bottle away. He never wanted to smell vanilla again, not as long as he lived.

Yet the demon within him cried out for more of what good sense told him to avoid. It caused him to hold her too closely, allowed mussed hair to tickle his nose. Let his rod stiffen anew.

Dammit.

He kicked open the parlor door, then deposited his wife on the settee. "Tweezers around here someplace," he muttered.

"In the drawer of the corner cabinet."

"What an organized little homemaker you are," he said snidely. "A place for everything, and everything in its place."

Georgia Morgan O'Brien, for all her proclivity for the forbidden, had kept a tight house. *History repeats itself.*

Jon Marc lit the lantern, then found the tweezers. Not resigned to the course of his life, he dropped down next to her—not too closely—and yanked a foot onto his lap. Yet he wasn't mean enough to wrest those stickers out of her feet. Gently as possible, he tugged one after another out of her flinching foot. Finished, he brought the other foot forward. This one wasn't a bad as the other. Nonetheless, she had a thorn deeply imbedded in her big toe. Just as he started to pluck it out, he noticed Beth's nightgown. It rode up sleek legs. This was the first time he'd ever seen them, really seen them.

The craving to run his tongue along that smooth flesh, to lave her knees . . . *Show her what that French phrase means!*

He wouldn't. Bending over his task, he tweezed the thorn out of her toe.

"Ouch!"

She jerked upward. The nightgown rode higher. The black triangle at the apex of her legs displayed itself.

He bit down on a groan.

"Thank you." She jerked the nightgown hem to her ankles.

"I'd better get some rags and wrap your feet," he said, his voice seeming to come from somewhere else.

"That's not necessary. I'll take care of myself from here on out. With your permission I'll retire to the bedroom."

"You're not going anywhere. Not on those feet. I'll get rags and soap, and whatever."

He left the parlor, collected supplies, and ducked into the bedroom to add a fresh nightgown to them. Returned to the parlor, he set a bucket of water on the floor in front of her. "Wash yourself. Wash yourself good. Get rid of the vanilla."

What his demon self wanted to do was watch her, but Jon Marc wouldn't. He turned his back. Heard the sounds of her toilette, later hearing her say, "I'm finished."

She'd even wrapped her feet. The nightgown, a flannel one too warm for this climate, was buttoned to the chin. She stood, but jerked when her bandaged feet made contact with the floor.

Pain greater than physical echoed in her voice as she whispered, "Good night, sir."

He knew bravado bore her out the door to the bedroom.

Slumped into the settee, he plunked elbows on his knees and rubbed his eyes with the heels of his hands. What a mess. What a damned mess. After all the trouble he'd gone to get a perfect bride, *this*. He laughed. Laughed and cried. What a chump he'd been, thinking he could do better than Connor and Burke had done. Thinking he might avoid the pitfalls of romance.

It was a curse, being the beneficiary of Tessa's well-meant wish on a magic lamp.

"What now?" Jon Marc said to himself, his gaze on the rafters. "What the hell do I do now?"

He couldn't have the marriage annulled, not after consummating it. He couldn't divorce her. The church would excommunicate him, and his soul would burn in hell. Nothing said he had to live with her, though. The rough part was, he didn't know if he could live without her.

Did he love her? He didn't rightly know. What was love, anyway? He'd never been in the vicinity of true love between a man and a woman. He did know he despised her. A poet once said that hate was but a spark from love.

"Forget love," he muttered to those rafters.

He'd expected her poetry and music to fill the air too often cracked by gunfire. All he'd heard were lies.

Yet he couldn't stop thinking about how she'd felt in his arms. When he'd realized she didn't have a maidenly shield, he'd wanted to pull out, thus saving a chance for an annulment. The hellion within him hadn't allowed it, not after Beth had pressed her breasts to his chest, then made green material seem to melt away. At the same moment she'd clutched him even tighter.

Damn.

Double damn!

*Your language is going to hell.*

He laughed insanely, knowing he'd reached the depths. Once more he was hard as a poker.

She was his wife. Why do without her? Why should he sit here, miserable, while Beth lay alone in *his* bed? Why not go to her? Why not take his fill of her, until she was out of his system? Didn't a wife have a duty to her husband?

"Don't push a woman where she doesn't want to go."

She'd pushed him further than he'd ever, ever intended to be pushed. "You owe me," he muttered, lowering his gaze to the open doorway. "If you turn your back on me, Beth O'Brien, I'll turn you off the Caliente."

That was when Jon Marc started shucking his clothes.

Too heartsick to cry, too pained to feel her brutalized feet, Bethany huddled in the sheets. How simple it seemed, before tonight, thinking she could bluff her way through a marriage bed.

*If he wants you to leave, you'll have to do it. You must.* Never to know his kisses again? Never to feel him inside her again? How could she leave? *No matter how badly you want to stay, you've got to think about Jon Marc for a change.*

He needed her.

Needed her to help him heal the wounds of the past.

No. She was simply another wound.

On the other hand, she would never do wrong by him. Not again. Oh, really? What about the rest of it? What about the fact she hadn't been Beth Buchanan to begin with?

"Beth . . . ?"

Jon Marc. What did he want? To turn her out in the night, as he'd been rejected in Memphis? Somehow, she would have to go, even if it meant walking away on these feet.

She swung toward the doorway. He stood there, night painting his body, his absolutely nude body, in silver relief. His staff protruded in full arousal.

Her pulse tripped wildly. Her womanly place stirred, went tight and moist, as if preparing for his entry. She wanted it. She would always want it.

But how long would he want her?

Well, she would be his for however long that might be. She lifted her fingers, offering whatever he desired.

"Get rid of the gown," he growled. "Take it off slowly."

She gathered up hems, easing them above her hips. His eyes followed her every motion. Her trembling fingers worked the buttons free, then she wadded the nightdress and dropped it over the side of the bed. By now he had walked toward her. How long would he stand there, taunting her, as her body ached for his?

The sinew and muscles of his lean frame captured her attention, her gaze then centering on his sex. His lovely long sex. His long, big sex. And then she saw it. A jagged scar that marked his abdomen, running parallel to his arousal. What had happened to him?

"I was gut-shot," he stated, reading her expression.

"When?"

"The war. Would've died, no doubt."

Bethany shuddered. A strange feeling, a terror lashed through her, as she considered how close he'd come to death. How awful her own life would be, if she'd never had the chance to meet him. No matter how their marriage turned out, she would never, ever regret whatever time Jon Marc allowed her.

"Thank God—" this was the first time she'd used such gratitude, she realized "—you're alive."

"I would've died. Was on the wrong side when Sherman burned his way to the sea. The magic lamp saved me. My aunt—Phoebe, that time—made a wish on the lantern. She wanted me to leave the war with my boots on. She got her wish."

That lamp. Did it have magical powers? Another quiver ran through Bethany, terrifying as well as intriguing her. She could not help but think of what a lamp like that could do. How could she get her hands on it, in order to make her own wish for forgiveness, acceptance, and happily ever after?

"Wanna know what I'd wish for?" he asked into the quiet. "I'd ask not to want this from you."

His knee dug into the mattress. As if climbing into the saddle, he swung a leg between hers. Then came his other leg. He levered above her, his elbows propped beneath her armpits. His thumbs hooked behind her ears, he lowered his lips to hers.

It was a kiss of fury, yet it eased into an embrace of desire that whetted her senses for more of him, even before his fingers trailed lower, his hands cupping her breasts.

"You're beautiful. Too beautiful. You let beauty ruin you." The pads of his thumbs circled her flesh. "It captivated me, watching you walk, and talk, and move about. Yet for all your beauty, you made this place a home. I can see you doing for me. And for Hoot's little girl. But how much of that is a lie?"

How could she form a lucid argument, when he was touching her thusly?

"Who else will you ruin, Beth?" he goaded while teasing the tightened peaks.

She must think, must speak. "I love you. You. Only."

At the same moment he squeezed her nipples, he lowered his head, trailing his lips to her navel. And lower. "Wh-what are you doing?" she asked, shocked at his exploration.

"Showing you what *mange-moi* means, like you don't know."

She tried to force his face away. Fingers clamped her wrists, holding them at her sides. Then she was beyond objecting. Scaling the walls of passion, she felt her heart beat in a savage staccato. Everything centered in the area that he flicked. Once more she reached the high point of ecstasy.

"Like what you asked for?" he goaded.

"Yes" came out in a hiss.

He moved upward to press his staff against that which he had teased. She writhed beneath him, out of her mind, as he surged upward again and again. Pleasure spasms radiated from where he lunged, rippling like white caps on a stormy lake.

Her legs wrapped around his back. He rode her hard. She reveled in it. In the second that pain met rapture, she bucked, crying out in her completion. Yet he wasn't finished with her. Still imbedded deeply, he sank his lips against her collarbone and nipped her, as a stallion would bite a mare.

She liked it.

She wanted to be marked as Jon Marc's.

Forever.

But, her passions afire as they had never before been aflame, she could take no more of quiescence. "If you would be a stallion, sir, I intend to ride you."

He went still for a moment, his eyes widening in the muted light. "What do you intend to do?"

Bethany shoved his shoulders, ushering him to his back. So as not to disturb their joining, she rolled with him. Atop him. Her hair a curtain to his chest, she bore down on his sex. Moaned. So filled, so filled. And then, as if she were on a race to the finish line, she gave it her all. Her womb convulsed once and then again. But Bethany never let go.

She needed control of her mount, lest Jon Marc ride away from her.

# Chapter Seventeen

Jon Marc rode from the Caliente before dawn. Without saying good-bye to Bethany. She hadn't figured he'd steal away like a thief in the night. But he had. Without listening to reason about vengeance against Hoot Todd.

At least he hadn't sent her away.

For that she could be glad.

She hugged her arms, trying to recall what it felt like to be enfolded in her husband's embrace. It just wasn't the same.

She supposed she should be thankful he hadn't left her alone at the Caliente. Isabel arrived, but Bethany, not wanting chatter or questions, asked her to go home, and stay there until sent for. Isabel left without argument.

After breakfast Catfish Abbott dropped by to say he would be "keeping an eye on the place."

Idly swinging a lariat, Catfish stood hatless in what served as the front yard.

The sun in her eyes, Bethany visored her brow with fingers. She took a long look at the mustachioed young man. Already she knew his age as twenty; Isabel had once mentioned it. His hair grew dark, the darkest of browns that matched his eyes, and curled to his shoulders. He was olive complected, not unlike many Mexicans around here.

She hobbled to the hitching post to lean against it, where the sun wouldn't interfere with her study of this ranch foreman who had links to the O'Brien family. Perhaps through Catfish, she could understand more about her husband.

"I'm told your aunt is married to Jon Marc's brother," she fished.

Catfish lassoed a pecan branch. "Yep."

"I believe her name is India."

"Yep."

This wasn't going to be easy. Bethany took a different tack. "Would you care for a cup of coffee?"

"No, ma'am. Got work to do. We got horses corralled down Salado Creek. Need to check on them."

"Surely that can wait awhile. You and I should get acquainted, since we're family now. I really do need to sit down. My feet, you see."

An eyebrow quirked as he wound the lariat into a circle. "Guess I could have one cuppa coffee."

He was kind enough to lend a shoulder to help her get to the kitchen. He did the pouring, too. They sat across the table from each other. Catfish didn't appear comfortable.

Bethany jumped in with nosiness. "Being strawboss of a ranch like the Caliente is a big job for a fellow your age."

He shrugged. "I've carried my weight since I was nine. Civil War, you see. Had to help my family run the plantation."

Having grown up in the Oklahoma Territory, before moving to Liberal, Bethany hadn't been touched much by the war, now seven years from the last battle. Of course, she'd seen soldiers leave town, many never returning, but Pa had skated around conscription. If the Rebels hadn't surrendered, though, his skates might have snagged. Nevertheless, she knew war had been horrific for many, especially those near battlefields.

"Did Jon Marc send for you, since he knew you're a hard worker?" she asked.

"No."

"Plantation life, at least after the war was over, must've been more exciting than the lonely life of a brush popper. I'm surprised you didn't stay in Louisiana."

He said nothing.

"Most cowmen want their own place, as soon as they can manage it. Do you plan to work for Jon Marc from here on out?"

"Nope."

If she was going to get anything out of this man, she must mold queries requiring more than a yes or a no, or dead silence. "What brought you to Texas?"

He fiddled with one end of his mustache. "Came to see my Aunt Persia."

"Aunt Persia? Who is she?"

"My aunt."

Bethany rearranged aching feet under the table and tried not to frown at the laconic Catfish. "Is she India's sister? Or sister to your father? And where does she live in Texas?"

"She and India are sisters. Persia lives in San Antonio."

Not once had Bethany heard Jon Marc speak of family in that city. Peculiar. "So . . . you went to visit your aunt in San Antonio, but ended up at the Caliente. How?"

"Jon Marc hired me."

"Was he visiting your aunt's home?"

"No."

This was like pulling teeth. Bethany ground hers before asking, "Where did you meet Jon Marc?"

"Uncle Tim was reading poetry at the ruins of the Alamo."

"May I assume Uncle Tim is married to your aunt?"

"He's dead now."

Which meant India O'Brien had a widowed sister living within a hundred miles of the Caliente. "Jon Marc had nothing to do with your aunt and uncle, I guess."

"He didn't cotton to Tim Glennie. Most men didn't. Sorta sissy acting, Uncle Tim. Ran a school for aspiring poets."

"Jon Marc was chummy with your aunt?"

"Never been a man who didn't have eyes for Aunt Persia."

Was she the widow Jon Marc got his experience from? If so, he evidently hadn't had enough "eyes" to ask for her hand. "Did your aunt have eyes for Jon Marc?"

Catfish snickered. "She has eyes for every man."

Fingers were pointing more and more to a connection between Persia and Jon Marc. If nothing had happened between the two, wouldn't he have said something, at least in passing, about family being as close as San Antonio?

Likely, her husband caroused with Connor O'Brien's sister-in-law, yet he expected Bethany to be pure as the driven snow.

Catfish drained his cup. "Gotta go."


Best to keep busy, Bethany decided after Catfish left. She refused to do too much thinking about Persia and Jon Marc, although it did irk her, his double-standards and virulent charges. What a rotten thing to do, cavort with a widow, then make Bethany feel even more rotten for giving in to blackmail. Men were like that.

She also didn't want to think about what her husband would face on his trip, or what they'd face as a couple upon his return. *You'll simply have to show faith in him.*

Yet her injured feet wouldn't allow manual labor, not for three days. Three long days. The fourth morning after Jon Marc rode out, Bethany scrubbed the kitchen and washed linens, set out vases of roses and picked up the parlor, where the water bucket and her discarded night-gown sat abandoned from the wedding night.

The wedding night.

She couldn't fault his experience.

Her wanton thoughts wandered down a worn path. *There once lived painted ladies at the Long Lick, who swore an untried cowpoke be easy t' pick; in bed he would jump, for a smooth hump; yet his stick would go off—way too quick.*

The widow Glennie had taught him not to do that. If everything were even, Jon Marc ought to be glad his bride hadn't spent their wedding night sobbing at the pain, or acting too modest to give the bridegroom a chance to fire a second round.

All things were not even.

That he wanted her body did give Bethany some hope for the future, though. She could count herself extremely fortunate Jon Marc hadn't discarded her, like used wash water. Whatever the case, her best chance was to show him her worth, both as a wife and a ranch woman.

She tossed the wash water, wishing mistakes and disap-pointments could be discarded with the same ease.

No matter how many chores she found to busy herself, she got more and more restless. Where was Jon Marc? Would he return as he had from the war, with his boots on? Or would he take another bullet? What if he returned, but—

*Don't bathe in dirty water, girl. Concentrate on how you can improve yourself, and this place.*

She inspected the smokehouse, and saw fish, fish, and more fish to go along with enough beef to feed an army. Jon Marc didn't like fish, either. Recalling the ham he'd scrounged for their ill-fated picnic, she thought of Padre Miguel's pigs.

This ranch could use a few pigs.

If nothing else, for fish disposal.

Her mind on how she could barter for swine, she wan-dered through the rubble of the Wilson home, finding a music box that still worked. After cleaning it up, she decided Sabrina might enjoy the tinkle of music.

Sabrina. Bethany needed something—*someone*—besides chores and too-frequent thoughts of Jon Marc to occupy her mind. Perhaps she needed to feel important to another human being, she wasn't quite sure, but she knew that a visit with her niece would be a breath of fresh air.

After lunch, she decided. This afternoon she would ride to town and visit Sabrina.

But that was not to be.

"Howdy. Been missin' your neighbor?"

"What are you doing here, Hoot Todd?"

"Visitin'." The outlaw who happened to be Bethany's brother shoved past her and into the kitchen, where she'd baked cornbread. He eyed the steaming skillet of bread, fresh from the oven. "Slice me up a slab of that, missus. I'll take a glass of milk, too, if you've got it."

Had Hoot come here to gloat about doing her husband in?

*You'd better not've hurt him. You just better not.*

Her years in the Long Lick Saloon had acquainted her with no-goods like Hoot Todd. Best never to show your weaknesses, never let them think they have you on the run.

"I used up the milk." Bethany folded arms over her chest, daring the bully to argue. "You want cornbread, you slice it."

Hoot rubbed a fingertip beneath his eyepatch, then got a knife from a sheath that was strapped to his calf.

*Excellent idea, telling him to pull a knife.*

He cut into the cornbread. "Looks good, Sis."

Sis? Why did he call her Sis? Reason surfaced. It wasn't unusual for Texans to call women "Sis." Of course, that was generally used in the familiar. Anyway, she wouldn't stand here while Hoot gobbled her lunch, not without finding out if Jon Marc had crossed his path.

"My husband's been looking for you," she said.

"Oh, that reminds me." Hoot peeled back his lips to smile unwinningly. "Congratulations on gettin' hitched."

Quite a wizard of etiquette, her brother. "Did you run into him?" she asked and held her breath.

"Naw. Sent Peña and Xavier off. Made it look like I went with them. Don't worry. They won't hurt your sweetie pie. My boys are gonna lead him around for a spell, then send him home tired. And beat."

She didn't know whether to believe him, but wanted to. Not that she relished the idea of Jon Marc chasing geese. "I should imagine your chums will have their hands full."

"He ain't no pussy, your sweetie, I'll grant." Hoot bit into cornbread, hummed with appreciation, then wiped his mouth with a shirtsleeve. "Figured old Jonny boy would come gunnin' for me, seeing's how I lightened his Rockport purse."

"Strange, your not trying to deny guilt."

"Wouldn't be no fun, claimin' otherwise."

Hoot slid the knife back in its scabbard, then straddled a chair, perfect guest that he was. He might look like Pa in his younger days, somewhat, but Hoot could benefit from a drinking habit. Alcoholism might elevate him to a better person.

"Gets me to laughin', when your man tries to outdo me," Hoot confided, like a schoolyard bully. "Never happen."

"From the looks of your nose, I wouldn't quite agree with that statement."

He got a nasty gleam in his single eye. "Things ain't always the way they look, wouldn't you agree?"

"Why are you telling me this?"

Using his fingers, he dug more cornbread from the skillet. "Don't want the bride worrying about her man, for one."

"Why would you care what I think?"

"You might say I've got me a vested interest in you."

"I don't think so."

"Doncha now?" Again he scratched beneath his eye-patch, probably at a flea. "Why don't you be a good girl and run get ol' Hoot a fistful of O'Brien money?"

"You've gotten enough already," she replied. "And I want it back."

"Sure you do. Greedy little thing, ain't you?"

"Quit talking in circles. What do you want, Hoot Todd?"

"Give me a fistful of O'Brien money."

"You take it on your own. Why do you need me to hand it over?"

" 'Cause it'll hurt Jonny boy more, if you give it to me."

Suspicions began to resurface. They didn't set her at ease. "I'll do nothing to hurt my husband."

"That so, *Beth*? You know, the way I look at it, you've got two ways to go. You can give me the money, then answer to your man. Or I'll just wait till he gets back from his snipe hunt, then call him aside for man-talk. He might be interested to know about my recent trip to Austin. And Round Rock."

Blood rushed from Bethany's face, pooling in her feet. It took all her strength to make it to a chair and plop down. "That's blackmail," she uttered.

"It is."

"I won't be blackmailed."

Once, but never again. What was she going to do? The breech-loader was in the house, on the bedroom wall. Hoot had a pair of guns and a knife, right here in the kitchen. She could scream, but who'd hear her? Catfish wasn't anywhere nearby. Albeit, guns and screams would show fear—what Hoot Todd expected. She needed to throw him off course.

"Do as you please, Hoot Todd. Tell Jon Marc whatever strikes you as clever. He won't believe you."

"All he'd need to do is mosey on up to a certain Catholic cemetery in Round Rock. Sis, one look at that gravestone—

you picked out a nice one, by the by—and he'll know you ain't never been no Buchanan.''

"May I be frank with you?" At his nod, she went on, proud of faked reverence. "Your reputation spread far and wide. Why, people as far north as Fort Worth are in awe of you. Robbing stagecoaches and stealing livestock, those are the tales that legends are made of."

She lowered her voice to one of pity. "Blackmail, of course, is no better than skinning cows and horses. Word gets out about it, people are liable to laugh at you. I know I'm disappointed. I was so frightened of you, I couldn't even bear to arrive in this town as Bethany Todd. Really, blackmailing is for lowlifes."

He drew up his shoulders, his mouth dropping.

"Would you like a cookie?" she asked sweetly, then went to the crock for one of the oatmeal treats she'd baked, hoping to have them on hand to sweeten up Jon Marc on his return. If he was of a mind for sweetening. "How about a cup of coffee to go along with it? Might taste a bit like 'horse piss,' but beggars can't be choosers, can they?"

He chomped down on the cookie, then slurped the coffee that she poured. Meanwhile, she took a gamble by going to the teapot, where she'd been keeping Pa's gold watch. Where she'd moved the filigreed bracelet that she would never wear.

Tucking the watch in an apron pocket, she said, "Yes, I was scared of you. So scared that I let Miss Buchanan talk me into trading places with her. But you don't scare me now."

"Not even a little?" Crumbles fell from his mouth.

"Not a bit. You're something that ought to be mashed under the heel of one's shoe. And I'm not talking about a higher form of life like a scorpion. Fishing worm describes you. Why, Pa wouldn't even be proud of you."

Hoot blanched. Apparently to change the subject, he asked, "How . . . how's the old man doin'?"

"He's in prison. *Wormed* his way into a church and robbed it. He's not the stuff of legend."

"Folks really call me a legend?"

She nodded. "They say writers will write books about you, someday."

"I be damn—darned."

"I've never read a book about a blackmailer, have you?"

"I don't do much readin'. Sissies read."

"Not so. Maybe someday, in your old age, you can tuck up in front of a cozy fire . . . and read about the dashing exploits of the legendary Hoot Todd. Anyone know your real name is Mortimer?"

He went pale as white flour. "You turning the blackmail tables on me, girl?"

"Me? Never." She was innocence itself. "Anyway, what difference does it make? No eager-beaver writer will track me down to get my opinion on a blackmailer."

"I don't want no one to know my name's Mortimer."

"I don't want Jon Marc to know my name was Todd."

Hoot screwed up that lone eye, assessing her. "Ain't never been said a Todd weren't good for his word."

The people of Liberal could argue that, but Bethany wouldn't.

She fixed him with a cool glare. "I'm not going to give you O'Brien money. Fact is, I'm going to forget you came calling, big brother. You're going to forget it, too, and speak of it to no one, including Terecita. After you return that money you took between here and Rockport, that is."

"I ain't givin' back the money."

More hardheaded than Hoot, she refused to quit, although she did wonder how far he could be compromised. "We'll table money talk, for now. But you will promise to keep your trap shut . . . Mortimer. And you'll leave my husband alone."

"Don't call me Mortimer."

Taking her gamble, betting on a hand of three's and four's, she closed her fingers around the watch, placed it in Hoot's palm, then fastened his fingers around the gift. *Insanity, girl! If Jon Marc can't forgive, you may need to trade this watch for stage fare.* No. She would gamble on Jon Marc.

"You willing to shake on our agreement?" she asked Hoot.

He lengthened each finger in turn, until all were straight and spread, and peered down at the golden fob watch that nestled in the center of his callused hand. "This is Pa's old watch."

"It is. And his father's before him. It's yours now. It's an heirloom. Keep it for good luck, not that it brought Cletus, or Grandpa, much luck. Maybe you'll change all that."

His voice had a strangely mellow content, when he confided, "Only been one other person done trusted me with anything of value." He swallowed. "You remind me of her."

"You hold on to this watch. Someday, give it to Sabrina. That's what decent folks do. For family."

"Why do that? She ain't mine."

Bethany couldn't help but laugh. "You must be blind in your last eye. One look at Sabrina's eyes—Those are Pa's eyes. My eyes. Your eye. And in case you haven't noticed it, it's like seeing Grandpa Todd—rest his soul—all over again, when I look at your daughter's nose."

"You reckon?"

"You ought to be good to that child," Bethany chided.

"I am good to her. Bring her an orange, ever' time I come back from Mexico."

"That's not good enough."

His shoulders hunched, his forefinger roofing his upper lip, he pondered Bethany's advice. "No. I ain't gonna change. Don't want no attachments."

She studied this brother, a bandit both fearsome and loathsome. He had a vulnerable side, even if he didn't realize, or wouldn't recognize, it. What made him want no attachments? What made him into a criminal?

"Fine," she replied. "Stay the way you are."

"Intend to."

"I'm attached to Sabrina." Bethany used her fingers to sweep cookie crumbs from the table, into the cup of her hand. "I want to spend time with her, here at the Caliente."

"Terecita won't let you. She hates your sweetie."

"Why?"

"He's too high-minded for 'er." Hoot reached for another cookie. "O'Brien's a strange bird, in case you ain't figured that out for yourself. He either wants something, or he don't. If he don't, ain't nothin' gonna turn him to it. Nothin'."

Chill bumps ran down Bethany's arms when she recalled how Jon Marc denied his family. Gracious, his family. When would Fitz O'Brien show up? Just what she needed, complications.

"Terecita ain't used to havin' men tell her no," Hoot further explained. "She ain't gonna wanna let her kid traipse around with the gal done got O'Brien's ring."

Reasonable. But Bethany wouldn't quit. She would become closer to Sabrina. And she needed to test her brother.

"You work on that, Hoot. You hear me? You ride on out, go see Terecita, and prepare her. Tomorrow I'm going to town to pick Sabrina up. For now, though, I'm going to ask you again. Are you willing to remain a legend?"

"I cotton to the idea."

"That means shaking hands with me. It means forgetting anything petty like blackmail. It also means I'll be very unhappy, should you continue to pester my husband."

"I'm willin' to forget you and me are kin."

"What about the rest of it?"

His mouth worked from side to side. He scratched under his eyepatch yet again, answering, "That's asking too much."

It probably was. "I'll make you a deal. You leave him be

for now. For a long now. And you return the Rockport money."

"Half of it."

"All of it."

"Weren't that much to begin with," Hoot muttered, as if to reconcile his capitulation. "I'm willing."

"You be here by midnight tomorrow night. Cash in hand. Understand?"

"Yeah, I understand." He clamped his right paw around her fingers, and shook them like a dog did a cat. Hard.

She let out her breath. This was the first easy breath she'd taken since he darkened the doorway.

Hoot quit the table. "Bethany . . . about Sabrina—"

"Don't call me Bethany. My husband is never to know you and I are related. Unless you want me to remember a few cowardly deeds. And your given name."

"*Beth.* Father Mike won't give her up."

"I can handle the padre."

# Chapter Eighteen

The next day Bethany hoped to see Jon Marc ride up.

When he didn't, she rode toward Fort Ewell to bring her niece back to the Caliente. Provided Hoot was good at his word. If he wasn't . . . she'd know soon enough.

Spurring Arlene past the nebulous city limits, she spied Sabrina down by the riverbank, at the pigpen.

"¡Hola!" she shouted to get her niece's attention.

Sabrina ran from the sty upon hearing Bethany's voice. "¡Amiga!" The girl's arms flailed with happiness—at the thought of visiting the Caliente? "Guess what!"

Bethany tried not to show disappointment when Sabrina gushed, "Jacinta, she has more babies!"

Had no one said anything to the child about . . . ?

Bethany decided not to borrow trouble, so she let her niece's enthusiasm carry her toward the new mother.

Indeed, the sow had expanded her family, Bethany determined, once she'd tried Arlene to a pigpen rail. Twelve piglets nudged Jacinta's ample belly. The sow wagged an ear at Bethany and Sabrina, giving a grunt of "be off with you."

"What a lovely family you have, madam," Bethany said, not put off by porcine dismissal. "You're fortunate to have such a nice young lady as Sabrina to bring you food and fill your trough with water."

Sabrina nodded, her braids flapping against her spare shoulders. "She is very greedy."

"Ah! It is the bride," said a male voice that had to belong to Padre Miguel. "Good morning to you, my child. How are you this fine day?"

A trio of Jacinta's older offspring ran between Bethany and the priest. And she got an idea . . . "I'd be much finer, Padre, if I could make a deal with you."

"A deal? And what would that be, my child?"

"I want twenty pigs. Preferably shoats. Of course, I'll need help with them." Bethany placed her hand on the crown of Sabrina's head. "If this *niña* is agreeable, I would love to have her stay at the Caliente and teach me about pig farming."

"What will your husband say about that?"

"He's gone. Trouble, you see. The matter of a theft."

"A certain *bandido*"—Padre Miguel cut his eyes to Sabrina, then back to Bethany, his meaning clear: don't mention Hoot Todd by name—"has affronted him again?"

"Exactly."

The priest's dark eyes grew crafty. "I might make a deal. Sabrina, *vete*. Go."

"Sabrina," Bethany cut in. "Look in the knapsack hanging on Arlene's saddle. It's for you. A present."

"For me?" Eyes widened.

"For you."

The girl scampered to rifle through the sack. A delighted squeal, not unlike a piglet's, rang when Sabrina eyed the sandalwood music box. She rushed back. "What is it?"

"Hand it here, and I'll show you." Bethany wound the key; the tinny sounds of "Oh, Susannah" floated through the air of the town that didn't have enough music.

"It is beautiful," Sabrina said in a breathy, little-girl voice. "It is really mine?"

*"Vete,"* the priest reiterated at the same moment Bethany nodded. "Take your toy and show it to Ramón and Manuel."

"Sabrina, the cookies in that sack are for the boys. We don't want to leave them out."

"Thank you, señora." She blew a kiss before tucking the treasure under her arm and turning away. "Thank you!"

"You will spoil her," was the priest's gentle scold.

"I intend to. I trust Terecita has spoken to you . . ."

"Ah, Terecita. Yes, she spoke to me."

Wonderful! Hoot would uphold his end of the bargain.

"Terecita," the padre said. "My lost lamb who would like to hear piano hammers instead of the clack of castanets . . ."

*You crafty dickens.*

Hands muffed in cassock sleeves, he reared up on sandals, then settled back on his heels. A rascally grin accompanied his bargain. "Pigs and a little girl . . . for a piano."

"I was thinking about something different. Such as teaching the boys to speak English."

"Ramón and Manuel do not need any language but Spanish. They are destined for La Casa de Nuestra Señora de Guadalupe, an orphanage in Mexico. This church—" a finger pointed at Santa María "—would benefit from your piano."

"It's not mine to give. Anyway, that piano is worth more than a score of pigs. And I'm not buying Sabrina. I simply want her for a while."

The priest pivoted on the toe of a sandal. His hands behind him, he paced the ground. Spinning around, the hem of his robe swaying, he said, "It troubles me, a lady of the faith who doesn't attend Mass. Where were you yesterday?"

Avoiding church. "Mass was yesterday? My days have run together."

"I have not heard your confession, Señora O'Brien. Not once. Do you not have sins to confess?"

"No."

"How can that be? We are all sinners, señora."

He dangled her from an invisible string; she knew it.

"Would I . . ." She licked her lips, recalling the incredible, invisible force that pressed down during the marriage ceremony, one she had feared repeating, had she attended Mass. Prudence demanded, Stay far from invisible forces. Impossible. How could she avoid Mass, without drawing Jon Marc's suspicions? Which meant she must beard the lion of religion. Or be bearded.

God's messengers could be bought off. This she knew, sure as the world. When the preacher at the Liberal Baptist Church got wind of the sticky situation at the Frye household, Oscar had slipped a handful of bills under the table. Oscar never had to worry about having the church door slammed in his face.

Bethany was in no position to buy anything. Nonetheless, her chin tilted toward Padre Miguel. "Would it settle me with the church, if I agree to trade the piano?"

"Have you forgotten the catechisms, my child? You should know Grace doesn't work that way."

Who was Grace? What was catechisms? Bethany could bluff her way out of this, she knew she could, but did she want to? If she and Jon Marc were to make a success of their marriage, she needed to be honest. She needed whatever Grace had to offer.

No.

If she and Jon Marc were to have a chance at lifelong happiness, she needed more than some woman named Grace. Certainly more than a magic lamp. She needed God.

Seeking religion would require his messenger, someone to speak with who knew she wasn't born a Buchanan. Hoot knew, of course, but he carried no divine messages, to be sure.

She sensed Padre Miguel trustworthy. It was somewhat on the order of honor among thieves, he being as wily as she was.

"Padre Miguel, you and I need to talk."

"What in tarnation are *pigs* doing, penned up at this ranch?"

Jon Marc shouted that question the same moment he shoved the parlor door open. He blinked at a completely rearranged room and a small girl who sat in the rocking chair, her legs crossed at the ankles, her hands clasped around some sort of box.

"*Buenas noches,* Señor Juan Marc. Good evening."

Sabrina. Todd's neglected love child, not that love had anything to do with her conception. Sabrina, no threat to Jon Marc. Minutes ago, before he'd the misfortune to catch sight of pigs between the stable and the river, he'd felt threatened. He'd seen his wife pass in front of the parlor window, her arms and hands in motion, as if in conversation. His mind had worked against him, making him think Daniel-type thoughts.

Jon Marc had prayed to every Catholic saint he could recall, plus everything related to his Protestant upbringing. He wouldn't start conjuring up images of his wife entertaining a man. It had worked.

Then he'd caught sight of swine.

"The pigs," Sabrina now said, "they are yours."

Jon Marc dreaded to find out why they were his, or how come the piano was missing, or what Sabrina was doing at the Caliente, way past visiting hours.

He stepped into the parlor. "Where is Señora O'Brien?"

"The bride, she has gone for milk and cookies." Sabrina scooted off the seat and, standing to set aside what now looked like Trudy Wilson's old music box, rubbed her tummy. "She makes very good cookies."

Yes, she did. And Jon Marc disliked the urge to find out just how good this batch had turned out.

A pointed clearing of throat to his rear signaled Beth's return.

He swiveled around.

The way his heart did a double-beat? He didn't like it. He wanted to have no feeling whatsoever for her. Yet he saw her as a desirable woman. Desirable. And hot to the touch.

She stood with a tin plate in one hand, a glass of milk in the other. Fixing her eyes on his, her lips trembling slightly, she moved not a muscle. Her hair had been braided into a single plait that fell over one shoulder. A burst of fire in his chest reminded Jon Marc of what that hair had felt like, brushing his body as she rode him to the throes of passion.

His veins expanded with a charge of heated blood. She'd been the essence of his most wicked dreams, willing and giving and hotter than a branding iron.

They needed to talk about passion.

Not with Sabrina around, naturally.

He turned back to the girl. "What are you doing here at this time of night?"

"I must take care of the pigs."

"Sabrina," Beth ordered, "go on to bed."

"And what bed might that be?" Jon Marc wanted to know, but suspected it was *his* bed.

"Go, Sabrina!" Beth shoved plate and glass into the girl's hands, but didn't make the connection.

Tin and glass clattered to the floor in a shower of milk, cookies, and in what became broken glass. The child wailed. Let go with a string of rapid-fire Spanish words that Jon Marc couldn't keep up with. Both she and Beth reached for the spillage at the same time. Foreheads knocked together.

"Get away," he ordered, "else you'll get cut."

Wide-eyed, woman and girl looked up at him.

Then Sabrina flew into the shelter of Beth's arms.

During his absence, Jon Marc had envisioned a host of scenes of how this evening would turn out. He had not conjured up images of milk-and-cookie chaos, much less the sight of Beth giving comfort. To the eye and ear, his wife gave the impression of being a decent person, but how much did the eye and ear deceive?

And where was that grand piano?

And why were those pigs suddenly his?

Answers had to wait. They waited. Beth put her arm around the girl, led her to the bedroom, and Jon Marc figured he might as well clean up the mess. This was one mess he could fix.


Her nerves skipped like Mexican jumping beans. Jon Marc, home. When they were in the parlor, she had yearned to rush into his welcoming arms and ask question after question about his odyssey, yet the look on his face had told her to stay back. Thanks to being thwarted in revenge? Simply because of Sabrina's presence, or the piano's disappearance? Because pigs rooted where long-horns were meant to roam? Foolish questions. He hadn't forgotten their wedding night.

That, Bethany expected.

The bad part was, she expected Hoot at midnight. Already she'd figured out what to say about the money, but how would she explain his presence?

Jon Marc, plus Hoot—enough to keep her mind off a troublesome event: Manuel and Ramón leaving for an orphanage in Mexico City. Would Sabrina—adored, precious Sabrina—leave with the boys?

Finished tucking her niece into bed, Bethany returned to the parlor. The mess was gone. So was her husband.

A dismal feeling bathed Bethany. How silly of her, imagining he'd wait for her. How very silly. She'd hurt him. To the core. Betrayed his trust. As with his family, he would exact punishment. His cold shoulder.

Odd, how life mixed triumphs with predicaments. Hoot at bay, a good thing. Her conversion to the religion embraced by Jon Marc in the offing, another good thing, thanks to an understanding Padre Miguel, who had promised to keep silent about her truths, while agreeing to give instructions in the faith.

Yet, according to the padre, the church didn't recognize her marital vows, since she had given false information. Texas did have laws, though. And Padre Miguel had informed her of one in particular. If she and Jon Marc lived as husband and wife for at least six months, they were married. In the eyes of Texas.

That was better than nothing.

Her intentions were to stay put, way beyond six months. Then she'd caught sight of Jon Marc's coffee eyes turned to petrified wood.

"Turn his eyes warm," she uttered, pining for one of the ardent gazes that had marked her beginning days at the Caliente. "Find him. Make it all better."

She found him at the river, in his bedroll. His shoulders bared, he lay on his side, sleeping. Did he pretend in order not to speak with her? Or was it feigned so that he wouldn't do as he'd done before their second coupling? Join with her when his heart warned him not to.

"*¿Querido?*" She shivered, recalling how his skin tasted as she'd kissed it . . . and how it felt when his lips tasted her own flesh.

"What?"

She stepped closer. "What happened on your trip?"

"Never found Todd." Jon Marc eased to his back and tucked a wrist behind his neck. His pose might be relaxed, but the edge in his voice told the true story. "Not an altogether wasted trip. Todd's *bandido*, Peña, met his fate.

Thanks to a showdown in the next county. He took my bullet between the eyes."

"You k-killed him?"

"Right."

Bethany shuddered. A man dead over money and an old feud. A pointless death, now that Hoot had relented.

How would Hoot react to the news?

Her lips moved in silent prayer. Moved as Padre Miguel had instructed her. She might be making peace with religion, but would there be no peace in La Salle County?

"You've got your answer," Jon Marc said. "Now I want mine. Start with why Sabrina is sleeping in my bed."

"She's teaching me how to tend pigs."

"Why?"

"Because we need them. For food. To clean up refuse. To trade for goods and services. Another thing, no self-respecting rustler would ever touch a pig. Or skin it."

"I'm not a damned *pig farmer.*"

Cattle ranchers considered it beneath their dignity, attaching their brands to anything other than cows and horses, but what was wrong with being practical? "I'll take care of the pigs. You can simply ignore them." Bethany, her knees weak, surrendered to it, sagging to sit a few feet from Jon Marc, her legs tucked under her. "No more about pigs. Not now. I can't talk about them. Not in the same breath we discuss death."

"Is this where you give me hell for taking care of what's mine?"

"I'm saying Peña was unnecessary. I've had a talk with Hoot Todd. He—"

"What do mean, you had a talk with Todd?" Jon Marc jerked up from his bedroll, exposing his torso. "*You* talk, Beth."

"I had a chat with Hoot Todd yesterday. He agreed to return your money."

"I'd like to know what the hell you said to 'chat' him into anything."

"He's not an unreasonable man, if you give him a chance."

"What did you have to give up, my lovely virginal bride?" Jon Marc asked in a voice filled with innuendo.

"If you mean to imply something illicit between me and Hoot, you are wrong."

"So, it's Hoot, is it? You sicken me."

Jon Marc's affront crawled up Bethany's spine. She had to work hard at tamping down her aggravation, her temper, her urge to get off the ground and stomp away. "Yes, it's Hoot. He dropped by, trying to upset me, but I decided to make peace with him. And a semblance of peace is what I made. Familiarity of address goes along with being neighborly."

"He's not a neighbor. He's a menace."

"Things can change. For the better."

"What in hell's name did you say to him?"

That, of course, she couldn't discuss. Yet she silently vowed that no more blatant lies would pass her lips. "Wording isn't important. The crux is, he agreed to reason. You might call it a good Catholic miracle."

"Jesus H. Christ."

Jon Marc's continued profanity dealt a blow. She was not to be respected. It might have been expected, her tightening of chest and throat, along with the drawing up in her veins and the burning behind her eyelids. But it wasn't. She would not, however, cry, nor act injured.

Only this morning, as she knelt before the altar at Santa María, discordance emitting from the piano, the padre had counseled her on accepting the guilt for her sins against her husband and a higher power. Padre Miguel would surely say she must bow her head and be blistered by the lash of her own making.

Her shoulders straightened, her nose hitching up. Unbowed, she said, "I'll thank you not to speak that way to me."

"You don't dictate what gets said on *my* ranch."

She rose to stand, indignity hurling her to Jon Marc's seated presence. "You intend to make me miserable enough that I'll leave, I take it."

"If you're wanting to leave, don't let the door kick you in the butt."

The difficult urge not to kick his behind assaulted her. "As I said before you left, I have no desire but to be a good and loving wife."

"By cuddling up to Todd, then offering his kid my bed? By bringing pigs onto a cattle ranch?" A moment tripped by. "By spreading your legs before marriage?"

Without warning, something skittered up her leg. Probably a lizard. Not squeamish about insects, she gathered her skirts up to flick it from her knee.

"If you're thinking to seduce me," Jon Marc said sourly, "think again."

She bent over once more. This time to gather a handful of earth. Her elbow drew back; she tossed dirt into his face.

Whirling on the ball of a foot, she meant to rush back to the house. Jon Marc grabbed her ankle, held her tight. She tried to get free. Couldn't. All her efforts got her? She tumbled atop him. Criss-crossing him.

She tried to get her bearing, which pressed her hips to his. For a moment she thought he met the pressure, responding to it, but he craned upward to roll her spine to the ground.

He sat back. Rubbed dirt from his face. "You and I need to talk."

"I'm in no mood for it."

"Tough. We're going to talk."

He meant business, she knew. Sitting up, she shuddered to think about discussing the reap of their wedding night. Thus, she would try to avoid it. "Jon Marc, about the piano—"

"Only one person wants that piano." He plucked a weed from the soil, then tossed it aside. "I reckon he's got it."

"Padre Miguel much appreciates our gift. He's been in a fine fettle. I've never seen such a smile on a man's face. Moreover, Terecita is beside herself with joy." Which was true. The dancer had devoted her efforts, outside the cantina, to practicing her music. Terecita did need practice. "She actually smiled at me, this morning at Mass. Afterward she thanked me for a 'blessed' gift. Music is what Santa María needs."

Bethany's announcement seemed to catch her husband off guard. "Terecita smiled at you?" he asked.

"She has a lovely smile. Sabrina got it from her."

"Sabrina is going back to the presbytery. First light, she's going."

She might be on her way to Mexico City. Pain went through Bethany's breast as she thought about losing her niece to an asylum of orphans. Terecita, despite her smile, had confided worries to the padre. She wanted more for her daughter than Fort Ewell could offer. What were the chances of the impossible, that Jon Marc might be convinced into helping keep Sabrina here?

"You resent her because she's Hoot Todd's child?" Bethany fished, with bated breath.

"I don't hold it against anyone, how they came to be on this earth. You ought to know that."

"Because of your mother and that Johnson man?"

"Which brings us to why I stopped you from leaving." Jon Marc jerked up from the ground. Glaring down at his wife, he said, "I've had ten days and nights to think about you and me. We're stuck in this marriage."

"I pray one day you'll not think of it as being stuck."

She figured he'd rage, would cast aspersions. It astounded her when he said, "That would be nice."

Her heart in her throat, she stared up at his looming form. "Is it possible we can go forward from here?"

"You ask too much, Beth. I don't have faith in you right now. Time goes by, maybe that'll change."

"Not fair! You were experienced."

"That's not up for debate," he said with a grate. "You either accept me as I am, as I must accept you, or we'll have to go our separate ways."

"We can't divorce," she argued. "It's not allowed in the church."

"Nothing says we can't live apart."

His statement stabbed her. Deeply wounded by the words she'd most dreaded, she forced a voice. "I won't accept that. I've given you my heart, my body, my soul. I'm not going to budge from your side."

Rising and stepping closer, she laid fingers against his throat. His pulse-surge heated icy skin. His scent rushed through her system. "I love you. You'll know that in time. And I want to be your wife, in every sense. Now and always."

"I have no desire for what you offer." He thrust her hand away. "I won't bring a child into this."

His statements hurt, like knives sticking into her chest, twisting. "What if we've got one already?"

"We best pray that's not so."

"That's sacrilege." Bethany knew enough about the church to know sexual congress was meant for conception.

"I converted to your religion, but I won't bring another me into the world." He stepped backward. "Go to the house. Don't bother me again. But I want to know when you get your woman's flow. Or not. Meanwhile, I'll sleep in my bedroll."

"You change your mind, you know where to find me."

If Hoot Todd didn't find him first.

Bethany left Jon Marc to his bedroll. One of life's ironies niggled. That bedroll could be the most sensible place for him, since he might not notice when her brother came to call.

# Chapter Nineteen

It was midnight. On the dot. Hoot Todd tucked his
Pa's watch into a vest pocket that already held a thousand
dollars, and alit the saddle. Guided by a light in the parlor
window at his sister's house, he made his tentative way
forward, his night vision rendering it a difficult course.
Damn fool thing to do, getting out in the dark at the
behest of O'Brien's wife.

But he liked her images of legend.

*That ain't all.*

More than legend, he'd felt Naomi Todd's presence,
sure as if she'd been among the breathing, when he'd sat
in Bethany's kitchen. It had seemed as if sixteen years fell
away, and he was again at Naomi's hearth, where she always
had a way of making him do right.

Right then, his foot connected with a rock. He tumbled
forward. Pain shot as a shoulder made hard contact with
a sharp, hard object. He tasted dirt. Hoot Todd wasn't a
man to cry. That was for pussies. Plus, it got his eye patch
wet and nasty. He cried.

He was thinking about Naomi.

She'd still been alive, up in the Indian Territory, when he'd returned from fishing a stream. A fried-fish dinner danced behind his eyes . . . before he found his stepmother. Like now, he cried. Held her dying body, and cried. Vaguely, he'd seen Naomi's little girl, standing by the log cabin, sucking her thumb. Crying, too. He hadn't cared about his little sister, but he'd begged Naomi not to die. Begging hadn't done any good. She died before Cletus Todd showed up, fresh from a buffalo hunt.

The two of them had dug her grave, Cletus and his son. That night Cletus got roaring drunk for the first time in his life, so out of his mind that he accused Hoot of not watching out for the family, like he was supposed to. And for being loved "better'n me." Hoot took that hard. It flat made him mad, having Cletus defile Naomi's memory by accusing her of infidelity of the mind. They fought, father and son. Fisticuffs that turned dirty, when Cletus crashed a chair upon his only son's head. Hoot left home the next morning, joined the cavalry. The army, where nobody hankered for anything but getting the best of Indians.

And so it was that Hoot had said good-bye to his adored stepmother and the false images that his father loved him. Love just wasn't worth it. It hurt too much when you lost it.

"Ain't nobody hurt me since," Hoot muttered, spitting dirt from his mouth. He eased against the ground, curling up into a ball. Yet he couldn't erase the image of Bethany O'Brien from his mind. Naomi all over again, she was, turning the tables on him. Making him a better person than he meant to be.

Bethany Todd could hurt him.

*You been hurt by something besides love.*

Drake Wilson, in Hoot's dumb years, had led an army recruit to believe he'd have a better life, if he left Fort Ewell—it had been a real fort back then—to devote himself to the Caliente. *Look how that turned out.*

Hoot pushed off the ground. Shaking his head, he tried

to clear his thoughts. "Ride outta here," he mumbled.
"You don't owe that *puta* nothing. She's married to that
asshole done stole this place from you. Just go. Save your
money."

Naomi wouldn't like it, if she knew he meant to renege
on a promise. Didn't a Todd did keep his word?

He brushed off his vest and chaps, then ambled on up
to his sister's house. Forcefully, he knocked on the closed
door.

A troubled look on her heart-shaped face, Bethany
answered his summons. "H-hello, Hoot."

He snatched a wad of cash from his pocket. "Here it
is." He infused a lighter tone. "Try not to spend it in one
place."

"That . . . this is good of you, Hoot."

"Ain't you gonna invite me in for a glass of milk?"

She shook her head. "Jon Marc is home."

O'Brien, home? Then where were Peña and Xavier?
They should have beaten O'Brien to La Salle County. Por-
tent crawled up Hoot's spine. He gave it a mental shake-
off. The boys wee probably getting liquored up in the next
town, having enjoyed dangling O'Brien from marionette
strings.

"Hoot. Thank you for this." Bethany tucked cash into
her skirt pocket. "You are the stuff of legend."

He chuckled. Tapping his finger against his cheek, he
said, "Then gimme a brotherly kiss right here, little Sister."

Like someone facing a last supper, and surely her last
chance to express sentiment, Bethany reached up on tiptoes and threw her arms around his neck. She squeezed
him tightly. Her lips pressed below the eye patch. "I
shouldn't have judged you harshly. Should've given you
the benefit of a doubt. Things might've been different."

He patted her back, then shoved her away. "Hey, watch
out. This ain't no puss—sissy you be talkin' to. You'da
showed up, presumin' to make a home with me, I woulda

sent you packing, girl. Ain't got no room for a sister. Not in this heart.''

She laughed, a tear trickling down her cheek. "You big phony. You great big phony. Oh, Hoot . . . I'm so sorry.''

He didn't have an idea what she meant, but figured hers was some woman's malady. He backed away. "Don't you go gettin' sentimental on me. This is Hoot Todd you're talkin' to.''

Again she chuckled. "That's right. Hoot Todd. Outlaw of legend.''

"Doncha you ever forget that.''

Kissing Hoot Todd. Beth was kissing Hoot Todd, her arms laced around his neck, like he were a lover. She stood right in the doorway of her husband's house, dallying with his enemy. Not even an hour had passed since Jon Marc sent her away, yet she was already cozying up to another man. This, on top of an earlier meeting. It took every bit of Jon Marc's strength not to charge up to Hoot Todd and break his nose again.

Which is what Daniel O'Brien would have done, sure as the world.

Before getting an eyeful of such a *tender* moment, Jon Marc hadn't been able to sleep. It bothered him, the hurt in Beth's eyes as she'd left him. Still shirtless, he'd checked the house to make certain the place was secure for his wife and Sabrina, yet if he'd found Beth crying, would he have dried her tears?

If anyone would be shedding tears, it would be Hoot Todd. Jon Marc would not allow him to tread on Caliente turf, making a mockery of territorial rights.

His booted feet eating up ground, he hurried to where Todd crawled into the saddle. "State your business," he said tersely.

The bandit's upper lip jerked. "Just having a word with

your pretty little missus. A word, and a matter of honor. You know about honor, doncha, O'Brien?''

"You kiss my wife, then have the nerve to speak of honor?" Jon Marc's right hand tightened into a fist. "Get off that horse, goddammit. I'm gonna beat the shit out of you."

"Get down from your high horse, O'Brien. I brought your friggin' money back. If you don't believe me, ask the missus."

Todd returned the stolen money, like Beth had said he would? What the dickens was going on here? "Why? *Why?*"

"Let's just say I like your missus better'n I like you."

Jon Marc was at a loss. After so much trouble with Hoot Todd, he couldn't equate decency with the man who had menaced this ranch for years. Unless Beth, as she'd done with him, had worked magic on this derelict.

That, unfortunately, made sense.

"Where's my men?" Todd asked. "Whatcha doin' home, when my men ain't?"

"Peña's dead, that's why."

Silence fell, a quiet as dead as the Mexican *bandido*. Then Todd asked, "Did you do it?"

"Damn right I did. In Campo del Fuego. He tried to bushwhack me. I outdrew him."

Jon Marc figured Todd would pull one of his pair of six-guns. Instead, the one-eyed hombre reached into his vest pocket, took out a small, white pouch. Shaking tobacco and rolling it into a cigarette, he ran his tongue along the long paper side. He stuck the finished product between his lips and flicked the head off a lucifer. The tip ignited. Todd drew smoke inward, then blew it skyward. "I need to kill you over this, you know."

"You've tried before. Give it your best, Todd. I'd love to kill you."

"You wanna showdown at dawn?" Todd took another drag. "In front of Short's post office?"

"Suits me."

"You ever stop to reckon what that would do to your missus? You got yourself a fine wife, O'Brien. Knows how to make a feller wanna do better. Too bad it ain't worked on you."

"What the hell does that mean?"

"Reckon it's a gift from The Man Above, her knowing what to say to make a body straighten up."

His head tipping to the side, Jon Marc squinted up at Todd. Reform and respect coming from him? This had to be one of the most peculiar moments in Jon Marc O'Brien's life.

And it was brought on by his wife. But he didn't want her charming men out of anything. Charm led to other things.

Todd scratched his cheek. "Sure would be a shame, you was made a sieve. Would hurt her, I reckon."

"You kiss my wife, then lecture me on how she react to a blood-letting? You're peculiar, Todd."

"She kissed me. Not the other way around. She kissed me, 'cause I gave back your friggin' money." Todd spat tobacco. "Beth's too good for you. You ain't the stuff of legend."

"Six-shooters at dawn. Fort Ewell post office."

Todd wrapped reins around his knuckles. "I ain't gonna draw on you. Got better ways to fix your bonnet."

With that, the outlaw spurred his mount and rode out, too yellow to accept a challenge. A yellow streak in Hoot Todd? Jon Marc had to shake his head, lest he believe what had happened. Todd didn't back down from fights.

Just exactly what sort of magic had Beth worked on him? *What about that "fix your bonnet" business?* Her magic might be potent, but Peña's death had overwhelmed it.

Too late for hindsight on the dead bandit, Jon Marc had to know what she'd said to Todd, even if it meant she got the wrong impression of his intentions. He found the bedroom and parlor empty, save for a small, sleeping girl.

Nor did he find his wife in the kitchen or stables. Where was Beth?

Had she left?

If she had, it was afoot. Arlene and the other horses were safe in the stables.

Where was Beth? Worry, damnable worry, got to him.

At last he found her, huddled beneath a craggy overhang on the banks of the Nueces. He braced a hand on the jutting rock above her head and bent down to peer into her hidey-hole. Clutching her arms, she shivered in spite of the balmy night. Her eyes had the aspect of a frightened doe's.

"You needn't be frightened," Jon Marc said. "I'm not going to strangle you for kissing a pig."

"You scare me, period."

Recalling Todd's transformation, before it got foiled, Jon Marc asked, "What's this game you play, wife?"

He waited for Beth's reply, dreading the answer.

# Chapter Twenty

"What game do you play, wife?"

Her husband's voice whistled like the cry of a wolf through the cavelike place where Bethany huddled.

What was the game Jon Marc played, finding her in this sheltered place by the river, where she'd hoped to listen to rushing water and find a semblance of peace amid the bedlam of his making? Probably he'd seen her kiss Hoot. If he killed for no more than dollars, what would he do to an errant wife?

"I play no games," she said, her nerve clattering from fear of how Jon Marc would retaliate for that kiss. And from what Hoot might do to retaliate for Peña.

Hoot, who had become more than she'd ever imagined. Hoot, who was still an outlaw, and dangerous. Hoot, who would surely raise the inferno of hell.

Jon Marc, who would meet that fire with his own hell.

"Come out from there," he ordered tightly.

She ground her spine against the overhang's wall. If only she could do as ordered, her head high, and tell the absolute truth: that hers had been a sisterly kiss of gratitude.

Jon Marc straightened; she saw no more than his denim-clad lower extremities.

"You figuring to leave Sabrina unchaperoned?" he asked.

At least he hadn't jumped right in with accusations. Bethany answered, "She'll sleep through the night. She's not used to clucking attention."

Jon Marc shifted his weight. "She has to return to the padre. Todd's not going to take Peña lying down."

"Perhaps you should've thought of that before you killed his man."

"It was Peña or me. Would you have preferred it been me?"

"No," she answered quietly.

A moment went by. "Why did you kiss Todd?"

"In thanks for his returning the money."

"Beth, dammit, if you and I have a future, you're not to slobber on men's mouths."

"I didn't slobber."

"What kind of magic did you work on Todd?"

"I-I simply appealed to his vanity."

Again her husband crouched down. Settling on the heels of his boots, he rested a forearm on a knee. His gaze delved into her soul. "You say whatever suits the moment, don't you?"

"Does that make me evil?"

"Does it?"

"I don't want to be evil, especially where you're concerned. You're my husband. I love you. But I'm scared of you. And for you."

He chuckled dryly. "I suppose you need to work more magic on Todd, then. Don't even consider it," he tacked on in an ominous nature.

"The only magic I want to work is on you. I wish I could make myself into what you demand. I wish you weren't hotheaded about Hoot Todd. I wish you'd never killed Peña."

"It's too late for wishes." Jon Marc swung from his crouched position to sit beneath the edge of the overhang. "There's going to be trouble. Big trouble. You'd best take cover. Laredo might be a good place for you to ride it out."

"What an ingenuous way of getting rid of me," she said, hurt anew. "Make me think I'll be safe in Laredo, then never fetch me. You do play games, husband. Listen up, know something, and know it well. I won't be shuffled off. Kicking or screaming, bound or gagged, I won't be gotten rid of. I am with you till the end, whenever that may be."

"You're a foolish woman."

"Perhaps. But you're . . . stuck with me."

"Yes, we are stuck, aren't we?" He laughed, the sound almost maniacal. Easing closer, he snaked an arm around her waist, drawing her to him. "If you must have a man's kiss lingering on your lips, it will be mine."

He inclined his head to press his mouth against hers. Fearful she might be of his capabilities, she couldn't and wouldn't deny him. *I want him.*

Her lips parted. His tongue parried with hers. Sighing, she laced her hands behind his naked back, his muscles tensing beneath her fingertips. Somehow, they were both on the floor of the overhang, Jon Marc in a superior position. Her husband grew hard at her belly.

She bowed up to him. The musk of desire flowed. Mindless desire overtook him, as she hoped it would. He kissed her ear, the column of her throat, the slope of a breast. His teeth teased the latter into arousal.

She ached for more. Her fingers prodded between their bodies, finding his engorged staff. He groaned as she worked the buttons of his britches. Her index finger capered with the tip of him, peeling back the foreskin.

Before she could free him completely of the confines, he pushed her away. But not altogether. He gathered up the hems of her skirts, parting her split drawers to rub a middle finger along the tender nub at the apex of her thighs.

"You want your little French phrase, don't you?" he taunted.

"Yes."

"How does this feel?"

How could she answer? Her head thrashed from side to side. She moaned low. He settled between her legs, drawing them over his shoulders. Then lips replaced his fingers.

Her fingers curled into the hair of his head, holding him to his task, loving it. The best part was yet to come. She bucked against his mouth, riding the crest to the stars. "More," she demanded as he thrust against her entry. "Fill me."

His tongue gave one last lunge. "No. No more."

He eased from her, rolled away. "Any more and I'd be filling you with a babe. I meant what I said earlier. There'll be no children for us. Not with things the way they are now. Never, if I can't learn to trust you."

The thrumming at her core subsided. She squeezed her legs together, hoping to sustain it. That wasn't to be.

Turning her gaze to Jon Marc, she saw him swiveling to his feet. He stuffed himself back in britches and buttoned denim. "Good night, Beth."

"Wait just one minute, mister. We're stuck. Let's make the best of it. You've got yardsticks for what'll make this marriage work. I've got mine, too. I refuse—absolutely, flatly refuse—to live in fear of losing you to Hoot Todd's bullet. Make peace. For me. But mostly for yourself."

"The hell, you say." Jon Marc bounded away.

She drew up her knees and buried her forehead against them. Staying in this position for hours, she mourned the hell of their existence.

\* \* \*

Hoot Todd, his thoughts scrambled from making peace with his sister and hell with her husband, rode into Fort Ewell to find Terecita. He found her, playing the piano in an empty church.

"You ain't much on that thing," he charged and scooted onto the bench beside her.

Terecita tried to slam the lid on his fingers, but he was too fast for her. "Do not criticize me, *chico.*"

"Don't give me no hard time, woman. I ain't in the mood for it."

"You're in a mood? What about me?" Terecita pointed at her bosom. "What about Sabrina? Padre Miguel says I should send her to La Casa de Nuestra Señora de Guadalupe, in the City of Mexico. He says I should think of her future. What he says is true. Sabrina must be educated, must know better than I give her. Unless I return to lifting my skirts. That is the only way I can afford to send her to a good school, in a fine city."

There she went, nagging, nagging, nagging. This was about the fiftieth time Hoot had heard this threat. "Terecita, you ain't that valuable."

She ground her heel into his toes. As he yelped, she blew up like a toad. "I do not know why I ever bothered with you."

"Wish you hadn't."

"Then why are you here? If not to lift my skirts, what do you want?"

"Talk. I got troubles, Terecita. O'Brien killed Peña. If I let him get away with murder, I'll be a laughingstock. Legends don't let nobody make a fool of them."

"Peña? I spit on Peña!"

Hoot left the piano bench. Sliding thumbs behind his silver belt buckle, he trod with head down, out the church. It wasn't that he gave a fig about Peña. Who would? That idiot had been more trouble than use, like when he'd torched Wilson's home.

But Peña was part of the Todd gang, and a leader looked out for his own. Which meant revenge.

Before his little sister got to him, Hoot would have licked his lips and smiled, making O'Brien dance to the tune of bullets. It aggravated more than it ought to, being caught between his promises to Beth and the vengeance he must exact.

What could he do, and how should he do it, avenging Peña, without paining little ol' Beth too much? There was no way.

In the moments before dawn broke, Bethany O'Brien came to a conclusion. Not really a conclusion, an affirmation. She loved her husband, had always intended to heal his broken heart, and she must not hide from the fruits of her ill-sown deeds.

But what about his violent streak? *He would kill at the drop o' a pin; never seeing it a sin; but for his troubled soul, my heart did beat, a greater truth ne'er been tol'.*

She brushed herself off, stretched the kinks out of weary muscles, and hiked up her chin. She'd see to Sabrina's breakfast and send her to chores, would go to Jon Marc, would face him down. Like a showdown at dawn. Love must be the victor, not bullets nor hatred.

Halfway home, she heard voices from over her shoulder. She turned. Looking from left to right, she caught sight of a fine coach as it wheeled down the trail from Fort Ewell.

Intuitively, she knew Fitz O'Brien had arrived.

He couldn't have arrived at a worse time.

He'd known the old goat was on his way. It had been too much to hope for, that Fitz O'Brien would turn back. Why was luck never with Jon Marc?

Wrung out from the near-miss of lovemaking with Beth,

he'd guarded her hiding place and kept an eye on the house, throughout the night. Each time his eyes turned to the overhang, he'd gotten aroused again. He wanted her with a fury like none known before, but he must not bury himself in all she offered.

Right now, he had to think of her safety, no matter what sort of fit she pitched. He'd put her on the next stagecoach to Laredo. Once he got rid of a meddlesome old coot.

Fitz's arrival was made worse by Beth running toward the coach, as if she welcomed the visitor. She was in no danger, not at this moment. Jon Marc took a different direction.

He had to find Hoot Todd.

To try to make peace.

Jon Marc owed Beth that much.

# Chapter Twenty-One

Bethany waved the coach to a stop, a good distance before it reached the house. The Caliente had more than one guest, as if they needed any at all, which she and her husband didn't.

The callers were led by a droop-eyed bloodhound. Even before the coachman proffered a step, the dog bounded from the coach to clump off to a chaparral, where he lifted a leg.

Bethany's gaze went back to the coach. She was surprised to see a youth take that step. Freckle-faced and dark-haired, the cowlicked boy appeared to be about twelve.

Could this be Pippin O'Brien?

Who else could it be?

"Hello to you, ma'am," he said, then hoisted a hand, like a coachman, to assist the next visitor.

A big fellow of undeterminable age, wearing the accoutrements of a gentleman, crowded the open door. Swarthy in complexion and emitting a foreign air, he had not a hair on his head. He did sport a golden earring in his left ear.

His nostrils expanding, he inhaled deeply, then flashed a tooth as golden as his ear jewelry. "Praise Allah, we have arrived."

It went without saying, this was the genie.

Did he have the magic lamp in a valise?

He lumbered to the ground. Bowing low, he said, "You must be the yield of my magic."

"Ye be a pretty lass," said another man.

She lifted eyes to the oldest-looking person she'd ever seen in her life. He crouched over a pair of canes.

The youth and the genie bracketed each side of the door, as if to aid the advent of royalty.

"May I presume you're Mr. Fitz O'Brien?" Bethany asked.

He nodded, the rumples of his face jiggling like jelly. He did not accept the twofold offer to alight. He didn't budge. Eyes green below bushy white brows accessed her. "May I presume ye t' be me great-granddaughter, by law?"

"I am Jon Marc's wife. Beth."

"Why did ye stop us short of yer castle? Is me grandson not of a mind t' be seeing me at all?"

The youth and the foreign-appearing fellow faded into the background, along with the bloodhound.

Bethany stepped up to the coach. "I stopped you for a reason, sir. My own reason. Before you see Jon Marc, I want to know what you want with him."

" 'Tis news I bring. 'Twill interest Jonny."

From what her husband had told her, the shrewd Fitz O'Brien would say anything for his will to prevail. *You should be able to identify with that, girl.*

"Sir, you and I must talk," she said.

He backed up. "Come ye into my carriage, lass."

She climbed the step and entered the plushest mode of transportation that her eyes had ever beheld. The scent of fine leather assailed her nose. A shelf of cut-crystal decanters banked one bulwark, each vessel filled with what had to be fine spirits. The sight of brocade upholstery

and fringed pillows took her aback at their luxury. She'd
veritably smelled money.

Money unimportant, she helped the old squire retake
his seat. She sat opposite. The door remained open.

"My husband isn't interested in removing to Memphis,"
she said bluntly.

A gnarled hand planted a silver-topped cane on the
coach floor, then waved it from side to side. "I willna
return without him."

In a perfect world Jon Marc would accept his supposed
grandfather's offer. It would take him from the hardscrab-
ble life of La Salle County, dislodge him from the trouble
Hoot was sure to raise. Somehow she couldn't envision
brush-popping Jon Marc cloaked in an embarrassment of
riches, his energies expended at a factor house. But that
was his upbringing, his heritage, as surely as the Long Lick
and a wealth of rotgut had been hers.

Where would she fit into Memphis life?

Memphis or the Caliente, her lot might be partially
determined by how Jon Marc reacted to Fitz O'Brien's
visit.

"Mr. O'Brien—"

"Granddaddy will be doing ye."

"Sir, you are a stranger to me. I wouldn't feel comfortable with such familiarity."

"Then call me Fitz."

"Fitz, it is." She studied the aged planes of his face,
wishing many things could be different, mainly that the
world could be perfect . . . here at the Caliente. "Jon Marc
won't listen to you, not if you make demands."

Fitz leaned back against the fine squabs, pondering her
statement. Just as he opened his mouth to speak, the bloodhound gamboled into the coach. Eyes as folded as Fitz's
gaped at Bethany. His tongue lolled.

" 'Tis Sham II, this beast," Fitz informed her. "Belongs
t' me great-grandson, Pippin."

Bethany stroked behind Sham II's ear, which pleased him. "Then I take it that young man outside is Pippin."

"Aye. A fine lad is Pippin."

Pippin, whom Jon Marc esteemed. His presence would be the good amongst the not so good, as her husband would see it. "Why don't you give your factor house to the boy?"

"'T' be a riverman like his da is what Pippin seeks, not cotton bales. An O'Brien through and through is the lad," Fitz expanded dolefully. "Set on his own course."

Bethany studied the old gentleman, her heart going out to him. He'd build a fortune from his factor house, yet none of his descendants appreciated his efforts. What ingrates they were, the O'Briens.

She'd loved her own grandpa, yet he'd left nothing but a gold watch to remember him by. She'd loved Grandpa Todd for his smile, and the way he told tales out of school. She'd loved his warmth. Was no warmth to be had from Fitz O'Brien?

He didn't look the least bit cold as he said, "I want me grandson back. Before me next birthday."

"You tossed my husband—a mere youth—to the lions."

Fitz's eyes turned sad. "Is a man t' suffer all the days of his life for one mistake?"

"Why did you make it?"

"Vanity."

He needn't say more. After what Jon Marc had told her, Bethany knew that Fitz had expected his grandsons-of-the-blood to follow in his footsteps. As a woman with many mistakes to account for, she understood this man's folly. "Yours is not an easy task. Jon Marc will not return to you."

"I will be going t' me grave unhappy, if I doona have an O'Brien t' take over me enterprise."

"What if you had a daughter and she had a son named, say, Smith or Williams? Would that son not be good enough?"

"My daughters doona have sons. They doona have children. Married too late in life, did Phoebe and Contessa."

"What if they had children? What does a name matter?"

"It matters not," Fitz conceded. "Matters not . . ."

Sham II rested his chin on Bethany's knee; she scratched his muzzle, asking Fitz, "Did you know Catfish Abbott is the strawboss here at the Caliente?"

Again the cane tip waved from side to side. A hint of a grin tugged at Fitz's mouth. " 'Tis Abbott I seek."

"Excuse me?"

"Give the factor house t' Abbott is what I will do."

"But," Bethany sputtered. "I thought you were here to collect Jon Marc. You said . . ."

"Jonny is me goal." Fitz nodded once. "But I know me grandson. He willna go without a fight. I will fight."

"I don't understand."

"Jonny is t' think 'tis Abbott I seek. 'Twill throw him the length of these United States, or me name isna Fitz O'Brien."

"Yours is a terrible and probably costly game."

" 'Tis me last chance. Run out of games have I. Jonny is destined for Fitz & Son, Factors. 'Twas ordained by God, through the decrees of John Knox. 'Tis time Jonny realized it."

John Knox? Who was he? She didn't want to imagine what such person had to do with anything. "I take it you intend to use Catfish as the bait? Is that what you're saying?"

"Aye. Do ye think I didna have a part in sending the lad here in the first place? Jonny told me naught, so 'twas the Abbott lad I sent t' do me hearing."

"So, you've had two spies at your pleasure. Pippin to write letters. And Catfish to send reports."

He nodded.

"And you did this solely to check on an errant O'Brien, one who had no right to the family name?"

Fitz laid the cane across his lap. "Nay. 'Twas because I love Jonny."

"He doesn't think so."

"I will be changing all that." Fitz set the cane upright again, this time to lean forward on it. "There be something I want t' tell ye."

"I'm listening."

He told her a tale that left her flabbergasted. Tears were in the teller's eyes.

"That's outlandish." Yet she appreciated the pain that his efforts had wrought. If she'd suffered any illusions about his purpose, they vanished, now that she knew how far he'd gone to reunite with Jon Marc. "My husband will never believe it."

"Ye are wrong. Wait and see, bonny lass. Wait and see."

"He won't allow you to stay long enough to find out."

"Then ye'll have t' help me with it, is what I think."

Bethany did her own thinking. How would her husband, troubled as he was, react to Fitz's astounding news? She felt strongly Jon Marc needed a reconciliation with family, no matter his reaction.

Scooting Sham II's nose from her knee, she got closer to Fitz. "If you love Jon Marc and want his love in return, sir, you must be willing to let him make his own decisions."

Fitz emitted a tsk of dismissal. "A fool is what he would be, if he chooses this scrap of a ranch over Fitz & Son, Factors. Buying time is what he does. He will be coming back t' Memphis."

It offended her, Fitz's disdain for this ranch that her husband loved so. It might not look like much to a richling from Memphis, but Fitz dismissed the Caliente without understanding the solace it gave to the man he had turned out in the night. Jon Marc had no business returning to Memphis, not with Fitz O'Brien. But shouldn't that be Jon Marc's decision?

"I do believe you've chosen a hard row to hoe, Fitz. A hard row to hoe."

But it might be Jon Marc's sole avenue, if Hoot Todd bore down like cattle on a stampede. *Maybe I ought to bake a lemon pie, and see what good it might do.*

"Would you care for a lemonade, husband?"

"I do not," Jon Marc replied, the sun fading to the west.

Glass in hand, Beth stood on the passageway between bedroom and parlor, a duo of seated guests crowding the wide covered shelter, one holding court in an invalid's chair.

The genie snoozed upright.

It would be preferable, sipping lye, rather than to socialize with a disappointing wife or with the O'Briens who figured "Jon Marc" was listed in Webster's under disappointment.

No one spoke. Except for Beth. "It's very good," she said. "Sweet. Fitz brought the sugar and lemons all the way from Galveston."

Why was she standing here, trying to fob lemonade off on her husband, when he wanted to be done with the uninvited guests, forthwith? For their own protection, if nothing else. For his own sanity, mainly. She should know that. Hadn't she once suggested that they would send Fitz on his way, without delay?

No.

Jon Marc recalled something about making the old man a bed, then sending him off the next day. *I should've thought about the implications of that.*

How long would it be before Fitz made his bid for Fitz & Son, Factors?

"Try the lemonade," Beth said.

"No lemonade," Jon Marc repeated.

"Where . . . where have you been?" She lowered the glass.

"Taking care of business" was his terse reply.

These folks needed to get moving, not engage in a brush-

country version of high tea. Already he knew Sabrina and
Pippin were down at the pigsty, the coachman and Sham
II with them. Why wasn't the girl back with Padre Miguel?
Jon Marc didn't have to wonder long. His wife hadn't
respected his order. Which might park Sabrina amid the
fury of her father's wrath.

Pippin, ah, Pippin—that boy didn't need trouble.

Fury did brew, Jon Marc, fresh from trying to find Hoot
Todd, was certain of it. Todd hadn't been at the cabin
he occasionally used, nor had he been at the cantina or
anyplace else nearby. Terecita, at Santa María, had banged
on piano keys and claimed no knowledge of his where-
abouts, although she did wax enthusiastic about the gift
piano.

It wasn't a bad idea, giving the musical instrument to
the church. Beth did have good ideas, perhaps a heavenly
gift. *If only I'd listened to her before I left . . . and found Peña.*

Jon Marc glanced around, his gaze resting on Beth. What
should he do about her?

He swung his eyes to the visitors. Jon Marc wanted nothing to do with what he'd left Memphis to be free of. Yet
Fitz was in no shape for a battle royal.

Eugene Jinnings? The sleeping eunuch, who'd lived for
centuries, had aged somewhat in the past four years. Without the magic lamp, Jinnings would die a mortal. That was
his own wish, to fade away an ordinary man, albeit a lazy
one cosseted by wealth and privilege.

He was mortal enough to die in the cross fire. Which
would break Tessa's heart. She loved this curious fellow.

Jon Marc couldn't turn his back on any of them. They
needed protection; he must give it. Unless he could get
them to leave—each and every one of them—without a
fight. And before Todd went on the rampage.

*Too bad the genie doesn't have the magic lamp. It might be
useful for a number of things.*

The lamp four years gone, Jon Marc faced facts. Fitz was
here, with others. Beth ought to be on her way to Laredo,

bound and gagged, if necessary. But they were all here, now.

Jon Marc strode to an empty chair, apparently hauled from the kitchen to await him, and sat down. Arms folded over his chest, he decided to ease into demands. "How-d-ya-do?"

Rousing, Eugene flashed a golden smile, the one that had charmed a maidenly Tessa but didn't hold water with Jon Marc. "Allah be praised, I am fine."

Beth took a seat.

"Do ye have not a welcoming word for me, Jonny?"

Jon Marc glared at Fitz, and got right to the point. "You are out of line, visiting without being asked."

"I doona need an invitation to visit an O'Brien," Fitz came back.

"You reneged on your word." Jon Marc scowled. "I wrote and asked you to leave me be while I got my wife." The family hadn't left his half brothers alone. He might have known he'd be no exception, the bastardy of his birth not carrying weight when it came to curiosity. "You got Pippin to do your answering. You said you wouldn't darken my doorway."

" 'Tis not ye I be here t' see, Jonny."

Right. Jon Marc bounced his gaze to Beth, who sat with hands in her lap, while he addressed his words to the grandfather who wasn't. "You're here to see what magic brought me." *And to lasso and hogtie me to that coach for a return trip to Memphis.*

Memphis, Jon Marc wouldn't bring up.

Eugene, sitting next to Beth, smiled anew. "A plum, bright and ripe, is your Beth."

Jon Marc's scowl settled on the genie. "Don't mean to be rude, Jinnings, but . . . go get those children from the pigpen. Take your time doing it. Wait for us in the kitchen."

Lifting his large body from the chair, Eugene dragged himself away, whistling a tune as he went.

"Where would we be finding Abbott?" Fitz then asked.

"He'll be here directly." Jon Marc didn't find it strange that Fitz would ask after India's nephew. "He's securing his cabin. And gathering my vaqueros."

"Hoot," Beth said succinctly.

Jon Marc nodded. "Right. Hoot. Todd isn't to be trusted."

"There's a thousand dollars in the cookie jar that says he isn't as bad as you claim. Of course, that was before Peña," she added, her voice trailing off.

It took biting his tongue for Jon Marc not to ask his wife to follow Eugene. He couldn't demand she leave. She was, after all, his spouse. She had a right to hear whatever he and Fitz had to say to each other. Again, Jon Marc wondered when the subject of Fitz & Son would rear its repulsive head.

He said to the old man, "You've come at a bad time."

"Aye. Yer wife told me. Trouble with the one calling himself Hoot."

"You need to pack up and get gone, Fitz."

"Ye ought t' know I doona run from fights."

"You're too old for this one."

"I can still fire a rifle, if Pippin will load it for me."

Jon Marc said, "You should leave for his benefit. It's going to get ugly around here." The boy, natural son of a now-dead trapeze artist and a woman not fit to bring a child into the world, had suffered before Susan O'Brien, then Susan Seymour, had rescued him from a circus. Pippin even knew what it was like to have his first father threaten to throw the child into a lion's den. "Pippin's had enough ugly."

Beth shot up, like a soldier raring for combat. "I won't allow it to get ugly. I'll find Hoot, and—"

"Sit down, wife! Now. You're staying put."

While she retook a seat, her eyes spoke: Bully, my methods are superior to yours. Jon Marc tended to agree. But

Peña was dead. They had to go from here. That wouldn't include cowering behind his wife's apron strings.

He asked Fitz, "How far to the rear are Tessa and Phoebe?"

"The girls dinna break their word. Contessa stayed in Memphis. Phoebe and her husband are cozy in New Orleans."

It was unfathomable, the aunties being unwilling to appease inquisitiveness, especially with Fitz making this trip. But they had. Jon Marc swallowed a smile, such an expression not what he wanted to convey at the moment. At least he could trust the aunts.

"Ye will be having another visitor, ye will," Fitz hinted. "No more than a day or two behind me party."

"My brothers?"

"Not at all," Beth said, and Jon Marc resented the hollow feeling that went through him, as well as the yearning to have brotherly love once more. Dammit. Did a man never learn?

"Who?" he wanted to know.

"A chap knowing how to handle a firearm, is me thinking."

"Don't talk in riddles, Fitz." The heel of Jon Marc's hand sliced the air. "I'm in no mood for it. Who is the mystery visitor?"

"Marcus Johnson."

Eugene Jinnings, eunuch, known in the Arabic lands as Marid, beheld a sty of swine and two beautiful youngsters, one as foreign-looking as the genie himself. "Hark, children. You must come with me."

Pippin O'Brien, older by several years than the girl, stopped filling a trough with what appeared to be chunks of fish. "Will Uncle Jon Marc let us stay?"

Having eavesdropped on the conversation at the house, Eugene tugged on his ear bob. Jones had not reacted well to the news that Marcus Johnson would make his presence known.

A mess that needed the grace of Allah, that was what this trip had unearthed. It followed that the Creator would grant no goodwill to heretics. This is where a genie needed his lamp.

Although no one was aware of it, outside Eugene himself, the lamp still existed.

At least a piece of it remained. The genie had retrieved a portion of the bowl, after the *Yankee Princess* went down in 1868. Not a soul knew that. Or that it was buried behind the O'Brien manse in Memphis.

Tired of toiling at the lamp's behest, Eugene couldn't breathe a word about the lamp's existence. He abhorred work. Or anything related to it. Wishes on the lamp meant work.

This journey had been too much for a lazy jinn, truth be told, which it had been fruitless to mention, Fitz having been set on the trip. A loyal son-in-law, Eugene had proven. Yet he would have preferred to be ensconced at the O'Brien lair in Memphis, tucked up with a hot mug of chocolate and a plump wife who accepted that his tongue was the hardest object that would prod her treasure trove.

Eugene licked his lips.

"Will Uncle Jon Marc let us stay?" Pippin repeated.

"I do not want you to leave." Shyly, Sabrina sidled up to the older youth. "You have much to learn about pigs."

"Aw, hush. I ain't here to learn about pigs."

Eugene sighed. "Do not say ain't. Susan would object."

The boy's face boiled with indignity. "Momma ain't here. Anyways, she's got sons of her own to teach not to say ain't."

Thick lips flattened. It was work, trying to make this boy understand his adoptive parents loved him, with no partiality toward their two baby sons. "She would object to your saying ain't. She has standards where you are concerned."

"Well, she ain't here, is she?"

Again, Eugene sighed. Why was it that so much trouble attached itself to families?

Why couldn't these O'Briens be happy with their lot?

Fitz on his never-ending quest for an heir.

Jones with bandit problems. If the genie could read unsettled faces, which he could, being a canny genie, he knew something smelled in Denmark, where the newly-weds were concerned.

Add that to Pippin's unhappiness at thinking he was odd son out—In the words of Eugene's old friend, Shakespeare, something was rotten in Denmark.

*Too much work, too much work.*

There was no rest for this genie. Pippin needed to know he was loved, so Fitz had demanded the boy come on this trip to "wheel me chair." The true reason? The patriarch knew his great-grandson admired the wayfarer Jones. Fitz believed the boy would benefit from being near his uncle. Possibly not.

Oh, for a cocoa, a cuddle, and a nap . . .

"Scoot, Pippin," Eugene suggested. "Go to the house. Work magic on your uncle. So we can be gone at the earliest."

"How'm I supposed to do that?"

"What is work magic?" Lovely eyes went round as pita.

Pippin cast her a look of disgust. " 'Brina, don't you know nothing about English? Uncle Eugene knows I'm the best one to make Uncle Jon Marc see the light."

"I do not understand. You speak too quickly." The girl bored hazel eyes into Pippin. "What is 'see the light'?"

*A beacon Jones will never see.*

# Chapter Twenty-Two

The last light of day faded.

Jon Marc lit a lantern, set it on the passageway floor, and wished he could retreat from his wife and nephew, plus Hoot's daughter, who'd gathered to catch evening breezes. Perhaps he just needed an excuse to be away from here, where he could think. Quietly, silently. And come to grips with the news that his begetter was on the way.

Too bad there couldn't be a limit on how many problems a man could tackle at once.

"Wanna play some checkers? Great-granddaddy brought his set along." Pippin grinned at his uncle. "Bet I can beat you."

Jon Marc swallowed a groan, knowing he could have Sabrina halfway to Fort Ewell by the time he finished a game of draughts. For his nephew's sake, he couldn't be rude.

"No checkers," Beth put in with the authority of a mother. "It's late. And you, young man, have had a long journey. Off to bed with you. You, too, Sabrina."

Already Fitz had settled into the parlor. Beth had insisted

old bones shouldn't sleep on a cot, even though Fitz had slept on a cot since leaving the steamship that brought his party to Galveston for the overland trip here.

Eugene would put up on that cot, next to the sofa. Beth had made a pallet for Pippin, next to the cot. When Sabrina asked where she might light her head, Beth smiled sweetly, assuring the girl no one would mind having her pallet beside their bed. Jon Marc would gladly strangle his wife for her suggestion.

She wanted to save face, he figured. If he took to his bedroll, it wouldn't bode well for their standing as newly-weds. Jon Marc would not light his head beside hers, face or no face.

Beth got a stern look. "Get ready for bed, children."

"Okayyyy." Pippin's grouse lost its fizzle as he clipped salutes to the hostess and to Sabrina. "Tomorrow we'll play checkers. I'll teach you, if you want, 'Brina."

No telling what the morrow would bring.

"Count Sabrina out," Jon Marc informed his nephew. "She's going home."

"I do not have a home."

"Yes, you do." Jon Marc crossed arms over his chest. "With Padre Miguel."

"But I want to stay with Tristan."

"Tristan?" Jon Marc and Beth echoed in unison.

"That's the name 'Brina picked for me." The boy slid a hand behind Sabrina's waist. "Momma and Dad said I could choose my own name, whenever I wanted to. Pippin just ain't proper for a grown fellow. My woman's got good taste."

Great, just great. On top of everything else, they must contend with puppy love. Jon Marc, before stomping away to gather a rope to hogtie Sabrina, bent his glare at an equally strong-minded female. *This is your doing, Beth O'Brien.*

* * *

"Husband?"

Why was Jon Marc not surprised at hearing Beth's voice? He might have known she'd follow him. He should have walked faster, since she'd no doubt try to stop him from his rope-goal. Turning to her as she fell into step, he sued for reason. "You've got to agree to send Sabrina back to Santa María. You've got to understand why it's necessary."

"I do. It's for the best. She'll have to go."

"Thank you."

"It's been a long while since you've thanked me for anything," she said in a hushed tone.

He knew what she meant. Once, he'd told her gratitude would accompany each kiss, but that had been in his gullible days. "So be it."

"Jon Marc, I know you have problems, but would you please listen to mine? I-I'm crying on the inside. For you, for me. And for Sabrina. I fear—especially now, with things unsettled around here—Terecita will send her away. Forever."

He studied his wife. Even in the darkness of night, he could read the anguish in her features. Beth, who loved that kid, and probably the hombre she'd tricked into marriage.

*Oh, Beth. What am I going to do about you?*

The meanest varmint in the county couldn't have denied her a comforting arm. Jon Marc surely didn't. He laced an arm around her shoulders. "Honey, Sabrina will be better off, away from La Salle County."

"Would you allow me to help her? Please! I'll repay you. I'm growing plenty of vegetables. I can sell them. And I could take in sewing. Anything! If I pay her tuition, she can go to school in town. At least I'd be able to see her occasionally."

"For your own good, you need to cut loose from Sabrina."

Beth's shoulders wilted. "I can't. I love her."

"She's not yours."

Balling her fist, she thumped it against her chest. "She is in my heart. Right here! And here she will stay."

Jon Marc took her shoulders and gazed into her eyes. "You may not have a choice in it. Her mother makes Sabrina's decisions. But . . . oh, Beth, if Terecita allows it, I don't see why we can't do what we can to educate the girl."

Complete reversal—this was the change in Beth's demeanor. Quick as a blink, she threw her arms around him, bracing on tiptoes to kiss his lips.

Hands that ought to know better slid into her hair. His mouth responded to hers. So did Mighty Duke. *Fool, stop. You don't know enough about this wife of yours.*

He set her away. "Enough."

"Yes, I suppose it is. I shouldn't push you." Hugging her arms, Beth took off to the right to study the ground, then the sky. She whirled around. "We should keep a distance, until you know I love you."

"That's right." His tone was crisp, his heart shaky. But he had to set something straight. "Beth, I want you to know something. I tried to find Todd. To make peace."

"You don't know how that pleases me," she said, her voice showing every bit of it.

"Let's hope it works. I don't know how to deal with a jackal."

"He's not as unreasonable as you might believe."

"Beth . . . I'd prefer not to discuss Todd with you."

"Maybe we should change the subject." She stepped closer. "Jon Marc, Fitz brought a message from your brother. Burke. You should ask about it."

"You tell me."

"Burke tried to write several times, but never felt he got the wording right. So he never sent a letter. Anyhow, he feels awful that he didn't get his feelings across, before you left Louisiana. You see, he got over resenting your shooting that madman. But Burke was so caught up in reconciling with his wife that he didn't express himself. He bears you no grudge. And hopes the two of you can be brothers again."

Eyes closing, Jon Marc dropped his shoulders. So, Burke wanted to mend fences. A thousand thoughts crossed his mind, one on top of the other. He settled for a halfhearted "That would be nice."

"I'm relieved you feel that way."

Trouble was, she didn't leave well enough alone. Having softened her husband up, she went in for the kill. "Jon Marc, Fitz didn't tell everything about Marcus Johnson."

The lousiest feeling caved through Jon Marc; it got more hollow. "I don't want to know what it is. My haven's been violated, infringed upon. Trespassed against. And the main encroacher has done me even dirtier. Why on earth did Fitz see fit to tell Johnson where to find me?"

Her fingers wrapping around the heel of his hand, Beth urged him to a stop. "Look at me, husband."

He did. And saw an artless face, silvered by moonlight. Beth, a magician who needed no magic lamp to work wonders. At least with outlaws, saloon dancers, and priests. Unless she was worked against, as Jon Marc had worked against her.

She said, "Fitz hired a sleuth to track Mr. Johnson down. A lady from New Orleans, I understand. A well-known sleuth who had a fine record for unraveling mysteries. Fitz thinks if you know the whole story about your mother and her paramour, you'll be more of a mind to . . . for family harmony."

"He wasted his time."

"Do you think it was easy for Fitz, to track down the man who caused his son's death? Doesn't that mean anything to you?"

In truth it did. Jon Marc had long known how deeply

Fitz had been crushed by Daniel's death, and despised Johnson.

"Jon Marc, would you be terribly offended if I put my arms around you?"

He tensed, not wanting her magic, yet his heart cried out for it at the same time. What would it hurt, one more hug? "As long as you know it'll go no further."

She moved in front of him to slide her arms around his waist. Her cheek nestled at his shoulder. It felt right, having her here. His wife. The Kansas beauty who had traveled to Texas to become his wife. Right now it almost didn't matter, the virginity business.

He longed to lace his arms around her. Enclosing her in those arms, he rested his jaw against her sweet-smelling hair, admitting, "I need this."

"We need each other, darling."

"The world has gone to the devil around us." He shouldn't expose his heart, yet he somehow couldn't stop. "Time like this, a man needs his wife."

"And vice-versa." Beth pressed lips to his turbulent heart. "Jon Marc, you *must* know something. Before it's sprung on you. Marcus Johnson isn't your father."

Shock. It had to be shock that weakened his pulse. Everything he'd ever known in his life about his parentage— none of it had been real. Yet reason kicked his veins.

"It's a trick, Beth," he muttered. "A dirty trick."

"I don't think so. Fitz told me—"

"I don't want to hear it. It's a trick. I won't be tricked. If there's anything worse than being lied to, it's compounding it with another lie."

Jon Marc took his arms from Beth. And set off to saddle León and collect that rope.


She kicked and screamed, howled to the night sky. Bethany, her heart heavy for her husband and his magnified problems, dashed after the mount that carried him and the screaming Sabrina away from the Caliente.

While she must stop her niece's terror, Bethany yearned to make everything right for her husband. Her husband, who thought it terrible to compound one lie with another. Her husband, who had known solace and heartache tonight. Her husband, who had married a fraud.

"Uncle Jon Marc, you're not very nice!"

Pippin. Bethany glanced over her shoulder. Barefoot, running toward León, the youth flailed his arms.

Jon Marc twisted in the saddle, shouting, "Beth, for God's sake, calm the boy!"

She hurried back to Pippin. Tears streamed down his cheeks. He rubbed a pajama sleeve beneath his watery nose. He was a troubled child. And, if Bethany was any judge, his troubles hadn't started with Jon Marc taking his playmate away.

"Shh." Bethany tried to comfort by patting his shoulder. "Be patient, Pip. He's not hurting Sabrina, I promise. There are many things you don't understand about this situation. Your uncle is very nice. And you are quite important to him."

"He's making my friend cry."

"You'll see Sabrina again. Mark my words, she won't cry."

"When will I see her?"

"Soon." Bethany squeezed his shoulders. "Trust me, Pip. I am good for my word." *Todds always are.* "I'm going to ride after her, make certain she's not crying when she reaches the church."

Pippin cocked his head, scrutinizing Bethany's expression. On a sigh he relented. "Then go on. Don't tarry."

She didn't.

Jon Marc wasn't the least bit pleased when Bethany and Arlene caught up with him and his unhappy burden, since she'd promised to keep an eye on the house. They were now less than a mile from Fort Ewell. Grudgingly, he allowed her to follow him, once she calmed Sabrina.

The bang of piano keys thundered through the air as they approached the church. Terecita was practicing.

"She hates you," Bethany pointed out, once they had dismounted and Sabrina had run into Padre Miguel's beckoning arms.

"Terecita will never tell you where to find Hoot. I'm in good stead with her at the moment. Let me talk to her alone. Please. I think she'll tell me where to find Hoot."

"I don't like this," Jon Marc muttered.

For the second time tonight, Bethany begged trust. "You've got to listen to me."

"If I agree, will you turn around and go home?"

She could lie, but wouldn't. "No. I won't. You need a partner, if we're to have harmony with Hoot Todd."

"Mine is man's business."

"You've got several platesful of business."

"I'm going back to the Caliente. Get my men."

"No! It's better if we speak with Hoot, just you and me." She took Jon Marc's hand, as she had before they left the Caliente. Again, he didn't pull away, which elevated her hopes for the two of them. "Darling, you're not going to stop me."

"I was afraid of that."


The candlelit church was empty, save for a pianist whose fingers never seemed to hit the right keys.

Bethany stopped for holy water, then strolled down the aisle. The big piano sat left of the rail where Bethany had pledged her heart to Jon Marc, even though God hadn't been listening. Her lips moved in prayer, that someday she would become a bride in the eyes of the Almighty.

If that day were to dawn, then accord must come to La Salle County. Terecita López might not hit the proper ivories, but she could hold the key to peace.

The dancer wore a cotton skirt, as scarlet as a painted lady's lips, and a white peasant blouse. Her long hair flowed down her back. She stopped striking keys.

Whirling around on the piano bench, she said, "Ah. It is the bride of Señor O'Brien. Wearing britches. Did you not know ladies should wear skirts?"

"Don't accuse me of being a lady," Bethany returned lightly. "I'd like to think of myself as simply a ranch-wife."

"I would like to think of myself as a lady. Or at least a good piano player." Terecita sighed. "What brings you to Santa María tonight?"

"We—I've returned Sabrina. She'll be safer here."

"Yes, safer."

Bethany approached the fledgling musician, then gestured to the bench. "Mind if I join you?"

"Sit down."

Scooting next to Terecita, Bethany touched an ivory, but not hard enough to make a sound. "When a woman is in love, it's peace she seeks. I love Jon Marc. Do you love Hoot Todd?"

"Sometimes."

That brought a chuckle. "Men can be aggravating, can't they? Occasionally they're lovable. Other times, we could pinch their heads off, couldn't we?"

"A stiletto slicing their throats is what they deserve."

"Would you kill Hoot?"

Terecita shook her head. "I wish *mi viejo* calm. It pleases me that you gave Chico pause to think about his deeds."

Bethany tried not to snicker at Terecita mixing "old man" with boy. Yet the import of that statement sunk in. "How much did he tell you?"

Terecita patted her hand. "Do not worry, *amiga*. I will tell no one."

Bethany would have to take her at her word, since she had no other choice. Terecita's promise didn't evoke a great deal of confidence, nevertheless. *This visit isn't about you.*

"Would you kill Jon Marc?" she asked.

"Many times I considered it. He embarrassed me in front of the other whores in Laredo. He shamed me so much that I couldn't stay there. I had nowhere else to go but here, where I am always reminded of my shame."

"I feel in my heart Jon Marc didn't mean to shame you. He did not share his body—" *not much, anyhow* "—before marriage."

Terecita's eyes rounded. "You mean it wasn't just me?"

"He thinks you're quite lovely."

A smile brighter than candlelight lit Terecita's round face. "Since he is married now, do you think he might be interested in a threesome?"

"He believes in fidelity of marriage."

"Oh."

"Terecita . . . do you know about Peña?"

"Yes. He is dead. At Señor O'Brien's hand."

"Unfortunately, yes. But my husband wants no more bullets to fly. That's why we must speak with Hoot. Where is he, Terecita? Where can we find him?"

"He and his *discipulos* gather at Salado Creek, at the cabin once used by Luis de la Garza." Terecita chewed her bottom lip. "Señora . . . Chico is a bad man in many ways, but he is good in others. He does not believe children should be touched by wicked hands. Tell him . . . tell him Peña wanted to buy Sabrina for a night."

Shocked—sickened!—Bethany murmured, "Surely you didn't."

"I would *never* give my daughter into wicked hands. I want the best for her. That is why she lives here at the church. That is why I decided to allow you to sew clothes for her. And to let my child visit the nice lady who smiles at her. I was wrong that day, when I ordered you not to help her."

"No hard feelings."

"Thank you, señora. I hope you understand why I must send her away with the orphans. For her own good." Tears glistened in Terecita's black eyes. "Someday, my Sabrina will be a lady."

"You needn't send her to the orphanage. Jon Marc and I will educate her, Terecita. We'll find a good school. There's no need for us to lose her."

"Do you mean that?"

"With all my heart. And with my husband's approval."

"My prayers are answered." The mother hugged the aunt, saying, *"Mil gracias,* señora. You are a fine lady."

Complimented to the core, Bethany smiled.

"Go, señora. Do good for Sabrina. And for us all."

There was no chance that Jon Marc would allow Bethany to confront Hoot on her own. She hoped whatever powers she'd used on her brother would hold, at least once more. She shoved up from the piano bench. "Good-bye, Terecita."

*"Vaya con Dios."*

"You, too, *amiga.* Go with God." Lifting her eyes, Bethany added a silent prayer. That He wouldn't turn his back, wouldn't make her husband pay for his wife's many sins.

*If You guide us through this, I will repay you. In whatever way You require.*


They found Hoot Todd and his desperadoes at a line shack on the Salado that rightly belonged to Rancho Caliente.

"We come in peace," Jon Marc said when a mean-faced brigand opened the cabin door; he and Beth stared at the business ends of a dozen or so six-shooters, including the leader's.

This was not the smartest undertaking Jon Marc had ever delved in. He didn't like the idea, especially with Beth at his side. Hoot Todd couldn't be trusted.

Nonetheless, Jon Marc had known if he hadn't agreed to find this lowly gang, she would have done it on her own.

"Raise your arms, O'Brien." Hoot did his showpiece

trick, twirling both revolvers on forefingers, then leveling them at Jon Marc. "Xavier, get his gun. Beth, you packin' a weapon?"

"None but my sharp tongue."

"Ain't she great?" Hoot grinned so big that his eye patch lifted a fraction of an inch.

"Yeah, my wife is great," Jon Marc answered, as Todd's minion divested him of pistol.

Bandits inched forward, a trio sidewinding behind Jon Marc and Beth. He stepped backward, but not soon enough.

Todd stirred one gun barrel. "Tie 'em up, boys."

Damn. *I should've gathered my men to back this up.* Jon Marc's fists flew; they did no good. The bandits descended like locusts, had him and Beth in strangleholds in no time.

Magic went only so far.

# Chapter Twenty-Three

"Hoot Todd, order your men to untie me and my husband. This instant!"

"Can't do that, Beth. O'Brien done us wrong, killing Peña. Can't let that go unpunished."

Hemp rope ate into Bethany's arms and legs, as she knew it must burn her husband. She turned a frosted glare on the *bandidos*, who jeered and laughed, while sucking down tequila and smoking cigars. Her cool eyes settled on Hoot Todd. One of those revolting stogies clamped between his teeth, he tilted a straight chair back on its rear legs, resting pistols and hands on his thighs, his forefingers not moving from triggers.

She and Jon Marc might be outnumbered, might be tied up like animals on their way to slaughter, but she still had her tongue. "Hoot? Would that be your given name?"

His chair snapped to four legs. "Now, Beth . . ."

"Tell someone to open a shutter." If only she'd listened to Jon Marc, Caliente men would have been outside, ready to make things right, in case they continued to go wrong. Every once in a while, a wife ought to listen to her husband.

"You're going to choke us to death with cigar smoke. Really, Mor- . . . Hoot, you don't want that on your conscience."

"Crack a shutter," he ordered one of the men, who didn't look much different from the rest, outside missing an arm.

"Thank you," she said primly, while Jon Marc cautioned her in a low voice to be careful. "Hoot, I'm going to ask again. Would you please have these ropes dispensed with?"

"Xavier, Morales, take off the ropes."

Jon Marc uttered, "Amazing."

When Bethany shook free of the bonds, she said to her brother, "We're here to talk peace, Hoot Todd. Just you, me, and my husband. May we have some privacy?"

A pistol waved. Hoot motioned his head toward the door. "Wait outside, amigos."

The desperadoes cried foul, yet they eventually took their leave.

"You want a drink, Beth?" Hoot asked, once the associates were out of the shack.

"Yes, I believe I do. Pour my husband one, too."

"I'm not interested in his liq—"

"We're just going to have a nice neighborly drink, husband," she interrupted, wishing she could thump Jon Marc's antagonistic head.

Hoot blew dust out of two glasses—Bethany cringed to think what might have roamed the bottoms—then poured generous shots of tequila. He handed them over.

She looked into the glass, not to check for small varmints. She recalled her wedding picnic, when last she'd tasted the potent juice of cactus. Would this night turn out better than that one? If her prayers were answered.

Jon Marc spoke. "Todd, my wife wants peace. I want it, too. What can we do to stop our feud?"

She was proud of Jon Marc for asking. It hadn't been easy, swallowing pride to beg his enemy.

"Peña weren't the smartest hombre to come down the pike," Hoot replied, "but he was ours."

"Your men would back down," Jon Marc mentioned, "if you gave the word."

"Nope. Won't do it. Did talk 'em outta skinnin' you. You can be thankful for that."

A shiver raked Bethany.

"What if I give that corral of horses, down the creek?" Jon Marc took a sip of tequila. "Would that call it even?"

"Nope."

"Look, Todd. I know you've had a bone to pick, ever since Wilson ran you off the Caliente. But you got the better of him, burning him out like you did. When is enough, enough?"

"Fires are such cowardly things," Bethany interjected. "Hoot, you're way too noble for fires."

Jon Marc slanted a look that asked if she'd lost her mind.

"That fire wasn't my idea," Hoot said slowly.

"Then whose was it?" Jon Marc wanted to know.

"That don't make you no never-mind."

"It's not too late for a showdown," Jon Marc challenged.

Bethany's heart tripped. "No more showdowns. The last one wasn't even a fair duel. Hoot, Peña ambushed my husband, not the other way around. The law of the West says a man has a right to defend himself. But that's not important right now. You ordered your underling to run Jon Marc ragged, but Peña ambushed him instead. Simply didn't listen to you, did he?"

"Peña was a mite hotheaded."

"Unruly minions can sure make a legend look bad."

Hoot rolled the cigar to the other side of his mouth. "You reckon?"

"I most certainly do. By the way, did you know Terecita says Peña was downright evil?"

Hoot took a thought-filled drag. "What did Terecita say?"

"Peña had a habit of buying young children for illicit

purposes." That was an exaggeration. But if he'd procured Sabrina, he could have very well done other children wrong. "I understand this sort of worm isn't even respected in prisons."

"Peña never did nothin' like that," Hoot objected.

Jon Marc looked as sickened as his wife had been at the church.

"Terecita swears he offered money for Sabrina." Bethany roused a suspicious mien in her brother. "You figure she lied?"

"Naw." Hoot's face went ashen. "Terecita wouldn't lie."

Jon Marc spoke. Quietly. "Seems to me, a man like Peña doesn't deserve to be mourned."

"Or to have his death avenged," Bethany appended.

Hoot shook his head. "I don't rightly know what to think."

"What time is it?" Bethany asked, the Peña ploy having gone awry.

Now both men looked at her as if she'd lost her mind, then Hoot got a knowing gleam in that single eye.

"Did you know your pretty little wife give me a present?" Hoot dug in his shirt pocket. "This."

The fob watch dangled from its chain, light from the lantern dancing off gold.

What was he up to? she wondered. Was this a challenge? A threat to expose her as a Todd? *Bad gamble, girl.*

Hoot looked at the gift lovingly. Jon Marc had never frowned as deeply. Bethany decided not to borrow trouble.

"I'm waiting for the time, Hoot," she said.

"Near on two in the morning."

"No wonder I'm so tired." She feigned a yawn. "Land's sake, the hour is too late for chats. Why, if I don't get my beauty sleep, I'm liable to be too tired to bake a nice lemon pie tomorrow." She paused while Hoot smacked his lips and Jon Marc flattened his. "Did you know we have company from Memphis? They brought enough sugar and lemons to make a dozen pies."

"Ain't et no lemon pie since the Oklahoma Territory. Nobody's ever got enough sugar 'round these parts to bake one."

"I've got sugar. Flour, too. You got any lard, Hoot? I haven't had a chance to render any. Must have it for pie crust. Maybe Padre Miguel has some."

"Would you hush about sugar and pies?" Jon Marc glared, his mind obviously on why she'd given Hoot an expensive gift.

"Sure would be a shame, if I was too busy fighting off a feud to bake pies tomorrow." She lifted her glass toward Hoot, as if in salute, but cast a glance at Jon Marc's wary countenance. "Husband, do you remember promising our vaqueros a feast to celebrate our marriage? Do you suppose we could get one organized in the morning?"

He jacked up a gold-dusted eyebrow. A moment slipped by before he twitched a shoulder, falling in a line, albeit crooked. "Don't see why not. Catfish Abbott is mustering the Caliente men, as we speak. He may have them at ranch headquarters already. May not stay put. Catfish being a worrywart, he's liable to wonder what's keeping us. You did tell our guests we were meandering this way, didn't you?"

Men! Why were they as difficult to handle as greased pigs? Here she was, skating like a hog on ice, yet her pigheaded husband made veiled threats. What could she do but support him?

"I did." She nodded, although she hoped it wouldn't set Hoot off. "I said we'd check your horses, here on the Salado."

Hoot sucked his teeth.

"Sure would be a shame, if they had to come all this way, just to turn around for a celebration," she said. "Why, I bet Padre Miguel would be so pleased at eating lemon pie he might even bless the meal. Would you like to join us, Hoot? Terecita and Sabrina are welcome. Your men, too. We'd be like one big happy family. A good Catholic miracle."

Hoot sighed. His eye woefully downcast, he holstered his six-shooters. "This county'd get downright civilized."

"Which no doubt will bring writers here, in search of stories about the wild days."

"That'd be nice," her brother murmured.

"We must add Isabel Marin and Mr. Short to the party list," Bethany said. "We wouldn't want to leave anyone out. Should we tell Liam to leave Stumpy at the post office?"

"I don't believe this," Jon Marc muttered.

"Tomorrow, would you be kind enough, husband, to read from one of your poetry books? I think entertainment would add the right touch." Provided Marcus Johnson stubbed his toe and fell in a well before reaching the Caliente. "Perhaps we should have the feast at church, since Terecita could play piano for us."

"You're dithering," Jon Marc said.

She cast him a shut-up glare. He had no idea how difficult it was, trying to change a miscreant brother into a solid citizen ... when she couldn't outright appeal to Hoot's sense of Todd.

"I don't wanna hear Terecita play nothin'. She's awful."

Smiling sweetly at Hoot, Bethany gave an alternative. "Perhaps we can talk her into a castanet recital. Any of your men handy with a guitar?"

"Jaime plays the violin. He's the one ain't got no arm."

"Mind if I ask how he does that?" Bethany inquired.

"Uses his toes."

"Jesus H. Christ."

"Hush, husband." She gestured toward her brother's clothes. "Be sure and tidy up before you come calling. Tell your men to, too. Our Memphis guests are quite refined." She angled a smile and a bat of eyes at Jon Marc. "Does your grandfather know any writers?"

"Hundreds."

"My boys won't wanna celebrate. Peña is dead. And he was one of us."

"You work on that, Hoot." Recalling something Isabel had once told her, she piled on rationale. "I've heard violent death is an honorable estate in the Mexican culture. Harks back to the Aztec days, when the winner in ball games had the opportunity to be sacrificed to the gods. You put it that way, and I'll bet your boys will see the light."

"I want them horses—all of 'em," Hoot announced. "Or we ain't made peace."

Jon Marc nodded. "They're yours."

Bethany smiled, relieved. And she couldn't help a selfish thought. Exactly what sort of peace would the perfect and saintly Miss Buchanan have brought to La Salle County? *I'm better for here than she would have been!*

The crisis was indeed averted. Jon Marc entered a fog of disbelief. Beth had dithered Hoot Todd into compliance. And he'd gotten his desperadoes to go along with it. A fine string of horses was a small enough sacrifice, Jon Marc reckoned. Peace would be nice. More than nice.

Her efforts tired Beth out. He heard yawn after yawn as they rode León and Arlene back to the Caliente.

Her husband knew a subject certain to open her eyes. "Where did you get that watch?"

"It was my father's," she replied, yawning.

"Why didn't you give it to me?"

"Must you argue everything?"

"Guess not," Jon Marc answered.

"*Querido,* I promised Pip he could see Sabrina again. We can't let him go, not until after the party. It wouldn't be fair."

"You're not playing fair."

"Seems to me, I get results."

"Braggart." Jon Marc turned León down the trail to

their home. "All right, wife. You win. Fitz and party can stay until after the get-together."

He expected her to say something, worried him when she didn't. Glancing to his left, he saw her . . . asleep atop Arlene.

Back at the house, he carried his wife into the bedroom—she never opened her eyes—and he stretched out beside her, too worn out for anything but sleep. Yet his last thought before snores took him was, *She is an amazing woman.* A good Catholic miracle.

Too bad she was out of bed when he awakened . . .

They might have tried a piece of peace.

By midafternoon, Padre Miguel had said grace over the laid-out feast. *Bandidos* gave an obligatory prayer for Peña's soul. *"¡Viva, Peña!"* echoed, after the last of the Todd gang made the sign of the cross on his chest.

Jon Marc figured it might get nasty, if honorable death were to lose out to good ol' brush-country revenge.

Not so.

Hoot Todd sidled up. "Made 'em see reason, like your pretty little wife done asked me to. You sure got a nice woman, O'Brien. Wish I could find me one like that."

Getting territorial, Jon Marc frowned. "Don't get any ideas about stealing mine."

"What? You crazy, O'Brien? She's my—" Todd thumped his chest. "She's the same as a sister, right here in my heart."

"Keep thinking like that, and maybe this truce will hold."

"Well, *cuñado,* that's rightly what I plan to do. Say, where's that feller done knows all them writers?"

Jon Marc pointed to Fitz. Todd sprang to the invalid chair and offered a cigar that was accepted.

Why had Todd called Jon Marc brother-in-law? That was not the sort of thing one quibbled about during a cease-fire, if Jon Marc had any sense. Anyhow, if Todd wanted to call himself brother to Beth, what was the harm in that?

Strolling away, Jon Marc chuckled. If anything didn't fall into order in his mind, it was the thought of his wife being sister to Hoot Todd.

He glanced at the sky. It shone like an aquamarine, set off by a canary-diamond sun. It was a fine day for a party. And for peace. Both in this county . . . and in a man's heart.

Beth O'Brien was a fine woman. A savior to this place, and to her husband. She'd made a mistake before marriage—she didn't recognize it as a misdeed, but as payoff to keep her father alive—but intuition had a word with her husband. Her value was higher than every aquamarine ever mined, every diamond ever polished.

He searched for her, but she shooed him out the kitchen, claiming pies had her busy. Funny, how a purpose could turn on a man. He didn't want her to be too much the working wife. They needed to do some working on each other.

Later.

He roamed the yard.

A pig turned on a spit, manpower provided by Xavier and Morales, bandits. Jaime rosined up his bow and set toes to work, playing tunes more appropriate to American audiences than to largely Hispanic ones. "Sally Good'ne" and "Ol' Man Tucker" seemed to be his specialties. He wasn't half bad.

Ten other bandits gobbled copious amounts of Isabel's freshly made tortillas, along with her specialty: hot sauce.

Liam Short and Padre Miguel partook of a home brew that the padre had been keeping to himself. Fitz drank a tin cup full, although Eugene declined for religious purposes. Jon Marc wasn't too holy to take several sips.

Catfish Abbott cast a wary glance at the Todd gang, but he eased down when somebody suggested a game of horseshoes. The Caliente vaqueros joined in, and had the foresight to lose. They paid off with whiskey, which the Todd gang took to.

Pippin did somersaults when Sabrina arrived, holding her mother's hand. Even before Terecita coerced Hoot Todd into a sensuous dance that involved her castanets, the youngsters took off for the pigpen, "Tristan" carrying the game board, " 'Brina" toting a felt bag filled with red and black checkers.

Just as the pig dripped fat, Stumpy eyed a bone that Sham II had squirreled beneath his paws. The mutt made a lunge for the bloodhound, who had been sleeping off the dregs of a bowl of chili and that beef bone, as house dogs were wont to do. Stumpy moved pretty fast, considering he did it on three legs.

Fur flew. Blood spewed. Liam Short doused them with a bucket of sand and the spew of his wrathful voice.

The music having stopped for the dogfight, Jon Marc, who knew *Evangeline* by heart, began a recitation. Both Stumpy and Sham II bayed through the first part. It wasn't long before the listeners, including the dogs, allowed their eyelids to droop. Hoot Todd's snores shut Jon Marc's mouth.

Well, poetry wasn't for everyone.

Jon Marc motioned for Jaime to fiddle, which perked up the revelers.

This was the best day La Salle County had ever known.

# Chapter Twenty-Four

"I've made enough pies for everyone in brush country," Bethany muttered under her breath. "Well, better for our cup to run over than for anyone to do without."

She shoved the last lemon pie into the oven, then blew a lock of hair away from her eyes. She should have been tired, having cooked while their guests made revelry, but she wasn't even winded. She felt renewed, pleased to have the chance to bake these pies. Her prayers had been answered.

How could she find out what to do in return?

"Need some help?"

"I thought I told you to stay out of my kitchen," she scolded softly as her husband entered the kitchen.

He wore denims over work-worn boots. The top two buttons of his rust-colored shirt were freed, the V baring the bronzed skin of his throat. Would he ever again invite her fingers to stroke that flesh?

"You'll work your fingers to the bone," he said, his ardent gaze welding to hers, "if you don't stop to enjoy your own celebration."

Disappointed that he hadn't ask for something of the flesh, she answered, "I'm almost through. I'm itching to get outside to enjoy the music and good cheer."

"Would you dance with me?"

There was a tender cast to his voice. What did it mean? She had her hopes, along with her gratitude for prayers answered.

"Wife, I'd love to dance with you. Right here, amid the oven and the mess of cooking. Just me and you."

"That . . . that would be nice." Should she anticipate more?

He ambled toward her, getting close enough for her to smell bay rum, yet he didn't offer that dance. He said, "You're a miracle, Beth O'Brien."

"I'm not."

"You are. I've never seen anyone who could turn things around like you can. There's never been anyone more special than you. You can be trusted, dear wife. And I trust you."

Praise rested heavy on her shoulders, like a hair shirt. She'd done nothing for glory. Her efforts were manipulation in its baldest form. Nothing to be proud of. A higher power had done the work, deserved the credit. If she said as much, she'd have to say more, would necessarily spill too much.

She cast her gaze to the earthen floor.

"You have flour on your nose," her husband murmured. "You've never looked as beautiful to me."

"Ah, ha!" Mirth forced, she said, "Now I know your secrets. You do seek a household drudge."

"No, Beth. I seek my wife."

Her heart seemed to stop. Was she hearing correctly, or . . . "Please don't toy with me."

"I intend to dance with you. If you agree." That was when he brushed a fingertip across her nose. "May I kiss you?"

A smile boosted her cheeks. "I'd be delighted."

"So would I . . ." His lips took hers.

He tasted like beer, which could be the reason he'd loosened up enough to kiss her. She wouldn't reason it out. She melted against his long, tall form, wanting more, more, more.

And he gave it.

He slid his palm to the base of her spine, taking her hand in his as she placed her left wrist on his shoulder. He whirled her around in the waltz that floated from Jaime's violin. Her husband danced with grace, within the tempo, as if he were a swain who'd escorted a thousand ladies to ballroom floors.

Surprisingly, Bethany had no trouble following, even though her only dancing had been with Cletus, when he hadn't been too drunk to dance. This was much better than dancing with Pa. This was wondrous.

And when the dance ended, she whispered, "Thank you."

Again Jon Marc kissed her.

This time he picked at her buttons. "I want to love you, wife."

No matter how much she wanted what he offered, or how much his surrender implied, he'd never declared his feelings. Was it silly to expect anything more than sweet talk? She was ignoble enough to ask, "Is that what you're doing, *querido*? Loving me?"

"I love you."

*Oh, Jon Marc, thank you! Thank God.*

Her husband ran a fingertip along her temple. "How could I not love you? I want to hold you in my arms and place you on this floor and bury myself so deep that I never find my way out."

She reveled in those words. Nevertheless, she wouldn't be his under false pretenses. Too much could never be told. With any luck, some things would never come to light. "Husband, do you know I'll never do you wrong?"

He eased her to the floor. "There's not a hateful bone in your body, wife."

But would he someday hate her, if he had second thoughts? "This kind of thing could make a baby."

"Let's hope it's a boy" was his comment.

"Or a girl. Or one or the other."

He laughed, deep and strong. "Aw, Beth honey, I'm the luckiest man alive."

That was everything she needed to hear. Rubbing her palm along the ridge in his britches, she wiggled against him and fiddled with his buttons. Jubilance turned to wifely teasing. "Draw on me, vaquero. Let's see what sorta weapon you pack."

It was as long as a Peacemaker.

As potent as the Colt arsenal.

And it went off like a cannon.

By the time the last pie had burned, the sacrificial pig had probably browned to a turn. Jon Marc and Bethany straightened their clothes to leave the kitchen.

"My turn to say thank you," he growled and grabbed her for another kiss.

Yet a niggling of worry jabbed her good cheer. It seemed somehow outrageous, being this happy when their marriage had yet to become legal in the eyes of anyone, save for the husband.

Not a half hour later, real trouble arrived.

A rider rode a white prancer onto the property.

The gentleman, not a youth by any means, reined in, near Terecita.

The big stallion reared to hind legs, the rider—wearing fringed buckskins as white as his silver-studded, ten-gallon chapeau—doffed that hat. His hair grew long and thick, curling to his shoulders. It was the whitest hair Bethany had ever seen.

She felt her husband tense beside her as the stranger gave a great whoop.

"Howdy, folks," the arrivee bellowed. "The name's Johnson. Marcus Johnson. Trick-rider and fast-draw artist. How 'bout I feed those dogs for you?"

Not unlike Hoot Todd, Johnson brandished a pair of pistols to twirl them. Crossing his arms skyward, he picked off first one, then another mockingbird that had the misfortune to fly into the line of fire.

The dead birds landed in front of Sham II and Stumpy. Both dogs had the decency to turn their noses up at the burnt offering.

"Goddamn the goddamn," Jon Marc muttered under his breath, his glare firmly on his dead mother's lover.

Marcus Johnson's arrival roused a commotion. No brush popper or vaquero, much less any bandit, had ever seen such an dime-novel version of a man of the West.

Fitz O'Brien, with Eugene's assistance, made his way into the house, obviously unwilling to speak with the man he'd summoned. Bethany knew how much it hurt Fitz, seeing the person responsible for Daniel's suicide.

Jon Marc stomped away, making for the river.

His wife followed, praying the wonderful part of this day hadn't reached an end.

"I don't want to talk," he said as they sat on the river-bank, their knees drawn up.

"I understand."

He reached for her hand, then squeezed it, not too gently. She inched closer and laid her head against his shoulder. His arm went around her. They stayed like this for a good while, as continued whoops, gunfire, and laughter rang through the air, from the proximity of their invaded home.

Then the music started again.

Bethany and her husband said nothing, but she knew he felt as she did. They were glad the show had ended.

"You two mind if I join you?"

That voice, belonging to Johnson, caused Bethany to straighten. It made Jon Marc heave to booted feet.

"You must be Mrs. O'Brien." Again, Johnson doffed the hat that no working cowboy would be caught dead in. Adjusting the turquoise garnish of his bolo tie, he said, "Pleased to meet you, ma'am."

She said nothing, feeling no need for social chatter. Up close like this, she couldn't help but notice red highlights in Johnson's white hair.

"Been a long time since we last met," Johnson said to Jon Marc. "I wouldn't have recognized you."

"Cut the small-talk."

"Would you like me to leave?" Bethany asked her husband.

"Anything I have to say to this man, you need to hear it."

"I'm the one with talking to do." Johnson set his hat atop a chaparral, with the care one might use to set a vase on a rickety table. "I hope you'll listen, son."

"Don't call me son."

"Fair enough. Since you don't belong to me."

Jon Marc's face hardened to the steel of a pistol barrel. "You forget who you're speaking to. I heard my mother taunt her husband with tales of her ongoing affair with you."

"We did have an affair, me and Georgia. Met her in Washington. Daniel O'Brien was stationed there in the army." Johnson squinted across the river, clasping his hands behind him, then slanted brown eyes at Jon Marc. "I was new to town. Had been selling my aim in the Opium Wars, over in China. Got hurt pretty bad. Those Asian fellows know explosives—" he patted each pearl-handled pistol "—even better than I know Pete and Repeat here."

"We're not interested in your history," Jon Marc said sourly, echoing his wife's sentiments.

She prompted, "Tell us what you know about my husband's mother and her husband."

"Daniel was a likable enough fellow. Meet him when I started representing a gun manufacturer. He invited me to their home for supper. I took one look at Georgia and fell in love. Never touched the lady, though. Not in Washington." Johnson flicked a gaze at his presumed son. "You were born some time later. But I had nothing to do with it."

Every muscle in Jon Marc's body went taut. "I don't want to listen to this."

"It's about time you did, since your mother—God rest her soul—did us all a disservice, claiming things that shouldn't have been claimed."

Bethany swallowed, knowing Jon Marc hated every moment of having his mother's dirty linen aired. Inconsiderate Georgia had been to her family, but she'd still brought him into the world.

Johnson strolled down the riverbank, then swiveled around. "When I moved to Memphis, Georgia was there. I took up with her. Wasn't right, but I did it. Had never gotten her out of my thoughts. Loved that lady. Sure did love that lady."

Jon Marc clenched and unclenched his fists as Johnson carried on. "Georgia and I talked about her getting a divorce. She stepped over the line, taunting Daniel into it. Claimed you were mine. Daniel believed it, since you and I both were born with red hair and brown eyes."

Bethany glanced up at her husband. From the look in his dark eyes, she knew he didn't believe this tale.

"That's right," he said. "We share coloring. I didn't resemble Georgia Morgan or her husband. I had you written all over me. I don't know what you expect to accomplish, Johnson, but I'm not falling for it. Why would she name me after you, if you hadn't been my sire?"

"Not unusual, a third son getting named for a family friend. Daniel and I did consider each other a friend at the time."

"It's too much of a coincidence for me," Jon Marc came back.

"You ever take a look in the mirror?" Johnson stepped closer to Jon Marc. "You're the spitting image of Daniel's sister. Phoebe's her name."

A flinch. A blink. Jon Marc retreated a half step. Shaking his head as if to toss out false images, he said, "Sheer coincidence."

"It's no coincidence, your being as stubborn as Daniel O'Brien. It's no coincidence you've got his nose. You recall his nose?"

"I don't."

Johnson sighed; so did Bethany. She figured the older man spoke the truth, but she feared Jon Marc would never accept it. Even if it wasn't true, her husband would benefit from believing he had blood ties to the O'Briens.

Some lies were worth making.

Jon Marc picked up a pebble to skip across the water. "It strikes me mighty funny, twenty-four years passing without a word from you. How much is Fitz O'Brien paying you to say all this?"

"Not a dime. I'm here on my own accord. And at my own expense, even though Mr. O'Brien offered to pay me, and well."

It was Jon Marc's turn to pace.

Bethany sighed. How difficult it must have been for Fitz, seeking out the man who had driven his son to murder and suicide, thus tearing the O'Briens apart in the aftermath. Could Jon Marc appreciate that?

She rose from the ground to follow her husband, as did Johnson, who said, "I've had a lot of time to think about Memphis, and what I'd do different, if I could do it over again. I wouldn't have run out of my house, when you and Daniel came to it. I wouldn't have left him dying and you crying. It was craven of me, but I was scared. Scared I'd get charged with killing him. And I was out of my head with grief over Georgia. I did you a worse disservice than she did."

Jon Marc might not recognize it, but Bethany figured it took guts for this man to show up like he had.

"When that sleuth lady found me in New Hampshire, at my exhibition, I could have said no. I'm not a rich man. I need the money ticket sales would've brought in. Furthermore, I'm not young. The trip from New England jarred these bones. But I saw a chance to pay my debt."

At last Jon Marc studied the sincerity in Johnson's eyes. "Then, you swear you don't claim me?"

"I'd like to claim you. You've done fine for yourself. Nice ranch in the West. Pretty wife. Everybody having a good time at your place. Those are the things I've always wanted, but never had. I've buried four wives, and one stillborn daughter. Girl was born in '38, before I went off to fight in Guangzhou. Never had any more children. I reckon that may have to do with—" Johnson imparted a sheepish look Bethany's way "—an injury I got, over in China."

"Mr. Johnson," Bethany said, "are you willing to swear on a Bible?"

"I am. As it were, I brought my own. Belonged to my mother. Been in the family for nearly a hundred years. Got a century of Johnson information. It's where I recorded my marriages, and the dates my wives and little daughter passed on. A man doesn't lie on a Bible. And especially against the memory of his family."

Jon Marc rubbed fingers down his mouth. He gazed at Bethany, his expression asking her opinion. She nodded.

He said, "Go get the Bible."

# Chapter Twenty-Five

It was all over but the mess.

Marcus Johnson left the Caliente by nightfall. Isabel threw leftover tortillas to the pigs, then joined the padre, Terecita, and Sabrina, as they departed for Fort Ewell. Fitz and the genie turned in early. Jaime packed his fiddle and bow, and he and the other bandits, led by Hoot Todd, went on their way, possibly to figure out how to expand the legend of the leader.

Tomorrow, Jon Marc and his vaqueros would ride out to trail the Caliente horses to their new owner. Fitz asked Catfish to stay behind. Jon Marc didn't find that peculiar, the strawboss having been part of the family for years.

Family.

What did it mean, now that Marcus Johnson had sworn on his Bible?

Jon Marc mulled it, while he helped Beth and Pippin gather the spoils of celebration. His mind still hadn't settled at bedtime. Beth then kept him too busy to think about family.

He awoke at the crack of dawn. Again, he found himself

too occupied to study on family, save for the idea of starting one.

Rather worn out, he at last dragged himself from bed. Already his wife had taken care of her toilette, had had her hair fixed, and was dressed.

"Woman, how can you not be tired?" he demanded to know, marshaling enough energy to grab her by the waist and to sip her earlobe.

She wiggled against him. "Tired? I could climb a mountain, fight a tiger, swim a raging stream!"

He got the feeling she meant to climb his mountain, wrestle his tiger, and swim his stream. He groaned. This was what he got for wanting a tornado in the bedroom.

Yet he grinned. Pep began to speed through his parts as Beth started rubbing his rear. Yes, he was one lucky fellow.

"How 'bout I ride into your valley?" he asked and guided her toward the bed. "And carry you to the stars?"

"Put your stallion where your brag is, sir."

He did.


Later that morning, mounted vaqueros gathered in front of the Caliente stable, ready to ride for Salado Creek and give horses to bandits. Jon Marc led León from his stall and outdoors, then slipped a boot toe in the stirrup.

Fitz shouted, "Gran'son."

He set his foot aground.

Pippin was wheeling the invalid chair from the house. Fitz had both canes across his blanket-draped lap. A blanket, despite the warmth of this summer day.

Jon Marc eyed León, wanting to hit the trail. His gaze advanced to his vaqueros, who needed to deliver horses. "You know where to find Todd, at your old place," he said to Luis. "I'll catch up later."

Luis de la Garza nodded, then pointed a finger southwest. The vaqueros rode out, dust in their wake.

It was time for Jon Marc to settle the matter of family. Tying Leon's reins to the hitching post outside the stable, Jon Marc ambled up to old man and youth.

He studied his grandfather. He couldn't remember Fitz being young or having his health. But he hadn't noticed how truly old and wizened the eldest O'Brien had become, until now.

"Why don't you let Aunt Beth to box up some of that leftover pie?" Jon Marc asked his nephew. "Take it to town. I'll bet Sabrina would enjoy another go at lemon pie."

"You really think so, Uncle Jon Marc? That'd be great. I really like 'Brina. I'm gonna marry her when we get grown." Pippin got a pensive look. "How am I gonna get to town? Great-granddaddy, can I borrow your coach?"

"There's a paint pony in the stable." Jon Marc tried not to think about how fast the Caliente horse-herd was depleting. "He's yours."

"Wow! That's great. Thanks! See, Great-granddaddy, he's not nearly as stingy with himself as you said he was."

Pippin, despite four years of seasoning, had not lost his tendency to say the inappropriate. Jon Marc laughed, nonetheless. "Go on, boy. Before I take back my offer."

He had never seen feet move that fast.

Then Fitz spoke. "Push me around these grounds. I want t' be seeing what all ye've got here. If ye wouldna mind."

Wordlessly, Jon Marc took charge of the handgrips.

As he wheeled past the ruins of the Wilson home, Fitz spoke. "That reminds me of me heart. Burnt. Burned it meself, I did. A fool 'twas I, tossing ye outta the house. Ye hafta understand why, Jonny. By rights, the factor house should've gone t' the eldest of me grandsons. If not Connor, then Burke. 'Twasn't you I resented, Jonny. 'Twas yer upstart idea, and yer youth."

Resentment couldn't just fall away. Jon Marc gritted his

teeth, then looked at the charred ruins. "Been meaning to have this lot cleared. It's an eyesore."

He gave the invalid chair a heavier shove, heading away from burnt reminders. Nothing more got said until he and Fitz reached the top of Harmony Hill.

Jon Marc stooped down to rock back on his heels. Rather than speak, he scanned the valley. He saw cattle and brush, the river and its branches. A mockingbird pushed its young from the nest of an oak tree, into a sky as wide as the heavens.

This Texan saw home.

Fitz rested one elbow on a chair arm and shelved his upper lip with a gnarled forefinger. It was coming, that bid for Fitz & Son, Jon Marc was certain of it.

But it didn't.

"Ye've done well for yerself," Fitz said in a voice that his grandson knew to be honest. "When I first got an eyeful of yer ranch, 'twas unsettling. Texas, especially this part, is a hard place. Worried me, Jonny, it did. Too hard a life did I see for ye. But ye'll make a go of it. Ye have, and ye will." Knowing old eyes tipped up to his grandson. " 'Tis ambition that fires ye, like yer brother Burke. Ye had t' work harder for yers, though. Just as 'twas for an immigrant from Belfast. Me two grandsons come by ambition naturally."

Jon Marc couldn't help smirking. Leave it to Fitz to try to take credit for whatever the O'Brien brothers accomplished. Wasn't that natural, too?

Whatever the case, Jon Marc found himself flattered by his grandfather's remarks. It was high praise coming from Fitz, the first O'Brien to launch into a cold world and make his place without help from anyone.

"Do ye think ye might be interested in turning yer ambitions t' the family cause?" Fitz asked to burst Jon Marc's mellow feeling.

"I might have known you hadn't given up."

"O'Briens doona give up."

"You'll have to quit this cause up, Fitz. It's lost."

The elder O'Brien studied the younger. Several moments went by before Fitz implored, "Tell me what ye think of this place, Jonny."

He had to make his grandfather understand why he must stay here. Never before had he wished more for the exacting, for the most poetic words to come to him.

"With tears I came to an unsettled place, where civil hands had ne'er to toil . . ." He wasn't a poet. All he could do was speak from the heart. "This is where I've planted roots. It's where I've known solace. And trouble. And great happiness, now that I have a wife to share it with.

"Someday I'll teach our sons and daughters to ride and rope on the land before us. And someday we may discover they have no use for it. But that's their choice to make. All we can do is love them, accept them, even if they seem not to want our love. If they fly away, like the birds in winter, Beth and I must let them go. In hopes they'll return in springtime."

A tear made a rivulet through the gullies of Fitz's face.

Jon Marc levered to his feet. "We have water for our thirsts, all our thirsts, and we have food for our souls as well as our bodies. God is here. When He calls us home, we'll rest on this very hill. It's a fine place to live. And die. And rest in peace."

Nothing more got said about Fitz & Son, Factors that morning. Nothing more got said at all. Jon Marc simply walked behind his grandfather's invalid chair and returned to the home he'd made with Beth.

Jon Marc left his grandfather with Eugene, then ambled over to León and climbed into the saddle, for the trip to Salado Creek. In his heart he knew Fitz would cease coercing him about that factor house.

He sensed rightly.

That afternoon, on his return, he found Fitz packed

for the trip to Memphis. The coach horses were hitched, Pippin's gift pony tied to its rear. A basket of food had been prepared by Beth for the first leg of their journey, and Pippin and Eugene awaited their chore of lifting Fitz into the plush interior.

Catfish Abbott, a knapsack attached to his saddlebags, stood off to the side, holding the reins to his mount. It was obvious to see. He would be leaving alongside the coach.

Instinct told Jon Marc that it had been planned like this from the start. It made sense now, why the Louisiana planter had wanted a job in the wilds of Texas. He'd been sent here to spy for Fitz. Jon Marc chuckled inwardly. His grandfather had never let him fly on his own. But that was just his way.

Jon Marc clipped a salute of good-bye to his strawboss.

Taking his wife's hand, he walked up to Fitz, who said, "We'll be leaving now, Jonny."

Strange. Now that the longed-for moment had arrived, Jon Marc hated to see his grandfather go. He recalled Fitz opening his arms, and not flinching from the pain of rheumatism when Jon Marc had jumped into them, that long-ago day, when the world caved in from two deaths.

Fitz may not have believed Jon Marc had ties of the blood, but he took him in, same as Connor and Burke, and gave home, heart, and love. Even sent a spy to watch out for him.

He'd even swallowed bile to face Marcus Johnson.

Jon Marc thought to extend his hand, but a force within him changed that. Leaving his devoted wife's side, he reached down to hug the old man, who still didn't complain about having his aching bones crushed by an embrace. "I love you, Granddad."

"I love ye, too, Jonny."

Neither grandson nor grandfather had a propensity for the mawkish, and neither wished to change. Fitz wiggled the kinks from his shoulders. Jon Marc stood to shove fingers behind his gun belt and stare off into the distance.

The younger O'Brien first felt the need to speak. "When you see my brothers, and the aunties, tell them our door is always open. It is to you, too."

"I'll be doing that, Jonny." Fitz smiled. "Yea, I willna be coming back. But me door is open t' ye and yers. Bring the babies t' see Great-granddaddy. I will be saving the strength t' hold them."

"That sounds like a fine idea . . . Granddad."

Beth let out a sigh, moving closer to Jon Marc. With a grin as wide as the Texas sky, she smiled up at her husband.

But Fitz hadn't finished speaking. "Jonny . . . I canna leave without telling ye the truth. Was a trick I was meaning t' play on ye. By dangling Abbott as bait. Meant t' lure ye, meant for ye think I would be giving the factor house t' him."

Everyone, Jon Marc sensed, expected an explosion of wrath. Catfish mounted up, fast, as if to make a swift get-away. Eugene retreated, until he backed into a coach wheel. Beth squeezed her husband's hand. She had a mighty grip.

Pippin, on the other hand, stepped forward. His dark cowlick catching a ray of sunlight, as well as his freckles, he boosted his twelve-year-old jaw and stood down his great-grandfather. "What are you gonna do about Fitz & Son?"

"Sell it, lad."

"No, you ain't. I want it. My dad has other sons to help him with his steamship company. He don't need me. I need you, Great-granddaddy. And you need me. I'm strong and I'm smart, and I can learn about cotton and how to sell it." Pippin wiggled his own set of O'Brien shoulders, albeit adopted. "You needn't worry 'bout love messing things up, Great-granddaddy. Me and 'Brina, we're already in love. She likes the idea of living in Memphis—I already asked her. We gonna start a whole new dynasty."

Jon Marc cut his eyes to Beth, who did what she could

not to laugh at the naivete of youth. Her husband, on the other hand, wondered how their lives would have turned out, had Beth Buchanan come into his life at Pippin's age.

"Great-granddaddy? What do you think?"

"Ye're too young, lad." Fitz tilted his head toward Jon Marc, who cast him a warning glower. A smile pulled up old lips. Fitz raised a finger, like he'd just had a brilliant idea. "But now that ye have me thinking, Pippin, I do believe there is a place for ye at Fitz & Son. As an apprentice, if yer parents doona object."

Beth left her husband to kneel in front of Fitz. "Work on that, sir. You can talk them into it, or my name isn't Beth O'Brien."

Fitz laughed.

So did Jon Marc, the latter shaking his head in amazement. "Too bad she can't go back with you, Granddad. If she can talk Hoot Todd out of a feud, Burke and Susan wouldn't stand a chance. Don't get any ideas of leaving, wife! You're right where you belong."

Four months later, Padre Miguel finished exerting his authority in the matter of Bethany's conversion to the faith, as was his privilege as a frontier priest. Not that he wouldn't have bent the rules, no matter his authority.

He served first Communion, in private.

It was All Saints Day, the first of November.

The wafer tasted bland on her tongue, as did the wine, yet the blessed sacrament gave her a fulfillment that she'd never known, outside her husband's arms. At last God would hear her prayers.

But He had in so many ways, ways too numerous to count.

Bethany had everything that she'd ever dreamed of, save for God's blessing over her marriage . . . or a child to hold in her arms.

"Amen," intoned the priest.

She rose from the rail. Padre Miguel opened his arms, and she went into them, to exchange a hug. The thieves had done honor to their clandestine pact.

"I must go." She wrapped a horse blanket around her shoulders to ward off the blue norther—unseasonably cold weather—that blew outside the church of Santa María. "I told Jon Marc I'd be home before nightfall. And I promised to stop by the post office before I left town."

*"Vaya con Dios."*

"I will. Thanks to you. And to God." She slanted her face toward the priest. "How can I honor Him?"

"You will think of a way."

[illegible] from the rail. [illegible] opened his [illegible] and she went into them, [illegible]. The [illegible] had come home to their [illegible].

[illegible] She wrapped [illegible] around her shoulders [illegible] off the [illegible]—that [illegible] and [illegible] And [illegible] before [illegible].

[illegible]

"[illegible] thanks to you, [illegible]," she [illegible] "How can I [illegible]"

[illegible]

# Chapter Twenty-Six

"Brrr!" Bethany, fresh from first Communion, sped toward home and rushed inside the parlor. "It's cold outside!"

Jon Marc, who had tucked up in front of a fire, poetry volume in hand, left the settee in the now-spacious room. He enclosed her in his arms, horse blanket and all. "You should have kept it for yourself, that coat you tailored for Sabrina."

"Don't be silly. She needs it."

The girl had not gone with Ramón and Manuel to the city of Mexico, as Terecita had promised. Lately, Bethany had tutored her kin. And she liked it. Yet Sabrina would go away to boarding school in the new year—oh, how her aunt dreaded saying good-bye, even for the semester. But it was for the best. Her niece needed proper education, if she were to become the lady her mother dreamed of. Perhaps to live on the Mississippi with Tristan O'Brien.

*I want my own child. Be it of my body, or adopted!*

"I feel like a churl," Jon Marc said as he led Bethany toward the rug she'd braided, that presently rested in front of the hearth, "wearing this sweater you knit for me, when you're cold. You're a paragon, Mrs. O'Brien. Knitting sweaters and mittens for everyone we know of, even Hoot Todd."

Despite the weather, Hoot and his band, astride fine horses sporting new brands, thanks to their crossing the C's from horse coats with a running iron, were currently on a campaign to rob stagecoaches in a more populated area, where writers were sure to tread.

She said, "Hoot looks good in chartreuse, won't you agree?"

"Wife, I have no idea how Todd looks in anything. Men don't ogle men."

She wiggled up to an all-male form. "He looks good. So do you." She smoothed fingers over her *querido's* woolen-clad chest. "I love you in damson purple."

His face went the same shade of purple. "Do you really think this is a good color for a man?"

"I most certainly do." She began to shed her wrap, since a network of veins were warming, thanks to Jon Marc's presence.

"Beth honey, I'm going to send to Laredo for a coat for you."

"That would be nice," she replied, no paragon by any means. "I've heard cashmere is warmer than down."

"Have you now?" he teased. "You could end up an expensive wife."

"Better get that herd to Kansas, husband. Else I'll flatten your purse."

"What you do is bulge Old Duke." His hand guiding her to the floor, they sat, her spine against his middle, one of her favorite places. Mighty Duke swelled.

Bethany closed her eyes to the orange fire, and wiggled against that which amazed her in its prowess.

"I oughta kick myself for suggesting you wear britches," Jon Marc muttered, his fingers delving into the top of denim. "There's a reason women wear dresses. Men designed them for easy access."

"Is that what the poets say?"

"That's what I say," Jon Marc replied with a growl, then dug at her buttons.

While his fingers eased trousers away from her hip, she squirmed out of them. In no manner was she cold.

His rid himself of his own britches, then she inched backward, again settling at Mighty Duke.

"I've never taken you this way," he murmured.

"You've done it many ways, why not this one?"

His fingers coasted beneath her shirt, stopping at the swell of her breasts. "I got more than I ever fancied in you."

"Same with me."

That was when she shoved her hips to him. He parted her cheeks, placing Duke just short of its goal. No! She didn't want this—had meant *this*. Oscar had used her thusly.

Jon Marc never used her.

He said, "It tempts me, but I won't. It goes against Nature. A man must penetrate the proper place."

"Do it."

He did.

To grant better entry, she planted her palms on the rug. And then he was in her, marvelously in her, as her desires demanded. His large sacs slapped her thighs, as he thrust into her, more times than any reasonable woman could count. All the while, he caressed her flesh, first her hips, then her waist, then her breasts. Luscious time passed— she relished every moment of it, her passions flying higher and higher. Sensing his completion, she felt her own. Her muscles tightened around his sex. With a snap of ecstasy he pressed one last time, planting his seed within her.

And then he rolled her backward, bringing his spine to the rug, her head to his chest. Still caressing her breasts, he whispered, "I don't think I could ever get enough of you."

"I pray you don't."

The Duke sagged out of her. She squirmed, releasing him, before flipping to her side. Her fingers slipping along Jon Marc's well-shaped hips, she cupped her palm over the blue-veined power, now listless. It was lovely. Thick and massive, even at slack.

A hunger lusted within her, the need to taste his jewel. Once, Oscar had forced her head to his spindly shaft, which roused nothing but counting sheep. She didn't find Jon Marc repulsive. Her tongue darted out, just a bit. "Would you let me do as you've done many times?"

He flushed. "Well, I, I, I don't know. Interesting. But what if I wasted our seed?"

"Couldn't we be selfish just this one time?"

His eyes showed that he would relent.

"Is it too soon for you?" she asked.

As if summoned, Mighty Duke nodded. "Not too soon," Jon Marc growled and pulled her head to it.

Eager lips surrounded the stout trunk. The tip of her tongue rounded the area beneath his foreskin, then she took him deeper. The tip pressed her tonsils, yet he still wasn't in. It took swirling her hips to accommodate him. He went past her throat, yet she didn't gag. Jon Marc's fingers combed into her hair, his groan filling the parlor.

"Geezus—never imagined!" he called out. "Good."

That was when she found his male nipples, and pinched them. His rear bucked off the rug. A high point overtook her, shattering, driving her wilder.

She sucked harder.

He pushed her face away. "No. In you. We shouldn't waste a drop."

He tried to drive her to her back. But it was too late. White pulsed against her cheek, then her hand. Her eyes were on Mighty Duke. In Liberal, she had thought the letting of male seed ho-hum. Presently, and forever, she

found it fascinating. It seemed to go on and on, so full
was her husband. This was what went into her, what filled
her so fully, what smelled delicious . . . and now, as her
tongue swept along Duke's head, tasted even better.

"We shouldn't do that anymore," Jon Marc lamented,
once he got his breath. "We should save it for making a
baby."

*"Querido,* I feel full enough for ten babies."

He bent over her, sliding his middle finger into a wicket,
wet with his previous stream . . . and the culmination of
hers. "Then why have we seen no evidence of a babe?"

"I-I don't know." Unless God wasn't a benevolent heart,
if He were the vengeful presence of Agatha Persat's religion. "Perhaps we haven't made love often enough."

"Beth, we haven't missed a day. Or a night."

That, she knew. "What if I'm barren?"

"Then we'll have to adjust to being childless."

The mere thought hurt, yet she tried to be reasonable.
"Would you mind terribly if we adopted a child?"

"You feel the need to ask that, given my background?
Beth honey, you don't know how many times I wished, as
a child, that some loving couple had taken me in."

She recalled the orphan boys, now south of the border.
"We should have gotten closer to Ramón and Miguel."

"It's too late for them. But if other children pass this
way . . ."

"I want them. Even if I swell with your child, I want all
children who need us."

"Fine with me."


Once they replaced their clothes and had shared bites
of dinner, Bethany glanced across the eating table at her
husband. His eyes were on her, as they had been when
she first arrived at Rancho Caliente. She grinned at his
ardent stare.

"You had me so engrossed for a while there," she said, "I forgot to mention the mail."

His palm found her knee under the table. "You want to talk mail, after . . . ?"

She knew what he meant. After their stunning bout on the parlor floor. Her insides tightened, recalling it. "We have the rest of our lives to enjoy the flesh's pleasures. But we must think about the world outside our door on occasion."

"Spoilsport," he teased.

"You got three dispatches."

"Did you open them?"

"You would accuse me of snooping?" she asked, returning his tease.

"Could happen."

"Not in this case. I didn't read your letters. But I know you have a post from Fitz. And one from each of your brothers."

"Where's the mail?"

She smiled, heartened at the strides Jon Marc had made since her arrival. "In my britches pocket."

Her husband rose from the table to stride to the denims that lay before the fireplace. He ripped open one missive, read it. "Pippin's parents will allow him to work at the factor house during summers, until his education is complete. Our nephew agrees with the terms."

"That pleased me," Bethany said serenely.

"Catfish will manage Fitz & Son till then."

"Good."

Jon Marc sliced open the next two letters. Handing one to Bethany, he pulled a sheet of paper from the other. "This is from Burke. He and Susan would like for us to spend Christmas at their home in New Orleans, celebrating Fitz's birthday."

"Your brother Connor and his wife say they're going to New Orleans. They want to make it a real family reunion. Do you think we can?"

"Doubtful."

Bethany figured Jon Marc's reply had something to do with the bad turn the Caliente had taken, thanks to the weather. There hadn't been a drop of rain in months. The Nueces and its streams were dried, the livestock suffering for it. No amount of money could buy water.

He said, "If luck is with us, and a good rain falls, we must get ready to launch that cattle drive to Kansas. We'll need to leave in February, March at the latest." He eyed her questioningly. "Unless you're in no position to travel."

She knew what he meant. If they had a child on its way.

Somehow she knew that no babe would ever grow in her womb.

*This is God's price for my lies.*

Bethany vowed to make the best of it.

The worst was yet to come.

# Chapter Twenty-Seven

The wind whistled like a mournful lover, the morning after those letters from kin arrived.

Jon Marc and his wife attended Mass to pray for the souls of their departed loved ones, on this the second day to honor the saints. Mostly, he gave thanks for a perfect wife.

Afterward, they accepted Liam Short's offer to stop by the post office for a cup of coffee.

The postmaster hovered over the potbellied stove, an Indian blanket draping his shoulders, Stumpy curling at his stocking feet. The dog stunk to high heaven, not unlike one of the pigs that Jon Marc still had no use for.

Liam said, "Shore be glad when this cold snap passes on outta here. Iffen I'd wanted to be cold, I'da stayed in Missouri."

Beth smiled. "Your troubles will be over soon enough, Liam. You know what everyone says. If you don't like Texas weather, stick around. It'll change in three days."

" 'Cept in summer. Then it ain't nothing but hot." Liam dug toes against Stumpy's ragged, fawn-colored coat.

"Iffen we don't get some rain, we might-uz well pack up and leave La Salle County."

"We've lived through droughts before." Jon Marc poured coffee and handed a tin cup of it to Beth. Worried he might be about the dried creeks, but he couldn't help smiling at the tingle that went through him every time he touched his honey. Since magic had given him a bride, he'd gotten a lot more calm about many things. "You just wait. The sky is going to open up soon, and we'll all be back in business."

Beth sipped coffee, then leaned to the left to peer out the oiled-paper window. Jon Marc's eyes were on the curve of one hip, and he recalled how it tasted on his tongue. He recalled how it felt to be tasted by her lips, and having Old Duke engulfed. He like to lost it. The coffee cup wiggled. He sipped deeply, scalding his tongue.

Her voice as dry as the cracked earth of their ranch, his wife said, "I do believe that's Hoot Todd riding up. Yes, it is. Terecita is running toward him."

"This is our lucky day," Jon Marc said, equally as dry, and gulped another swallow of Liam's bitter brew that was supposed to be coffee.

Not long after that, Hoot Todd kicked open the post office door. He let in a draft of frigid air that sent Stumpy into Liam's lap.

"Close the door," Jon Marc barked, not too interested in the return of La Salle's bandit supreme.

Todd nearly slammed the door in Terecita López's face. The dancer turned piano player—her talents had improved almost to acceptable here lately—shoved her weight against the barrier and burst in. Spanish eyes blazed. Too bad they couldn't warm this clapboard structure.

Everyone shivered from the cold.

"You," the dancer snarled at Todd.

Guilt over an unnamed source affected him not.

"Dad gum writers," he complained while huffing over to the stove, "they ain't looking for a legend. They's just looking for another Robin Hood. What's Robin Hood? I ain't never heard of such a thing."

Terecita apparently felt no need to explain the exploits that harked from a faraway place called Sherwood Forest, in bygone days. Perhaps she didn't know.

"Where have you been, Chico?" She adjusted her hair, then slipped fingers beneath her poncho. "It has been weeks, but I have heard nothing from you. You said you would give me money for Sabrina's education, but you have given not a *centavo!*"

Beth glanced at Jon Marc; he met her regard. Apparently the dancer-cum-musician had said nothing about the O'Brien promise to educate Sabrina.

Well, couples did play games.

Jon Marc had played his own. Giving over school money would have to wait until the upcoming cattle drive to Kansas filled the family coffers. Provided the Caliente outfit had any cattle to drive to Kansas.

Jon Marc wouldn't worry his wife with the honest-to-God truth. But if rain didn't fall and soon, their herd wouldn't survive the winter.

Without a word of comment to the mother of his daughter, Hoot Todd, gracing Terecita with a glare, warmed his thorny hands above the stove. In a tone contrary to his abrupt arrival, he inquired, "Anybody miss me?"

"Why, yes." Beth set her cup on the floor. She had one of those conciliatory looks that her husband had come to understand more than well. "How have you been?"

"Sick as a dog."

"What is wrong?" Terecita, forgetting aggravation, rushed to her man to try to offer comfort.

"Dad gum it, get away! Don't need no woman-problems."

When Todd grappled to free himself of his lover's clutching fingers, Stumpy got the wrong idea. The dog leapt from Liam's lap and took a hunk out of the bandit's thumb.

Which, of course, caused Todd to bring his knee up

hard beneath Stumpy's chin. The dog tossed from his
master's lap, landing on his ear to howl. Liam thrust off
his blanket, took hold of a fire-poker, and tried to whap
it upside Todd's head.

Bethany went for the already-crippled dog.

Jon Marc caught the poker short of its mark.

Terecita stepped between Todd and Jon Marc, but
Stumpy got the wrong idea. He chomped into her ankle.
Blood spurted. Which rubbed Todd the wrong way.

"Friggin' dog," he yelled and connected his fist to Liam,
instead of his intended canine target.

The postmaster flew backward, the Indian blanket soar-
ing against Beth's middle. She threw off the restraints to
bind her arms around the canine and shush him with her
own brand of charm, not inconsiderable.

"Enough!" Jon Marc shouted.

Everyone went still.

Stumpy then laved Beth's ear.

A visage as woebegone as Stumpy's worst countenance
swept over Todd's face. "Can't even get no respect in my
hometown. I'm leaving. For good."

"You are leaving? Ha!" Terecita accepted the clean
handkerchief Jon Marc provided, and began to wrap her
ankle. "You will not be the first to leave." Terecita lifted
her nose toward the ceiling. "*I* am leaving. I will take my
daughter and my talents with the piano, and find a more
appreciative audience."

"What about Sabrina?" Beth asked, her voice not dis-
guising her concern. "Where will you take her?"

"Mexico City, perhaps. I will find an adoring man—a
true protector!—to pay for my daughter's education."

"Terecita, I told you, be patient." Standing, Beth had
a worried look. "My husband and I will help."

"I am out of patience." Terecita swept out the door,
leaving it open to let cold air in.

"Well, god—" Hoot, eyeing Beth, bit off his curse. "Dad
gum it, you just cain't trust women to love on you when

you need it. Always gotta think of theirselves, women. Dad gum it.''

If not for his wife's woeful, downcast face, Jon Marc might have chuckled at Todd's view of himself as he related to women. What a contrast in view versus action.

"I won't want her to take Sabrina away," Beth whispered, all eyes.

Moving his line of inquiry from one person to the next, Todd wanted to know, "Anybody got any idea what Robin Hood is?"

"He ain't you." Liam grabbed Indian blanket and snaggle-toothed dog. "You ain't nuttin' but a saddle sore, pure and simple."

Beth closed troubled hazel eyes. Her shoulders hunching, she crept closer to her husband, whispering, "I love that little girl. I don't want to be without her."

As if the weather weren't enough to worry about, Jon Marc had to consider his wife's feelings. Poor Beth. He nestled her cheekbone against his shoulder. She hadn't been quite herself here lately, no doubt because no sign of a babe had come their way.

It worried Jon Marc, too, the reason their many matings hadn't brought what they should have. This wasn't the moment to worry about young O'Briens. He couldn't let Terecita hare off with the little girl who meant so much to his wife.

"I'll go after her," he said and went for the door.

"What did you say?"

Jon Marc asked that question in Santa María Church, the reason for this visit falling away. He sat on a pew beside Terecita, who sobbed into a rag.

"Chico has not been the same." She blew her nose into the white confines. "Not since your señora filled his head with ideas of legend."

"That's not all you said." Jon Marc laid a wrist on the

pew in front of them. "What did you mean, 'By appealing to his family honor'?"

"*Es un cuento largo.*"

A long story was it? Did that make sense? "What do you mean?"

"They are not really related. It was a hoax. A ploy." Terecita buried her forehead against twined fingers that rested on the forward pew. "Your wife has been good for this place, but I sometimes wish she wouldn't tell so many tales. She was never Chico's sister. She lied to mold him into what she wanted him to be."

"Is that so?"

"She is *una buena mujer, su esposa.*"

That Terecita couldn't express herself in English troubled Jon Marc. She had a grand understanding of the Anglo tongue. Something had made her revert. Did it exclusively have to do with a lover who wouldn't provide for his get and gal?

"You call my wife a good woman, but I don't want to be sent sidetracked by nuances. Speak English."

"She is not sister to Chico. She told him so only to get on his good side."

"Beth got the idea to call herself sister to Hoot Todd?"

Terecita nodded. "When she called him Mortimer, it changed him. He was an hombre after glory."

This woman's confidences struck Jon Marc as strange. Could it have to do with suspicion at its most stark? For the past few months, since Beth had given Todd a watch, her husband harbored a curiosity, one no happily married man should have.

Once Jon Marc had gotten over the visit from his grandfather, he had a chance to think about that gift watch. Three days after Fitz left, it came to him. Aaron Buchanan decried timepieces. The Kansan claimed to be a true man of the West, telling time by the arch of the sun and the moon's position in the heavens.

Aaron Buchanan hadn't carried a watch.

Which, if Jon Marc thought about—not something he wanted to do—preyed on his mind. As was his custom, he found excuses. "Family honor" had to do with Beth's campaign to curry favor with the outlaw, for peaceable reasons. Didn't it?

"They aren't related," he stated without stuttering.

"*Es verdad.* It's true." Again Terecita blew into the rag. "It was all a ploy to make him think they were brother and sister, calling herself Bethany Todd. I do not know how Beth found out his name is truly Mortimer, but it worked."

Jon Marc wrinkled his brow and studied the cuticles of his thumbs. How did Beth find out Hoot's given name? One thing about it, she knew the truth that night in the bandit's shack.

How long had she known it, and why hadn't it been important enough to mention to her husband?

Jon Marc intended to find out.

# Chapter Twenty-Eight

"How did you know Todd's name is Mortimer?"

Somewhat in the neighborhood of three dozen answers came to mind, yet Bethany hesitated to answer her husband. A good while back she'd vowed never to lie to him again.

Rather than make up a story, she took up the fire-poker and rearranged logs in the hearth. "We've been home for hours. Long enough to change into work britches and shirts, and to take care of several chores. You haven't said one word about Sabrina. Is her mother going to take her away?"

"I don't want to discuss Sabrina."

"But you went after Terecita, for the very purpose of—"

"Beth, you didn't answer my question."

"You didn't answer mine, either." She rubbed her upper arms. "Such a chill. Warm toast would be nice. I could brown those leftover biscuits from breakfast. Or shall I pour us a tot of whiskey?"

"Cut the folderol. I don't want a servile wife. I want the

truth.'' Jon Marc loomed into her path. "Beth, answer me. How did you know Todd had another name?"

Nothing would be the same, ever the same, if she confessed. Her gaze ascended to her husband's sharp regard. Trouble etched brackets at his mouth. She had the eerie suspicion that he, like any good interrogator, knew the answer before asking it.

"I'm interested in a shot of whiskey," she said.

Somehow she sidestepped Jon Marc to make for the corner cabinet. Her hand shook as she poured a generous shot into a glass. That hand trembled even more as she brought the fiery contents to her lips. It burned down her gullet. Perhaps it was the conflagration of what was yet to come, she decided. Was there any way to avoid that fire?

She had to try.

With a wan smile plumbed from the very depths of her essence, as if she could ever smile again on her own, she said, "Before my traveling companion succumbed—" fingers moved to make the sign of the cross "—we discussed Hoot Todd. Miss Todd mentioned his given name. I believe Mortimer is Celtic for sea warrior. Quite elegant as a surname in England, I understand. 'O, how stalwart is thee Mortimer, who sails the seas as mine heart does purr.'"

"That's awful."

"That's not fair."

Jon Marc set his feet wide apart and crossed arms over his chest. "I could mention you've never recited for me before now, but I won't. Let's leave it at: you're awful."

His assessment made her flat offended. She had no right to call herself a poetess, but her verse had a certain ring to it. At least she hadn't added anything bawdy. "I'd like to hear you come up with something better."

Her husband took the glass out of her hand to fling it to the hearth. It shattered. "You knew his name. How do you claim? As a wise soothsayer? Or as an untruth-relayer?"

"Is relayer a word?"

Smoke might as well have plumed from Jon Marc's nostrils and ears, so incensed was he. Yet he got still. Very still. His eyes changed from fiery to as cold as the temperature outside their home. "I think I've been made a fool."

"You're not foolish. Not in the least."

"I didn't question you too much about why your eyes weren't blue. Or why your hair didn't curl. Did I call you on why you didn't object to a 'foreign' priest? No. And never once did I mention anything about Aaron Buchanan not carrying a fob watch."

What could she say, but "true"?

"Let's don't even discuss why you don't eat fish on Fridays. But I do, by damn, wonder why you appealed to *Mortimer's* sense of honor."

"To make peace for us all."

"At what price, Bethany?"

"What price is too high?"

The moment she gave that answer, she knew she'd given herself away. Her heart plummeted. Her blood rushed from her face.

Beth Buchanan would never have replied to "Bethany."

Jon Marc looked equally as stricken. The strength seemed to leech from his formidable body, his shoulders hunching. He dropped his jaw. A lock of old-penny hair fell over his brow. "What has happened here? What did you do? What are we?"

He shoved up his gaze. And it was as if he were seeing his wife for the first time. "Who are you?"

"A good wife."

"What I wanted was a true wife. I wanted Beth Buchanan. You're an imposter. A liar."

Beth whirled around to stare at the floor. How could she argue the truth? Her only hope was to throw herself on his mercy. She pivoted to face his disappointment and confusion. "I'm sorry, Jon Marc. So very sorry. All I can offer is myself. I pray I'll be enough. Because I truly love you."

He stood without moving, until his hands dropped to the side. "You are in fact Hoot Todd's sister?"

"I . . . I wish I weren't."

Jon Marc slammed shut anguished eyes and reared his head back. His lips moved silently. And then he glared at the woman who had vowed to love, honor, and obey him, until death did them part.

The distance in his eyes caused Bethany to shiver, even harder than before.

"Where is my bride?" he demanded.

Her hand went to her heart. "I am your bride. I love you, husband. I'll always love you. Forever. And beyond. I would give my life for you."

He retreated, the heel of his hand slicing the air. "I don't know you. You're a stranger."

"That's not so! You know me. I've given you my everything. I have cleaved to you. I'll never be anything but a faithful and loving wife to you."

"How can this be?" He shook his head, as if to clear cobwebs.

Bethany understood his stupefaction, his antipathy, his quest for honesty, yet the whole of her yearned to be everything he demanded. That couldn't be. She hadn't been born a Buchanan.

"My only thought was to make you a fitting wife," she whispered. "If you'll listen to what I have to say, maybe you'll understand how I came to be here."

"Nothing you can say would interest me, *Bethany Todd*. You're not what I want."

Heartstrings threatened to break. Why hadn't she thought of how deeply she might hurt him, with this black-hearted scheme?

"But, Jon Marc, I am your wife."

"I pledged to Beth Buchanan, not to Hoot Todd's sister."

"I am, for all intents and purposes, the woman you sent for."

He wasn't convinced. "What happened to my bride?"

Jon Marc clamped his hands on Bethany's shoulders, as if to shake her. The seeking stare that she had once cowered from, later relished, now ate into her, leaving her without defense.

She wasn't able to look at him, when he implored, "Tell me, wife. And I don't want any of your stuff and nonsense. Where is Beth Buchanan?"

"She's dead."


"I feel as if somebody walked on me grave."

"Oh, Daddy, don't be talking about dying." Tessa O'Brien Jinnings dimpled a smile at her elderly father, not that she wasn't approaching elderly herself. "You're just cold. That's all. Do you need another cup of this nice hot cocoa?"

Eugene Jinnings swallowed a groan. He didn't want to get up and fetch Fitz's chocolate. Truly didn't. With the servants having turned in for the night, Tessa would likely send her husband to the kitchen.

The genie burrowed into the lap shawl, closer to Tessa's plump side.

This was a blistering cold night in Memphis. A fire had been lain in the fireplace of the O'Brien family home, where Eugene nestled on a horsehair sofa in the drawing room with his wife, her father in his invalid chair, the latter's feet toasting before the fire.

"I wonder how Jon Marc and his little bride are doing," Tessa said, her mind never far from her nephews or their families, unless it was to think about Eugene. "I do hope they'll join us at Burke and Susan's home for Christmas."

"A rancher is Jonny." Fitz gave his second daughter a kindly smile. "Doona be disappointed if they canna make the journey. 'Tis a cattle drive he is wanting. Ranchers canna leave at the drop of a hat. Another time, Contessa.

If we doona see them on me birthday, we will another time."

"I can't wait to see Jon Marc. Or to meet Beth." Tessa got one of her stubborn looks, then turned it squarely on Eugene. Her silver ringlets bounced pertly. "I think we should visit. Daddy says we're welcome. I have every right to see what my wish brought dear Jon Marc. I have sat still long enough."

Not another trip to Texas. Not another! Eugene was still worn out from the last one. He'd never catch up on his naps.

The trouble with living as a non-working genie, he got older. Which had been the foremost wish of Eugene Jinnings, formerly having served as a jinn, the genie to grant wishes. How could a man live in retirement, or expect a pleasant death, if carriage wheels were forever bouncing his bones to pieces?

Eugene oiled a smile at his wife. "Let us not be hasty, milady. And do not despair. Jon Marc and his bride may end up in New Orleans. If we leave, we might pass them in the night."

"I do wish they had a telegraph office in Fort Ewell." Tessa's diamond bracelet sparkled as she fluttered a hand. "Why, we could be in touch in no time."

"Contessa, go be getting yer old da more of that cocoa," said Fitz.

Her rosy, wrinkled cheeks turning up to Eugene, Tessa cooed, "Genie, my pumpkin, would you . . . ?"

"Contessa, do it yerself, please." Fitz meant business. " 'Tis a word I'm wanting t' have with yer husband."

"You men. You never want to say anything in front of me."

" 'Tis because ye are the next best t' a telegraph office, Contessa. Canna have a confidence one, not with ye nosying about, passing along every word t' yer sister."

"Men." Grumble she had, but Tessa laid back the covers and headed for the cocoa.

No sooner did she leave than Fitz spoke. "Eugene . . . something bad is happening with Jonny and his bride. I feel it in me bones. They ache. Same as they ached before me grandson gave back his heart t' us."

"You sense it in your bones, Fitz?" Eugene had his own intuition. "Or is it something you know?"

Fitz picked up one leg, then the other, to set them on the floor. "There's something I have been meaning t' tell ye. That postmaster lad—Liam Short, I believe is his name—said something at Jonny and Beth's to-do. Been drinking the priest's beer, had he, which loosens a lad's tongue. Said he worried about Jonny. Relieved he was, Jonny being happy with Beth. Said he hoped Jonny never found out the truth about her."

"What truth?"

"The real Beth Buchanan is dead and buried. Methinks Jonny's bride is a woman named Bethany Todd. 'Tis my thinking, and that of the lady sleuth I sent to Kansas. You know her. Velma Cinglure of New Orleans. Used to be Velma Harken. Had her check on Beth. Velma followed Beth's trail. And found out our gal is an imposter. Run out of a town called Liberal, Bethany Todd was. Isna good. Isna good."

It certainly wasn't.

" 'Tis also in me bones that Jonny's bride is a good one." Fitz wiggled into his blanket. "Mrs. Cinglure spoke with folks in our Beth's hometown. A schoolteacher, and the wife of an attorney, vouched for our lass's good character. Jonny's wife was a victim of circumstance. The ladies said she was a good girl, a hard worker, before events turned her bad."

"Is that so?"

" 'Tis so. Ran her out of town, did the ladies of Liberal. But they had a change of heart, once truth came t' light. The Baptist preacher turned on a lad named Frye, exposing him as a scoundrel. His wife kicked him out of the house. 'Twas too late to help our Beth, Mrs. Frye and the schoolteacher thought. Not so. They begged indulgence from Velma Cinglure."

Eugene Jinnings, having lived before the age of Queen Victoria, found nothing titillating in the tales of Liberal. He recalled ribald days in the Renaissance, in the Dark Ages, and all the way back to Roman bacchanalia. He yawned.

Fitz continued speaking. "Done wrong our Beth may have, but I know she loves Jonny. And will be a wonderful wife, like me departed Edna."

He forever equated fine women with his one and only wife. Of course, he'd never been acquainted with the plum who'd married Julius Caesar.

The genie had never met long-departed Edna, but he did agree with Fitz. Jon Marc's wife seemed a good one.

"Eugene, 'tis help I need. Ye've got t' give it."

Work was in the offing. Allah, help! The genie said nothing, but he knew Fitz meant toil, knew it as surely as he knew every crevice of Tessa's body. The Creator be praised, Fitz didn't have a clue that the magic lamp still existed.

There was no time to rest on that comforting thought, since Fitz said, "Ye need t' let me have a go at the lamp."

Surely the crafty old man didn't know . . . Surely!

Eugene shrugged. "I can't help you. The lamp is no more."

" 'Tis not what me gardener says. He showed me what he dug up in the petunia bed. Seen enough of that lamp in the past. I knew a portion of it, when I saw it."

Desperation roused sweat on Eugene's upper lip. "Where is the lamp? If it falls into someone's hands . . . ! Allah, do not do this to me!"

"The lamp is right where ye left it, doona worry. Go get it, Eugene. I'm wanting me three wishes."

Why not again claim the lantern held no more magic, that its powers had sputtered to nil in the explosion that ripped it apart? Because Eugene held his father-in-law in high regard. And why not? Fitz provided a fine life for his daughter and her husband. Moreover, they had been friends for many years. More than friends. Eugene knew Fitz considered him a son.

How much did he owe the old man?

"Go dig up the lantern, Eugene. I want it. Now."

And so it was that Eugene Jinnings peeled aside his snug blanket and trudged to the petunia garden in the dark of night. A cap didn't do much to warm his bald head, nor did gloves keep his fingers warm. But he shoveled earth from the ancient treasure, brushed clumps of dirt from it, then tucked it under his arm to return to the drawing room and Fitz O'Brien.

Tessa had also returned, a fresh mug of cocoa sitting untouched on a silver tray next to her father. Her blue eyes were big as a sultan's treasure chest.

"More magic," she said breathily and wiggled against the sofa back. "Oh, Daddy, what will you wish for?"

"Do not be hasty. Either of you." Eugene frowned. "I will grant three wishes, but you both must agree to something. Once the wishes are made, the lamp will be no more. Forever."

That was a challenge to the lady whose wishes for her nephews had started all this, in a seaside town on the Mediterranean. Like her sister, Phoebe, Tessa had many ideas on how to improve the lot of this person or that. Yet she bit her lip and nodded. "The lamp will be no more."

"How can we be rid of it?" Fitz asked.

"Send it to a smelter."

Tessa again nodded. "That's a good idea."

Fitz reached for the jagged piece that had once been part of the lantern's etched-brass bowl. He palmed it, gave it a long study. His opposite thumb clamping an edge, he began to rub the bowl-piece. "I wish . . ."

A force that had plagued Eugene Jinnings for hundreds of years took hold anew. Power billowed within his veins. Servitude prostrated him to a knee in front of Fitz O'Brien.

"Your wish is my command, master."

"I wish t' live t' see Pippin grown and taking over at Fitz & Son. That me family will never again be torn apart from within. That Jonny accepts his bride. If not, I wish for Beth t' find a way t' make him accept her."

"Daddy, no!" Tessa blanched. "That's four wishes."

Lips peeling back into a grimace, Fitz slammed closed his eyes, groaning at the blunder.

His daughter steepled her fingers. "Good gracious. The wishes are made. There isn't any backing out. Let's pray God will answer at least three."

The folds of his face jiggling, Fitz nodded. " 'Tis in God's Hands, all 'round."

Yes, Allah must intervene. Perhaps in several ways. Fitz, like his daughter before him, hadn't been specific enough in his requests. He should have added "immediately" to the third wish, and left it at that.

Now . . . none but the Creator would have a say in the marriage of Jon Marc O'Brien and the brunette calling herself Beth.

# Chapter Twenty-Nine

Jon Marc didn't know what hurt the most, being played for the ultimate fool, or not knowing the woman once thought to be his wife. No. He knew the hardest part. It was the grief. He'd lost more than the pious young lady from Kansas.

He lost every anchor to count on.

Jon Marc couldn't decide what to hate or whom to mourn. But he'd never get his wits together, standing here while Bethany Todd tried to explain Beth Buchanan's demise.

"Save your breath." He paced the parlor floor, passing the place where Beth Buchanan's piano had sat. Beth, who could no doubt have played with the capacity of Chopin. "I'm better off not knowing."

"But, husband—"

"Am I?" Was he? Was he legally tied to this stranger?

Her eyes filled with sorrow, Beth—no, Bethany—rushed over and tried to take Jon Marc's hand. "You may have written to Miss Buchanan, but it's me you fell in love with."

He shoved her fingers away. Whom did he love? Bethany

or Beth? The line has fuzzed somewhere along the way, yet he knew the difference between image and reality. "What is love? I have lust for you. Dammit, I could take you right here, on the parlor floor. Like last night. And have no problem with it."

The bad part was, he could have. Fire still burned in his loins for this wanton. The wanton who had inflamed him now made a little O with her lips, as if in surprise. And perhaps delight. *She's got you just where she wants you.*

Fighting the force of her powers, he said, "Love ought to be more than tossing around naked. It has to mean respect and trust. You ruined that for me, Miss Todd."

The face that had paled now turned ashen. "We can work this out, Jon Marc. Together, we can. You might not see it that way tonight. I understand."

"Do you, *Bethany?*"

She'd never looked this scared—hell, had she been scared, since that first day at the stagestop? Jon Marc didn't think so. She'd blithely set about to deceive him, had never looked back while lying time and again.

He stomped to the fireplace to rivet his gaze to flames as chaotic as his wits. "You're like Georgia Morgan. She could look someone in the eye, someone she claimed to love, and tell tales to change a person's life forever."

Agony stabbed his heart, when he equated the two most important women in his life. Both had let him down. Bad. Getting gut-shot in the Civil War hadn't hurt like this. It damned sure hurt worse than witnessing his parent's deaths.

"Husband, listen to me. Your mother was an adulteress. I'm not." His supposed wife walked over broken glass; it crunched beneath her shoes. "I could never lie with anyone but you."

"Why am I not laughing? You weren't a virgin."

"You weren't either. I don't fault you for that. Things happen. It's what develops after a couple falls in love that matters. I'm faithful to you. And always will be."

When he'd discovered her lack of chastity, Jon Marc had promised himself not to ask the particulars. That promise popped, not unlike the flames he gazed into. He turned to the woman standing like a soldier, to his right, ready to leap into the fires of battle. Ready to be fired upon.

"What were you, Miss Todd? Before you showed up here?"

"An outlaw's sister."

"Had to have been more than that."

"All right. I was the daughter of a drunk. I was a cook and dishwasher in a saloon, raised by whores. I know bawdy rhymes. Have made a few up myself. I'm a fallen woman. I let a scoundrel barter me out of what I should have saved for my husband. I had to. I had no money to pay for a lawyer."

"You sold yourself."

"I had to try to save my father. From going to jail. Pa is in the penitentiary at Huntsville. He is a thief of church funds. But he's still my father. And if I had it to do over again, I wonder if I would do differently."

After the blow taken over her identity, Jon Marc didn't find it shocking, that a jailbird begat her. Nothing would ever shock him again.

"Real nice bunch," he said sourly, "the Todds."

"I suppose you mean that as an asperity against Hoot."

"Now that you mention it. Guess we ought to be thankful, not bringing a child into this. I'd hate to think my son or daughter called that one-eyed no-good 'uncle.'"

That made her mad. "You've got gall. How can you stand there and decry my brother as a no-good? You'd have been better served to be Marcus Johnson's son. At least he has courage. Daniel was such a coward that he killed his wife, *and* himself! At least Hoot doesn't kill people."

As soon as the second syllable of "people" was out of her mouth, she slammed fingers against her lips.

Jon Marc said facetiously, "That's right. They won't write

any books about Daniel O'Brien. That 'honor' will fall to
the venerated Hoot Todd."

"I'm sorry, Jon Marc. I didn't mean to be cruel."

"I did." Yet it bothered him more than it should, his
defense.

"I don't blame you," she said. "I am to be scorned. Do
it. Scorn me. But don't forget who loves you. And that you
love me. I couldn't be that wrong about you, Jon Marc. I
know you love me. *Me.* Not the lady you sent for. She was
a wonderful person, I'll grant that. I held her in the highest
regard and respect. Saintly—everything of her letters and
more—that was Miss Buchanan. So saintly that she would
have preferred to become the bride of Christ, than to
marry you. But she would have. She was good at her word."

Real respect issued from the imposter's tone and expression. Jon Marc remembered the letters. Their poetic references, the mentions of pianos and a convent education.
What a prize he'd lost, when Beth Buchanan had died.

Oh, really? Hadn't his fiancée evaded saying yes to his
proposal to arrive on April twenty-first? She would have
preferred the veil.

"From the moment I met her," Bethany said, "I've
wished I could truly be Beth Buchanan."

Jon Marc studied the woman who had been his wife for
nearly six months. She had never evaded him. He'd
thought as much, in the beginning, but hadn't she
accepted him, without stipulations or hesitations? Or had
it been another of her hoaxes, her means to charm?

"Can't say you didn't try being Beth Buchanan," he
allowed.

Bethany Todd, never prone to give up or in, did as she
always did. She tried to make things better. "Once you've
thought about our situation, you'll see I love you. That
I've been a decent wife to you. That I want your happiness."

Something inside him wanted to believe her. He thought
back on her many good deeds . . . and how much the two

of them had pleasured each other, when good deeds were the farthest from their thoughts.

That was the thinking of a chump, someone as thick-headed as a log. Too much, Jon Marc had been a chump. "If you think you can charm me, think again. This isn't Hoot Todd you're speaking to. You may've made me a fool, but I'm not stupid enough to eat out of your hand. Not anymore."

"You won't grant me a second thought?"

Jon Marc parked his palm above the fireplace. "That thousand dollars you talked Todd out of is still in the cookie jar. There's more in the strongbox at Roca Blanca." *Would've been easier, if you'd paid her stage fare, the day she showed up.* "Take it, Miss Todd. Take it and leave."

"I'm not Miss Todd. I'm your wife."

Was she? Jon Marc knew he must speak to the priest. Probably, he would need to consult with an attorney. The thought sickened him. Too often he'd eaten disgrace. Too often.

"You would throw me into the night?" Bethany asked.

Could he do that? He recalled what it was like, being cast aside like so much refuse. He didn't want that for this woman. A part of him yearned for her happiness. The smarter part warned not to become a bigger fool.

The dumbest part caused him to take her elbows. "You always ask too much, Beth. Bethany. Too much. Always."

"Maybe I do." She gazed up into his eyes. "Maybe I do."

Her palms trailed up his vest, her fingers curling behind his neck. Her breasts pressed against his chest. Undeniable lust lashed through him, spurring reason away. His hands found their way to her back, her derriere.

"Give in to this, Jon Marc." Her voice embraced a heady purr. "Make us both happy."

"You'd like that, wouldn't you?"

"Yes."

When she wiggled against him, he nearly lost track of anything but desire.

"I need you inside me, Jon Marc. Please."

How many times had he been there? Too many to count. Many wonderful ones to recall. Never had they started a child, but they might have. One could be on its way.

Their babe.

How could he have maligned the fruit of their love? No child should pay for the sins of his parents. Or grandparents. Or uncles.

Bethany arched against him, like the cat that she was. "I'm not the lady you imagined, but I want to be your wife and woman. Forever and ever."

His rod met that bowing. *I don't want a lady.* He wanted her, whoever she was.

At least once more.

No!

If for no other reason, to prevent a child.

She peeled his vest and shirt aside, her serpent's tongue laving his nipple. God! Why did such a thing feel so good? Man wasn't meant to nurture children. Why did a craving wind to Jon Marc's lower back and settle in his male organs? Why did he even wonder?

This must have been how his father had felt. Let a woman fool you. Let her seduce you. Or let yourself be seduced. Then howl for more.

If he gave in, it would be forever.

He couldn't live with that. Wouldn't be another Daniel. Wouldn't have a liar making a mockery of marriage.

He counted to ten. Then twenty. His rod shriveled, feeling the cold of November and the slap of reality.

The muscles in his hips contracted as he thrust her away. So did his heart.

Bethany clutched her arms, her shoulders sagging. "Please don't let this be the end of us. Give me a second thought, Jon Marc."

Was this the sort of thing Georgia had said to Daniel?

Probably not. Georgia had wanted to be done with her husband. But Bethany had her own set of deficits. She wasn't Beth.

*Who is she? What does it matter? You don't care about piano playing, or blue eyes, or curly hair. That fob watch is nothing. Who cares?*

Jon Marc O'Brien cared. He'd come late to Catholicism, but marriage was a sacrament, not to be undertaken in deceit or misrepresentation. This woman had laughed in the face of his religion. And Beth Buchanan's.

He went to the settee, crumpling into it. "Bethany, we need to make rational decisions. If you've got a babe in your belly, I want it. I'll raise it."

Her face brightened. Sweeping over to him, she knelt at his feet. "You won't be sorry." Fingers gripped his knees. "I'll be a good mother. A good wife. You won't be sorry."

"You don't understand. You aren't part of the picture."

The light in her eyes died. She ducked her chin. A laugh as hollow as a log rent the parlor. "Here I go, trying to deceive you. No more of that. I should imagine a child is something we needn't worry over. I am barren. I know this. I was meant to be alone. To pay for my sins."

No, she wasn't meant to live her life without loved ones around her. For all her mistakes, Jon Marc knew this was basically a good woman. She just wasn't the woman for him.

Which didn't mean he had no sympathy for Bethany Todd.

"Find someone else," he said, hating those words. "Be yourself. Don't lie. Put this behind you."

A long moment stretched taut before she shoved to stand. "I'll be on the next stagecoach."

He nodded. "Till then, I'll stay away. Way away."

Jon Marc left the home they had shared, riding hard for Santa María Church. If ever there were ever a time for spiritual resuscitation, it was now.

# Chapter Thirty

"Let not your heart be troubled," Padre Miguel said to Bethany, reminding her of that long-ago advice given by Mrs. Agatha Persat. "Come to Santa María, my child. Let me hear your confession."

"Yes, Padre. I will." Bethany, standing several hundred yards from the river, put down the slop bucket that she'd brought to lure pigs from their sty. Out of hearing range from Diego Novio and the other vaqueros, she said, "Tomorrow."

Tomorrow. The day the stagecoach would arrive from San Antonio, on a southward course to Mexico City. Even though Hoot Todd had relented, had given Terecita ample funds for their daughter's schooling, mother and daughter would be on that coach, as would Bethany.

The mere idea of climbing into that conveyance sent a shiver of hurt through her. She had come here, desperate and having no other choice. She would leave, desolate and having no other choice.

Money would not be a problem, even though Bethany would leave Jon Marc's money behind.

Yesterday, Hoot Todd had shown up. He'd handed his sister a velvet sack, saying, "You need these. Sell them. Make a life for yourself."

Her eyes had rounded upon catching sight of a fortune in jewels. Diamonds, rubies, and pearls that Naomi Todd had given to her stepson for safekeeping. Once upon a time, Bethany would have been elated to receive her mother's heirlooms.

Then and now, she simply felt sorry for herself.

*You brought it on yourself. Face up to it. Get on with it.*

"Today," she said to the padre, "I must deal with dead cows."

Brutal weather had felled a half-dozen cows, their carcasses lying between the river and the adobe house that had become no more than shelter for a weary head. Throughout this day, with help from Padre Miguel and a trio of Jon Marc's vaqueros, Bethany had been herding pigs.

"Juan Marc will be pleased," the padre commented. "Your pigs disposing of the remains."

Bethany doubted that. She, however, tried to inject a light tone. "They don't call them pigs for no reason."

"It was farsighted of you, wanting to raise *los puercos*. I have counseled my son Juan Marc on your goodness and efficiency."

Oh, why didn't the priest simply shut up? The fewer reminder she had of her husband, the better she was able to deal with it. No. In no form could she deal with the chasm separating her heart from the trouble of getting from one moment to the next.

In the four days that had passed since Jon Marc found out about Bethany Todd, she hadn't seen anything of him.

Diego Novio had assured her of her husband's welfare. He stayed at Hacienda del Sol at night, and spent his days digging a well, in hopes of bringing water to his dying herd.

She said to the padre, "Jon Marc would've preferred I

played piano and wrote poetry about sunsets and love . . . perfect love that does not exist on this side of the Mississippi River. Save for God's love."

"Tck, tck." Padre Miguel leaned down to clap his hands and send an errant shoat back toward its mission.

The pig squealed, but tightened its curled tail and waddled off.

Straightening, the padre muffed his hands in cassock sleeves. "Juan Marc asked my advice on the validity of your marriage. He, as a good Catholic, entered the marriage in good faith. He cannot shy from the sacrament. I mentioned that you have been confirmed in the faith, that you are a practicing Catholic now. I also mentioned something else. That you are married in the eyes of Texas."

"You did exert your 'authority,' didn't you? We were a couple weeks shy of calling each other husband and wife for six months. You fudged."

Padre Miguel smiled, a rascal to the core. "*Un poco.* A little."

"Did you tell him God doesn't acknowledge our marriage?"

"Señora, one must share some things with God and his confessor. Only."

"You wicked dickens."

"Not I!" The priest's eyes widened, as if in innocence.

To wipe her brow with the back of a hand, she shed her gloves and stuffed them into a skirt pocket. No more would she wear the britches Jon Marc had purchased for Beth Buchanan.

Her gaze went to Padre Miguel, who helped with this repugnant but necessary chore of carcass disposal. Almost daily, during the norther and afterward, when the weather had been cold but not frigid, he had listened to her nebulous plans and very real heartaches.

She said, "I came here with a dead woman's wardrobe and dowry. I will leave with what is mine alone." And a broken heart. "That's the way it should be."

"You do not even own a coat. It is cold. There are a few ponchos and serapes at the church. Please accept them."

"I'm not cold," she protested. Toil kept her warm, as warm as one could be at a time of anguish. "I never owned a coat in my life. Why should anything be different now?"

"What will you do with your newfound riches?" the priest asked.

"Give it to charity."

Although some ideas of future came to mind, Bethany knew not what she'd face in that foreign city called simply *México*. But the next northbound stagecoach wouldn't pass through La Salle County for another two weeks. Stay here that long? No. She wouldn't do that to Jon Marc.

*You mustn't think about him.*

Seeing a boulder that invited a tired behind, Bethany walked to it and plopped down. Funny, how everything now drained her.

A strand of wayward hair blown from her cheek, she eyed Padre Miguel, who roosted on a similar boulder. "The nights have been long, very long," she said. "I've had time to consider my future. You know, and don't try to argue it, Jon Marc can have this marriage annulled by a court of law."

Even as she said those words, her heart cried out to deny them.

Padre Miguel sighed. "Then you have no hope to reconcile with him?"

"The choice isn't mine. Padre, I must stop thinking of myself. I'm still young. Only twenty. I must consider how I will live the rest of my mortal days. I think I should devote myself to God's work."

"Can you do this without the heart-regrets that would be mocking the Father, as well as His Son and the Blessed Virgin?"

"Yes," Bethany replied in honesty, but jumped when a clap of thunder rent the sky. She glanced upward. Dry lightning. Just dry lightning.

The priest lit a cigar. Past a curl of smoke, he said, "I know you love children. Always, there will be children who need Grace. Many live at La Casa de Nuestra Señora de Guadalupe. They need the helping hand of those who vow to take no earthly gain. There is a convent in that city. It is outlawed, yes, because of Benito Juarez's edicts, but it exists. My child, you might consider entering the sisterhood."

A wan smile, the first time Bethany had smiled in days, came over her face. "Thus is my thinking exactly. You see, I always wanted to be Beth Buchanan." She glanced heavenward, seeing another arc of lightning and feeling that an angel smiled widely from above. "She wanted to become a nun. I believe God wants me to fulfill her wishes. I should walk in her footsteps, as I tried to. I will devote myself to the good works Beth Buchanan would have taken, had she not been obligated to do as Aaron Buchanan, and Jon Marc O'Brien, wanted."

"Is that what *you* want, my child?"

"It is what I pledge to God."

The moment she answered, lightning jagged downward. Hit a dead mesquite tree. A boom erupted. Fire cracked. Flames arced through, and from, the tree. It sparked to a rain-deprived copse of chaparral.

Fire!

It could be the death knell to Rancho Caliente.

Bethany shot to her feet. So did Padre Miguel.

"Blankets, sand, buckets, whatever!" she bit out. "We must put out the fire!"


Fire!

Jon Marc threw down a shovel. *Beth's over there!*

He jumped into León's saddle, his helpers following suit on their own mounts. Jon Marc rode hard toward the inferno.

He couldn't let anything happen to his herd.

No.

He couldn't let anything happen to his wife.

Not far from his goal, he caught sight of Hoot Todd, ahead of him, and riding toward the red-blue horizon, apparently to help. Strange, how things could change. Forever. Such as Hoot Todd becoming an ally.

The outlaw jumped from the saddle. Unbuckled it from beneath his mount's belly. Grabbed his stallion's blanket. Ran forward.

Jon Marc did the same.

León bolted.

Arrived at the burning chaparral that threatened to spread licking fingers to the cattle cornered between the Nueces and its nearest branch, Jon Marc rushed forward. The crisis could be put down, if God were with them.

Then Jon Marc saw Bethany. Wearing skirts—where the hell were her britches!—she had a slop bucket in hand. Scooping up earth, she tossed it. A blue finger of fire, as if in defiance, thrashed at her.

She jumped backward.

"Go home," Jon Marc shouted. "Get away from it!"

But she didn't.

Hoot Todd beat the burning scrub. So did Padre Miguel. Heat, too much of it, pushed at Jon Marc when he slapped León's blanket to fight aggressive fire. Black vapors billowed into his eyes. It was a good feeling. Smoke meant the fire from this chaparral was dying.

Indeed, the crisis was averted.

Between Padre Miguel, Hoot Todd, the Caliente's owner and the woman who had vowed to be his wife, the fire hissed and almost died. It was under control.

No.

Just as Bethany scooped another bucketful of dirt, one last flame swelled outward.

Licked her skirt.

Orange and blue bounced, parrying, like a native dancer gone even wilder.

Bethany shouted.

Her clothes caught fire.

"No!" Already Jon Marc rushed toward her.

At the same moment the sky opened up, rain pouring.

The sounds of rain mixed with Bethany's screams. Or were they her husband's?

# Chapter Thirty-One

She was dying.

Two days ago, Jon Marc carried his wife to the bed they had shared in love and lust, where she lay prone. Already, Padre Miguel had recited last rites.

No one said so, but her husband knew a coffin had been sent for and that Luis and Diego were digging a grave on Harmony Hill. *I can't leave her there! Not yet. Not till we're both ready to go!* Jon Marc couldn't stand the idea of a long life, without Bethany.

On a straight chair at her bedside, he sat. Tears dripped down his cheeks and onto the sheet that draped her inert, bandaged form. With her breath shallow, with her face as white as the pillow that it rested on, he gazed at her. An awful, crushing weight slammed against his chest. A grief. A grief more powerful than any sorrow he'd ever known.

There wouldn't even be a single red rose to place in her casket.

His eyes closed, remembering, remembering . . .

Her face, when she first saw Trudy's roses. Her face, looking up at him during the wedding ceremony. Such a pretty face. Such a good woman, always ready to be everything she thought he wanted.

Funny, how a lady could make an hombre feel better about his lousy self.

Once, he had felt better about himself.

Before that awful night, when he'd confronted her.

It had been hard to take, reaching the church and finding out that Padre Miguel had known all along. Liam Short had known, too. Jon Marc had turned inward, his mind reverting to what his father must have felt when Georgia Morgan's infidelities became common knowledge.

But Georgia Morgan had never been an admirable woman. Jon Marc's mother foremost, and otherwise, had thought only of herself. Bethany considered anyone but herself. First came the good of Jon Marc. And then Rancho Caliente. And then Sabrina. The latter two, not necessarily in that order.

"Oh, Beth," he whispered and cried for what they had known, and lost.

This was the lady who had seen beauty in an unbeautiful ranch. He recalled when she'd grinned at his big nose, had assured him it was attractive. Such an elation he'd felt, as if he were ten feet tall. As well, he remembered their times of loving, when she'd been the wanton of his most wicked fantasy.

There would be no more fantasies.

*O'Briens doona give up.*

Fitz's words buffeting him, Jon Marc sniffed back tears. He would talk her out of dying. "I planted your orange trees. I expect you to make orange marmalade, once we pick fruit. Do you smell your potpourri, wife? Terecita put bowls of it, around this room. We're running short. You need to make more. I'll bet Hoot would loved to have lemon pie. And I'm hungry for cookies. You don't want your man to go wanting, do you?"

She gave no response.

"I want to see your fingers—" No. Her fingers would never work a needle again. "You could pour me a whiskey. I could sure use one right now."

Those fingers had never tinkled piano ivories.

What were ivories?

"Pianos make sounds, that's all. They don't make a wife. And they don't compare to your sweet laughter. I expect to hear it, during our cattle drive to Kansas. You do want to come along, don't you?"

Jon Marc studied the bandages on her hands. They were the messengers of the heart, those hands.

Her body wouldn't be the same, would forever bear scars. Two of her fingers were gone. Those hands had caressed her husband, had fed him, as well as greedy pigs. Pigs that had cleaned up the mess of drought and cold weather. Swine that Jon Marc had denounced. Not a bad idea, pigs.

Not a bad idea, Bethany.

Jon Marc centered his gaze on her closed eyelids. How those hazel eyes had danced with fun, had softened with sympathy, had rounded in horror when life had reared its ugly head. Mostly, he recalled her avowals of love. She loved him.

Without a doubt, she had loved him.

"I love you, wife. Live!"

If ever a person deserved a second chance, it was Bethany Todd O'Brien.

She gave a shudder, a faint "Oh" issuing from her throat.

He felt a hand on his shoulder. He glanced up into Terecita López's sad eyes. "Juan Marc, it is time to let her go . . . to a better place."

"For the love of God, live!" Jon Marc cried, touching his wife's cheek. "Live for me. Marry me, Bethany. Let me be good to you."

* * *

Was it a blessing, that she lived?

Bethany chose to think so. Forever, she would carry scars, but shouldn't she think of them as a reminder of her misdeeds? As God's reminder of her sins.

"I do not want to leave," Sabrina complained, standing beside the chair that Liam Short had set on the ground for Bethany, this last day of 1872. A gray, bleak day.

They were waiting for a stagecoach. Padre Miguel stood offside, along with Terecita and Hoot. Thankfully, Jon Marc wasn't with them.

In the weeks of Bethany's recovery, she had asked not to see him. Her wishes had been respected. As pleased as she was at Jon Marc's forgiveness, she had promised God to give her crippled hand to Christ. Todds didn't go back on their word.

"Hee-yah!"

A driver's voice, that.

Hooves. The turn of wheels. The stagecoach was arriving.

Gentle hands helped her stand. Hoot's and Liam's. The two men steadied her as she took small steps toward the stage.

"I'll put you aboard, Sis."

"I know you will, Hoot. Thank you." She compelled a smile, recalling the many evenings he and Sabrina had sat at her bedside. "You've been a great comfort to me, brother."

"Maybe I'll come see y'all, down Mexico way."

"Do that, Hoot."

Bethany knew he'd proposed marriage to Terecita, only to be turned down. Yet the pianist hadn't asked for Hoot to stay away from her or their daughter. Terecita simply wanted to become a lady, and the father of her child had too many rough edges.

"Woof!"

Stumpy hobbled up. The grizzled dog lifted his snout

at Bethany, peeling back his lips to expose his missing incisor. It really was rather pitiful, Stumpy's smile. It was as if to remind her that nothing had ever been quite right in La Salle County.

"He is a funny-looking dog." Sabrina patted Stumpy's head.

Held tightly by Hoot and Liam, Bethany fixed eyes on her niece. "Not a bad one, though."

"Oh, Tía Bethany, you always see the best in people and things."

"Is that a terrible thing, Sabrina?" she asked and felt warmth in a ragged heart, hearing the girl call her aunt.

The girl, dropping her chin, shook her head. "I hope I can be like you, Tía Bethany."

"Be anything but someone like me."

Sabrina approached the stagecoach's step, but turned. "If I live in Mexico City, will Tristan be able to find me?"

"Yes, he will. Be worthy of him, when he does." Bethany reached the three remaining fingers of her right hand to touch her niece's cheek. "Keep yourself chaste, Sabrina. Unto your own self be true." A clutching pain tightened, even more powerful than the outcome of a fire. "Don't lie to anyone. Especially to your loved ones. That's the same as lying to God."

"Hey, y'all. Get aboard." The driver didn't seem the least amenable. "Ain't got no time for cripples."

A tall, lean figure ambled toward Bethany. He wore Sunday best, a frock suit and string tie above polished boots. It seemed as if ten more years were etched in his wonderful face.

"Don't leave," Jon Marc said shortly. "I need you."

"Good-bye, Jon Marc. *Vaya con Dios. Mi querido.*"

"Is there nothing I can say to change your mind?"

She shook her head.

He shoved something into her withered hand. "Read it. Read it, then decide if you must leave."

Bethany looked down at the sheet of paper. It had been folded in half.

"My child." That was Padre Miguel's voice. "Do not think God has a higher place for you. Your place is here in La Salle County, at Rancho Caliente."

"It is," Jon Marc concurred.

Her stiff thumb managed to open the message.

> *"An angel of mercy you turned out to be—*
> *There's no other angel in my heart, don't you see?*
> *Give me another thought, angel mine—*
> *Even if this doesn't rhyme."*

She laughed at his feeble poetry, but not at the sincerity of his declaration. A smile on her lips, she gazed at her beloved, who looked strong, handsome, and wounded. "I'll keep this forever. It will be my only treasure."

"That wasn't its intent. I was."

Padre Miguel unmuffed his hands to say, "Give love where it is needed. Give it to this man. He needs to be your husband."

"But my promise to God—"

"You must first honor your promise to your husband," the priest argued, ever ready to twist matters to his own authority.

Her heart tripped like a repeater rifle as she studied Jon Marc.

His hungry look drilled into her. "We'll find children who need us. You needn't leave to find those who need you."

Turning to the priest, she asked, "Would God smile on it?"

"Yes, my child. God would smile."

The sun broke through the clouds.

# Epilogue

*January 1, 1879*

"You sure you got all that down right?"

Hoot Todd had to know. Hunching over the shoulders of a lady writer from Baltimore, he watched her scribble into that journal of hers, recording the exploits of a very successful Robin Hood.

"Did you get the part where I give money to that orphanage in Mexico City?" he asked.

The crone—way too skinny for Hoot's taste, this one—drew up spare shoulders and tossed down her pen. "If you've told me once, you've told me twenty times."

Hoot scooted around to the other side of his sister's dinner table and plunked down. "Just want you to get it right."

Millicent Bagwell crossed arms over her paltry breasts. The old maid had a look in her blue eyes that could have melted the icicles that hung from eaves outside this house. "Mr. Todd—" her voice rose and fell on his name "—have you ever considered taking a bath?"

"Millie, you sound just like my sister, always tearing into me." Which caused Hoot to smile. "She wants ever'thing up to snuff, but I'm too old to change all my ways."

"You ought to listen to her." Again, Millicent picked up her pen, then tapped it on the table. "I should imagine your aroma is what frightens people out of their purses, not the threat from you or your gang of blackguards. You smell like a can of ashes."

"Better to stink than to be so clean you smell downright dead, like you do." Hoot grinned and poured a big glass of milk. "Wanna gimme a bath, Millie? I'll even let you dust me with fou-fou powder."

Her pinched face, looking every year of her thirty-five, pulled into disgust. "I'd rather bathe a skunk."

His mouth twisted. An itch under his eye patch caused him to scratch it. "That ain't very nice, Millie."

"I'm not here to be nice. I'm here to write a book. If I'd known your sister and her husband wouldn't be in residence, I would not have agreed to stay with you."

"Well, you're here. So am I." Hoot eased the chair to its two hind legs and dug a cigar out of his vest pocket. "Ain't this the life?"

"You light up, and I'm going to stuff that nasty thing in your mouth."

"What nasty thing are you talking about, Millie?" Oh, how he loved to tease Millicent Bagwell. It was more fun than robbing stagecoaches and trains. Rolling the cigar to the other side of his mouth, he asked, "One of them little-bitty titties of yours?"

"You are incorrigible." Shaking her head in exasperation, Millicent bent over her task once more. "Let's see now. You support the House of Our Lady of Guadalupe. What about your own child? What have you done to shelter Sabrina López?"

"Adopted her. Done give her my name. She's Sabrina Elizabeth Todd nowadays." His sister had asked for Elizabeth to be tacked on, in memory of her special friend up in heaven. "Sent Sabrina off to a fancy school in Switzerland, I did. She'll be finishing up in a few years."

"Isn't your sister active in raising money for the orphanage?"

"Yep, Bethany spends a lot of time, collecting money and clothes for them kids."

Hoot eyed the dining room. Jon Marc had built a new house, back in 1873, after their successful cattle drive to Kansas. It wasn't a grand place. Bethany hadn't wanted grand. She had, though, insisted on several bedrooms so that she and her husband would have plenty of room to take needy children in.

Millicent said, "Your sister and her husband don't have any children, I understand."

"Wrong. They've got three. Tykes what didn't have no parents of their own. Jon Marc and Bethany love those kids, just like they'd been born to them. They're up in Memphis, as we speak. The O'Briens have a get-together, ever' year, 'round this time."

"Is that so? A close family, are they?"

"Couldn't be closer." That was true. "The visit they made a year ago was the most special, I reckon. Celebrated Fitz O'Brien's hundredth birthday, they did." Hoot tapped the unlit cigar against his chest. "Went with 'em, I did. Wanted to see how the other half lives," he said with a chuckle.

"So, how does the other half live?"

"Purty doggone high on the hog. Even the dog eats outta a silver bowl." Hoot clicked his tongue. "Boy howdy, I could sell that silver stuff for a fortune. Them orphans in Mexico could sure use some of that wealth."

Back a long time ago, Hoot hadn't cared a fig about anybody but himself. It was a fine delight he now got from seeing smiles on little faces when he provided the necessities, as well as a toy here and there.

He'd done good for himself, these past few years. His

exploits were legend, he had a fine bond with his daughter and sister, and a writer was taking down his memoirs. What more could an hombre ask for?

He ogled Millicent's flat chest. Why, her breasts had beaded up against her bodice. He wouldn't mind giving one of those raisins a try. "You know, someone once told me—anything over a mouthful is wasteful."

Ink splattered on her bosom, so fast did she try to cover herself. "You deplorable, double-negative-speaking lout!"

"Now, now, Millie, my raisin."

"One would think—at your age!—you'd been too grizzled for womanizing."

"I ain't but forty-one. And the only gristle I got, well, it's the kind what gets nice and hard when it needs to."

"Oh, please. Let's do get back to business. How did the celebration turn out?" she asked, yanking his attention to her mouth.

It wasn't bad-looking, now that he got to thinking about it.

"What? Oh, that. Well, it was okay. Got kinda sad, though. The same night Fitz O'Brien turned over his factor house to his heir, he croaked. Right there in his invalid chair, in front of the fire in his drawing room. Old rascal had a smile on his mug. Said he could die happy. All his wishes were answered. 'Just lay me t' rest next t' me Edna' were his last words. 'I'll be resting in peace.' "

Hoot took a lucifer from his pocket, struck it, then sucked smoke into his mouth, which caused Millicent to feign a cough and bat her hands in the style of old maids everywhere.

He ignored her, choosing to stare up at the ceiling instead. Yes, old Fitz had found peace, thanks to the bonhomie within his family. Someday, Hoot would have an even stronger connection to the O'Briens, when that young fellow in Memphis made good on his promises to Sabrina. Those two didn't need magic to get things going, no sirree.

While in Tennessee, Hoot had heard about that strange lamp, the one that brought both heaven and hell to the O'Brien clan. It was gone now, the lamp. Everyone had said, "Good riddance."

But the magic lived on.